BEAUTY AND THE BOUNTY HUNTER

ONCE UPON A TIME IN THE WEST
BOOK ONE

LORI HANDELAND

CHAPTER 1

bilene, Kansas 1870
A new customer strolled through the front door of
Letty's Sporting House. Short, swarthy, stocky—the three *S's* of
ugly—he sported a ridged scar around his neck. Nevertheless,
nearly every woman in the place straightened, preening for his
attention.

Cathleen Chase didn't waste time. She stepped forward. This
was her man.

A hand clamped onto her arm. "Sissy!"

Cat fought not to cringe at the foolish name she'd adopted.
What *had* she been thinking?

"We don't choose them." The whore tightened her grip, talon-
like fingernails pressing sharply into Cat's skin. "They choose us."

Cat raised her gaze from the hand on her wrist to the once-
pretty face. As often happened when Cat let people see what lay
beneath, the girl took a quick step back, wrapping her bare arms
beneath her satin-shrouded breasts as if she were cold. Since she
was revealing more flesh than she was covering—hell, so was Cat
—it might have been true.

1

LORI HANDELAND

Shrugging, the young woman glanced away. "One's the same as the next to me."

"Not to me."

Her skirt swished just below her knees as she sauntered toward her quarry. Cat had chosen a garnet dress to complement her long dark hair and green eyes. Her skin as pale as any Irishwoman's, she'd been spared the red hair and freckles of so many of her relatives. Cat resembled her mother—God rest her soul and the souls of everyone else she'd ever loved.

Cat had altered her bodice until the neckline dipped dangerously low, so that her breasts practically burst free with every breath. As she moved across the room, she discretely tugged the garment lower.

When she reached the man his gaze went directly to her chest and stayed there. "How much?"

"Five dollars." On the high end but not unreasonable. Still, he hesitated, and Cat lifted one finger, tracing it back and forth across her skin.

His eyes followed the movement like the pendulum on a clock; then he grabbed her hand and dragged her up the creaking oak staircase without ever once looking at Cat's face.

Sometimes she was so good at this, she scared herself.

"Which one?" Voice harsh, his breath came in short gasps.

Cat reached past him, making sure to brush her breasts against his arm as she opened the door to her room. Shrouded in shadow, she'd left it that way. Why bother to turn up the lamp? The less he could see—the less she could—the better.

She hadn't taken two steps inside when he kicked shut the door and yanked her around to face him. The man made a beeline for her cleavage, fingers crushing the soft flesh as he lowered his head and lifted her to his mouth.

Cat contemplated the peeling floral wallpaper and let him have at it. Her time would come.

When he began to drag up her skirt with one hand, reaching for his belt with the other, Cat murmured: "Hold on there, soldier," tempering her denial by palming his erection, tightening her fingers just enough to make him moan. "You get what you pay for with me."

"Wha—?" He couldn't form the word, could barely think, if his slack expression was any indication.

"What's your name, sugar?" It was always best, before she moved on, to be sure.

"C-c-clyde."

Cat's lips curved, and she kneaded him through the stiff material of his trousers, running her thumb over and back, over and back, across the throbbing head. Leaning in, she increased the pressure and the rhythm. "You don't want just a quick poke now . . ." She squeezed him once, just short of pain, and he gasped. "Do you?"

His head thrashed back and forth.

"That would be no to the quick poke."

Continuing to touch him just enough to keep him interested, not enough to finish him off, Cat removed a rope from the pocket of her dress with her unoccupied hand. Clyde was so far gone he didn't notice her looping it around his wrists until she pulled the knot tight.

"What the—?"

"Shh." Cat unbuttoned his pants, then dropped to her knees; her hair cascaded over her face.

Clyde's breathing picked up when she peeled back his open trousers. Inching closer, she "accidentally" bumped his hands with her head, drew back, frowned. "Maybe I should tie these behind you."

"No."

"No?" The pout in her voice was almost as convincing as the moist rush of her breath trickling over him.

Cat knew men; the threat of her displeasure wasn't half as

3

convincing as the threat that she might not follow up on that moist trickle.

"All right."

Her smile hidden by her hair, Cat untied his wrists, and he turned. She stayed on her knees, giving him the illusion of control, while at the same time she kept the promise of her mouth on his pecker alive. Cat yanked the knot tight, pressing her gambler's gun to his spine as she rose. "Now, Clyde, repeat after me: you or her?"

"Wha—?"

Cat placed the barrel against his temple. "Say it. You or her?"

"Y-y-"

She closed her eyes and, as it did every time she reached for it —and sometimes when she didn't—the past returned.

She couldn't see through the blindfold, couldn't move for the bonds. But her ears . . .

Her ears worked just fine.

"You or her?" Clyde blurted.

Cat's eyes snapped open. It wasn't him.

Disappointment flooded her, so stark, so deep her legs wobbled. How long could she keep doing this? How long before someone got the drop on her? How long before she let them?

Cat shoved aside those thoughts. She'd made a vow, and she would not stop until she kept it. No matter how long that took. No matter what she had to do. So far she'd done plenty.

After testing the knot that bound Clyde's wrists—never could be too careful—Cat nestled the gun more firmly against him. "Let's walk."

Applause exploded from the shadows, and Cat started, nearly putting a bullet into Clyde's back.

A man swam out of the gloom. His Colt strapped down like a gunslinger's, she couldn't see his face beyond the brim of a dark slouch hat. His hands, which were still applauding—slowly, sarcastically—were shrouded by black gloves.

There was something familiar about those hands.

"I've never seen anything quite like that before," he said.

There was something about the voice too—an odd cadence, an accent she couldn't place. She was good with voices—had to be—even better with accents. That she couldn't decipher this one caused the itch that had started up when she saw his hands to intensify.

"Who are you? What do you want?"

She half expected him to say he'd been waiting for her, that he was one of Letty's regulars, sent upstairs to have a taste of the new girl. A common enough occurrence in this business; it would be a simple matter to promise him she'd be available soon, then disappear.

The newcomer kept his head canted so that the shadow of his hat concealed his face, and that bothered her. What was he trying to hide and why?

"Fucking bounty hunter," Clyde spat.

"You nearly did, my sad little friend."

"Nearly did what?" Clyde's voice was mystified.

"Fuck the bounty hunter."

Cat's eyes narrowed. How did he know?

Clyde glanced over his shoulder, and Cat shoved the derringer more firmly against him, lest he try anything funny.

"She's nothing but a whore."

The other man stepped forward. Cat had time only to tighten her grip on the gun before the body she was threatening it with crumpled. It took her several ticks of the clock to understand that the first thud she'd heard had been a fist connecting with Clyde's jaw; the second had been Clyde hitting the floor.

"Well, hell. How am I going to get his sorry ass downstairs now?"

When she received no response. Cat glanced up. The intruder leaned against the wall as if he hadn't a care in the world, or a place to be in this century.

5

She turned her gun on him. "What'd you do that for?"

"I didn't like his tone or his language."

"Names don't bother me."

Men like Clyde did. She'd devoted what was left of her life to bringing them in, and if she checked each and every one to see if he was *the* one . . . Cat gave a mental shrug. It was nothing less than she deserved for *doing* this job.

"Obviously not since you use so very many."

Cat stilled. Did he *want* her to kill him?

The man flicked an elegant, dark finger at the lightly snoring Clyde. "Which one did you give him?"

"I'm—" Cat's mind groped for the name she was presently using and came up blank.

"That is often the problem with lies. So difficult to keep straight. Shall I help you to remember, Cat?"

Her trigger finger itched. Should she set it free? This man had seen what she'd done; he knew who she was. She really didn't have much choice.

"You plan to kill me with that?" A dip of his stubbled chin indicated the derringer pointed at his chest.

"You *have* been asking for it."

Laughter erupted, as startling as the applause had been. "Kitten, that wouldn't even slow me down."

He might be right. She should get closer.

"They say Cat O'Banyon always gets her man." He gestured toward the gun, the bound Clyde, then the room with a languid twirl of one gloved finger. "Is this how?"

"This?" She smoothed a hand down the satin-covered ladder of her rib cage, brushing the uncorseted weight of her breasts with her fingertips, curving her palm beneath one ripe swell. "Sometimes."

If she kept his attention on her body, he wouldn't notice anything else. Like how close she was getting. Just another step and—

He snatched the gun and tossed it onto the bed. His other hand came down on hers where it still rested beneath her breasts. Then he whirled her into the shadows, his large, hard male body aligning with hers.

Cat wanted to shriek and kick. Instead she went still and quiet. She'd learned disguise from a master, and it involved not only the outer trappings but also the spirit within. Cat O'Banyon wouldn't panic at the brush of a man's thigh along hers. Cathleen Chase on the other hand—

Cat shuddered, deftly turning the quiver from fear to arousal with the almost undetectable addition of a moan. She wasn't stronger; she couldn't fight. Not with fists. So she placed her mouth on his.

She'd planned to take charge, to ensure he thought of nothing beyond this until the time he no longer thought at all. She failed miserably as, soft and gentle, his lips countered hers. Slow and easy, as if he had aeons of time to do anything that he wanted, and what he wanted was her.

This was nothing new. Men had desired her—it was how Cat made a living, or at least how she pretended to often enough—but they hadn't desired *her*. Because she wasn't Sissy the whore or Betsy the barmaid or Dorothy the dance hall gal. She was Cat— the woman who'd been born from the ashes that had tumbled across Billy's grave nearly two years ago.

A sob almost broke free. She trapped it in her throat, and the stranger set his hand there, as if he'd heard, as if he knew, as if he cared. His tongue flicked out, testing the seam of her lips.

Lust flooded in and, shocked, Cat gasped. He slanted her head with clever fingers, letting his thumb trail across her chest, leaving gooseflesh in its wake.

She wrapped her arms around his shoulders. Funny, but when she touched him he didn't seem so broad, and she had to reach higher than she'd thought, as if he were taller than he appeared.

Her brow furrowed; memory flickered—a mirage—there and then gone and then—

He deepened the kiss, and he tasted like blue night, something dangerous but exciting, something that pulled you in even when you knew you had to get out. She drew in a breath, his scent reminding her of places that were green and sunny and gone. Warmth rolled off him; she wanted to bask in that heat like her namesake.

Besides, as long as he was kissing her, he wasn't paying attention to her hand, which had, seemingly of its own accord, slid across his shoulder—definitely more lithe than large, how peculiar—down his arm, across his oddly slim hip.

Her sigh masked the shift of her palm from his body to her own, the arch of her spine, the press of her breasts into his chest concealing the track of her fingers as they disappeared beneath her skirt.

His tongue traced her lower lip, tickled her teeth, slid through and danced a bit with her own. What would it be like to give in? To feel something more than nothing for a minute?

Cat was tempted, and because she was, she got careless. She concentrated on his mouth when she should have been concentrating on his hands. Ain't that always the way?

He cupped her breast, one finger dipping beneath the lace and trolling across the nipple. A sharp tug shot through her, awakening sensations she'd forced into slumber long ago. That sob she'd been stifling erupted, becoming a howl of fury as it flew from her mouth. She yanked up her skirt and reached for the Arkansas toothpick strapped to her thigh.

"Looking for this?" He pressed the tip to Cat's throat, and she froze.

She didn't much care about living, but she wasn't ready to die yet either. Not until she found the owner of the voice that whispered through her nightmares. Even if the interminable searching made her feel as if she were just chasing the wind.

Cat was prepared to beg if she had to. She'd done it before. Then her eyes met his, and everything changed.

CHAPTER 2

$\mathcal{C}$at kicked him in the knee. "Goddammit, Alexi, what are you doing here?"

Tall, dark, and gifted, Alexi Romanov would command all eyes wherever he went. He was that pretty. Smooth, sun-kissed skin, wavy black hair, deep blue eyes, and hands that could make a violin sing or a woman moan. He could also lie to an angel and cheat the pants off the devil himself. He had taught Cat everything she knew.

Cat shoved him. Alexi stayed right where he was, although he did lift the knife from Cat's neck a little, probably afraid she'd skewer herself just for spite.

"Move," she ordered.

"Make me."

She lifted her knee, fast and sure. He blocked the attempt to unman him—permanently—with his hip; then he grasped her waist and yanked them together in an effort to preserve certain parts he would no doubt need later. For someone else.

Cat rolled her eyes, pretending boredom. At times it was the only weapon she had.

"What," she repeated, voice tired now instead of angry, "are you doing here?"

"If I let you go, will you shoot me?"

She didn't point out he'd already taken her pistol. She should have known right then who he was. He'd once taught her how to disarm any fool who ventured too close with a gun. Snatch the barrel while turning to avoid the bullet, then twist. The element of surprise and quick hands had thus far guaranteed every weapon Cat had tried it on had become hers.

"If I shot you, Alexi, I wouldn't have a friend left in this world."

"I am not your friend." He stepped back.

"I know."

As Alexi moved away, he ran one finger along her forearm, that single touch reminding Cat of a hundred and one nights in his bed. She'd come to him broken, bleeding inside, and he'd mended her somehow. Not completely, but enough to go on. She'd begun touching him back as payment; she'd stopped touching him for the same reason.

Cat didn't think his name was Alexi—or Romanov, for that matter. But that was the wonder of America. If farm wife Cathleen Chase could become the legendary bounty hunter Cat O'Banyon, then an Al could become an Alexi.

Alexi was a confidence man. He crossed the country lightening the loads—and the pockets—of the citizens. He insisted he didn't steal and, in truth. Cat had never seen him take anything that wasn't freely given—even if what he gave back was often more mud than magic.

Cat ran her gaze from his dark slouch hat, past the shoulders that seemed broader than they had been, on down to his overly dusty boots and understood why she hadn't recognized him right away. Alexi's talent lay in making people see whatever he wanted them to.

"You're supposed to be a bounty hunter?" Cat's lip curled.

Alexi smirked. His disguise had worked and he knew it. Alexi didn't merely *pretend* to be someone else; he *became* someone else. She'd never seen anything like it. She was good, but Alexi . . .

Alexi was better.

He lounged against the wall, head tipped so that his hat again concealed his face. With gloves covering the hands she knew so well, dirty denims combined with a white cotton shirt and the scratched grips of some mighty big guns peeking out of their holster, not to mention the three days' stubble across his chin . . .

He *was* a bounty hunter.

"You keep playing around in things you don't understand," Cat said, "you're gonna get killed."

Alexi snorted. Though the body beneath the costume was lithe and slim, it was quick and much stronger than it appeared. However, his body wasn't what made Alexi dangerous, but rather his clever, clever mind.

Cat eyed him now. He seemed half asleep, but she knew better. The last time she'd seen Alexi, he'd *been* asleep. Naked in her bed as she'd tiptoed into the night and never looked back. Now he was here. That couldn't be good.

"How'd you find me?"

"*Mon Dieu*," he muttered, sounding exactly like a Frenchman. "You think no one knows what you're doing? That a woman can trounce hither and yon, snatching up men and disappearing with them into the sunset, with no one noticing?"

"Say what you mean, Alexi." *Dear God, just once, say what you mean.*

He came away from the wall with cougarlike speed, one instant languid and sleepy, the next tense, edgy, and so close he made her tense and edgy too. "A female bounty hunter attracts attention. But a female bounty hunter no one can identify . . . " Alexi shrugged. "She becomes a legend."

Cat shrugged too, though hers wasn't half as graceful. "So?"

"The problem with legends is that everyone wants a glimpse of them."

A chill trickled over Cat's neck. She wouldn't put it past Alexi to capture her and place her in a gilded cage.

"Come one, come all," she murmured. "Step right up and see Cat O'Banyon in chains."

His beautiful face creased. "I'd never—"

"Of course not." Nevertheless, Cat moved closer to the gun on the bed. She even risked a glance in that direction, her gaze landing on nothing but sheets. "How do you *do* that?"

"Do what?"

Cat didn't bother to answer. "Why are you here?"

He certainly hadn't come for a kiss, amazing as it had been. Alexi's kisses were always amazing. And they were always a prelude to getting what he wanted. Cat didn't think he'd ever kissed anyone for the sake of the kiss alone. Of course, neither did she anymore.

Alexi's eyes flicked to the window. "We should go."

"I'd love to. Unfortunately, you knocked my bounty out cold, so I'll have to wait until—"

"Leave him." Alexi headed for the door.

"No."

He paused with his hand on the latch. "What was that?"

He no doubt expected her to shiver and shake at the menace in his voice. Everyone else did.

"I'm not leaving him behind so he can waltz out of here and do again to someone else whatever it was he did that got me sent after him in the first place."

Alexi peered over his shoulder. "You don't know?"

"I don't care."

He turned away from the door. "Come with me now, *Katzchen.*"

One of Alexi's most appealing—or was it annoying—traits was his use of foreign endearments when addressing a woman.

13

Cat had concluded that he did this so he didn't have to concern himself with learning all of their many names.

"I'm not leaving without him." Cat eyed Alexi's black gloves with suspicion. She'd thought he wore them to cloak his distinctive showman's hands, but considering Clyde's lack of consciousness, maybe the gloves concealed his henchman's favorite pair of brass knuckles.

Alexi wasn't much for hitting. His hands were as precious a commodity as his face, his body, and his brain. Which was why he rarely used them for anything other than—

"Fine," Alexi snapped. "We will bring him with us to St. Louis." He bent and reached for Clyde.

"No."

Alexi straightened. "Why the hell not?"

She stifled her smile. When he was annoyed, Alexi lost all hint of refinement.

"I need to deliver him to Rock River, Kansas, for the bounty."

"Fuck the bounty!" Alexi exploded, and her hint of a smile faded.

"Why are you here?" she repeated.

He glanced again toward the window. "We need to go."

Though the curtains hung limp, a chill wind blew over her. "What have you done?"

"Me?" He set his black-gloved hand against the creamy shirt covering his chest, eyes widening in a poor attempt at innocence.

"Dammit." He'd sold her out. But to whom? *She* wasn't wanted.

Cat didn't waste her breath with more questions. Alexi wouldn't admit a thing without persuasion, and the way he was behaving—obsessed with the window, insistent on getting gone —she didn't have the time.

Though she hated to do it, she'd have to leave Clyde behind and capture him again later. She'd need a different disguise, but like Alexi, she had plenty at her disposal. Clyde wouldn't see her coming until she was already there.

As she went past, Alexi snatched her elbow. She tried to shake him off. "Let me go. We need to—"

"Too late," he whispered, then pulled her against him, curling his elbow about her throat and placing her own blade to her chest.

The door burst open; three armed men crowded in. At the sight of Cat and Alexi, the shortest and fattest narrowed his already small eyes to slits. "We're lookin' for Cat O'Banyon. She—"

"You think a bounty hunter of such acclaim is a woman?" Alexi's laughter mocked, and their weapons, which had lowered slightly, lifted again.

"That's what we heard." A sullen sneer marred the short one's thin lips.

"Think, gentlemen, if you're capable of it," Alexi continued.

The two silent men frowned, whether with the effort of trying to follow his suggestion or recognition of the insult, it was hard to say.

"Of the three people you've found in this room, who is the best bet for a legendary bounty hunter?"

The first man considered the unconscious Clyde, then the captive Cat, before finally settling on Alexi. Slowly he smiled.

After that, things moved very fast.

Alexi's wrist twitched. The front of her dress split, and Cat's breasts spilled free. In the half-light her skin gleamed like pearls beneath clear water.

Then the hand at her breasts, the arm around her throat, the body at her back was gone, but not before he whispered, "Play the part, *mi gatito*. You *are* Sissy."

The thud of a boot was followed by the whoosh of what sounded like wind. The yellowed lace curtains fluttered past her cheek.

Cat's gaze stayed on the three men. Theirs were fixed unwaveringly on her breasts. They hadn't even noticed yet that Alexi was gone.

Cat let them stare to the count of ten. Then she gathered the tattered remnants of her gown. "There he goes!" She pointed at the window, hand shaking, lips trembling. "Cat O'Banyon broke in here. He hit that man. Said he'd take him in dead or alive."

The spell of her breasts broken, the three hunters blinked. Still, there was an instant when she thought they might decide to forgo chasing "Cat" for a taste of her publicly displayed charms.

She'd shoot them first. *She* chose who and when and why. Unfortunately, she no longer had a gun.

"Come on," the leader ordered, and they clattered down the stairs, then slammed out the front door. Whoever had paid them to find, capture, or perhaps kill Cat O'Banyon must have paid them very well.

But why?

* * *

ALEXI RELEASED the windowsill and landed lightly on the roof of the porch just below. A few steps to the edge, then he dropped to the ground and blended into the crowd. With Cat's exquisite breasts to divert the bounty hunters' attention and the route he'd planned before he'd even walked inside, escape was easy.

They would follow. He wanted them to. Then, while he led a merry chase across the prairie. Cat would take her blasted bounty and get gone.

Sometimes it was all Alexi could do not to strangle her. She took so many chances; she courted death every day. He'd hoped some time on her own would make her less impulsive, but he'd been wrong.

Memories flickered—desire and fury. He'd made her come, but he'd never made her his, and it burned.

Alexi rubbed a hand over his face, wincing at the scritch of stubble against his gloves. Too much thought, too much emotion got people killed. He'd learned that the hard way.

When he reached the end of the street, Alexi glanced back. The three men were already following, though slowly, checking each building, every alleyway. They weren't as stupid as he'd thought, and this worried him. Oh, they wouldn't catch *him*. But that they'd nearly caught *her* . . .

That was a problem.

He slipped into the stable and retrieved his horse. The animal was still saddled, as ordered; he hadn't planned to be here long.

Alexi had hoped to convince Cat to join him in St. Louis. He should have known better. If she'd wanted to be with him, she would never have left him in the first place. Another thing that burned.

But he'd dropped enough hints while he was with her to ensure that when she finished with Clyde, she would come after him and discover all that he knew.

Despite the circumstances, Alexi looked forward to it.

* * *

CAT STARED out the window long after Alexi and his pursuers had disappeared into the crowd on the street. Even at this time of night, heat seemed to rise along with the dust, giving the clapboard houses and stores, the moon-shrouded horizon a dreamy quality.

Nearby cattle milled in pens ready to be loaded onto the trains that chugged east, their lowing mournful, as if they knew what awaited them at the other end, their scent so thick it seemed to float just below the clouds like a coming whirlwind.

Someone in the crowd began to hoot and holler, pointing at Cat, who had been leaning out the window, her breasts spilling free from her gown. She jerked inside, narrowly missing a smart rap of her head against the casement.

Clyde mumbled something unintelligible, and Cat considered knocking him out again. However, it would be easier to get him to Rock River if he could move on his own. Certainly she could enforce the dead provision of Clyde's "dead or alive" bounty, and she would if he gave her one good reason. But Cat had discovered she couldn't kill someone just to make things easier for herself. If the law wanted Clyde dead, they had plenty of ropes.

She needed to change clothes and find another weapon. Clyde wouldn't come along peaceful-like if she didn't have a gun.

Cat slid the torn dress from her shoulders but when the material hit the floor, it thumped. Cat knelt and patted the garnet satin. In one pocket she found her derringer; the other held her knife.

"How does he *do* that?" The man's hands were quicker than his tongue.

Her cheeks heated at the images conjured by that single stray thought. Considering what she'd done today to capture Clyde and what she'd done on any number of occasions to capture others just like him, Cat was more shocked that she could still blush than at the idea of what she'd been blushing about.

She dressed in dark wool trousers and cracked leather boots, dropping a long-sleeved homespun shirt over breasts she'd quickly bound. Atop that she added a jacket she'd padded at the shoulders to add manly breadth, then tucked her hair under a slouch hat very much like the one that had shaded Alexi's face. They were common enough, having been worn by both the North and the South during the war.

After waking Clyde with a few shakes and slaps as well as the remains of a stray glass of whiskey tossed into his face, they left by the back stairs. The only person who saw them was the maid. Cat tossed her a coin and a sharp "Keep your own counsel, gal," using the gruff male voice she'd perfected long ago.

Took them a week of hard riding to reach Rock River, but they got there. The first few hours Cat traveled with a rifle in her lap, expecting the bounty hunters to discover Alexi's ruse, as well as her own, and track them down. But by the next morning, she settled in. No one had ever figured out any of Alexi's ruses. She doubted that would change with those three, as they'd appeared to possess a single working brain between them.

The trip would have been forgettable if not for the sting of a nick Alexi had left just below her left breast. An accident, perhaps? Or a reflection of his annoyance that her stubborn insistence on following through with her plan had ruined his?

Whatever it had been.

The cut wasn't serious, would probably have healed in a day if the cloth Cat used to bind her breasts hadn't rubbed against it, breaking the scrape open over and over, staining her shirt red. She looked to have been wounded, which was not a good thing when traveling with a man like Clyde. If a lawman came upon them, Cat would be hard-pressed to explain who she was before he shot them both.

Cat timed her approach into town for nightfall. Just because people liked to spread the legend of Cat O'Banyon didn't mean the sheriff wanted to be caught employing her. Even if he was her brother-in-law.

Rock River, which wasn't far from Wichita, lay south of Abilene. The town had hopes of becoming part of the Chisholm Trail, and many thought it soon would be. Ben had been hired as the sheriff and moved here, about thirty miles away from his first lawman's job, a few months before Billy's death.

As always, Ben Chase answered the knock fully dressed, gun belt around his waist. Cat had stopped wondering long ago if he slept in his clothes. She didn't care either way.

"Cathleen." His Southern lilt caused a trickle of nostalgia, one of the reasons Cat had trained the same accent out of her own speech. Every time she heard a Georgia twang, she remembered.

Though she hadn't been by in a month, had gotten the information for this particular bounty from one of Ben's associates in another Kansas town, Ben wasn't happy to see her. He still hadn't gotten over Billy's death. Who had?

Ben's gaze flicked to Clyde. He didn't ask, didn't need to. If Clyde was still breathing, he wasn't the man she'd been searching for. That didn't mean someone didn't want him.

"Come for the bounty?"

Cat didn't answer. She certainly hadn't come for the company.

Ben indicated she should precede him down the steps that led from the living quarters above to his office and the jail below. She retrieved Clyde, whom she'd left hog-tied at the front door.

Ben quickly confined the prisoner, found the record of the bounty, paid it, then headed for the door. Once outside, he paused. "You coming up?"

The faint light of the crescent moon revealed, if Cat had perhaps forgotten, that Ben was everything Billy was not. Light hair instead of dark, blue eyes instead of brown, short instead of tall, alive instead of dead.

"I'll come up." She didn't have much choice. Everything she owned was there, and she needed to change.

She'd just removed her coat when Ben's gasp split the tense silence. Cat whirled, palm slapping the butt of her gun. But no one lurked in the shadows. Unless you counted Ben.

He pointed, and Cat glanced down. Her shirt was a bloody rag.

Cat crossed to the pitcher and basin on the washstand, poured some water as Ben moved to the window and stared out. As there was only one room above the jail, this was all the privacy Cat could expect.

Quickly she unbuttoned the shirt, unwrapped the bindings, and set to work washing away the blood. The water was cold and felt heavenly across her sweaty skin.

"Why do you do this?" Ben asked.

"Because you won't."

That was unfair. No one else knew the voice. No one *could* do this but her. Still, she'd had enough of Ben's judgment. Sometimes, especially when she was hot and tired and bloody, Cat just had to wound him too.

"I'm a lawman, not a vigilante."

"He was your brother."

"You're going to get yourself killed."

She could only hope.

"He wouldn't want that."

Cat wasn't so sure. She was no longer the girl Billy had married. That girl had died when he did. Would he even recognize her?

Cat tossed the bloody cloth into the equally bloody water. "You have no idea what he'd want."

Ben spun; his gaze went to her bare breasts, but Cat didn't bother to cover herself. Any modesty she'd once had died when she began to use her body as . . . What? Leverage? Distraction? Currency? Sometimes all three.

She'd learned on that long-ago night—or perhaps from Alexi; it didn't matter—that she couldn't think of her body as anything other than flesh and bone if she wanted to keep moving forward. Every day, every bounty, every man brought her one step closer to *the* man. To find him, she'd do anything.

"Where did you put my belongings?"

Face flushed, Ben lifted his chin, indicating the chest at the bottom of his bed. She wondered where the trunk had come from; it certainly wasn't hers. However, when she lifted the lid she saw that everything inside was.

On the trail for the past year, in constant pursuit of evil men, Cat couldn't drag along her ever-increasing array of costumes. She could have bought a new set for each new guise, since she still possessed most of the money she'd earned as a bounty hunter. She had little to spend it on, living the way she did. But why buy new ones when the best worked again and again?

Cat dug through several outfits she'd worn in saloons and whorehouses over the past year, tossed aside a serape, chaps, and a gambler's vest until she found more cloth to bind her breasts and another homespun shirt.

Once she resembled the person she'd been when she arrived, less the blood, she rooted around until she unearthed a costume she hadn't worn in a very long time, then stuffed it into her saddlebags.

After a few minutes spent returning everything she'd tossed onto the floor to its former place, Cat closed the lid.

Ben stared again through the window as if he might find the answers to everything on the prairie.

Hell, maybe he could.

CHAPTER 3

*C*at boarded the train to St. Louis dressed as a lady. She'd found it safer to journey by train or stage as a woman. She was accorded a respect she wouldn't get in pants.

Though traveling this way was safer, it certainly wasn't easier. The crinoline she'd purchased that morning—she couldn't very well carry such a contraption on her horse from Rock River to Kansas City even if she'd had one in Ben's trunk—added a fashionable bell shape to the rear of her teal silk skirt. But it was difficult to manage. She bumped into things and people whenever she turned and sometimes when she didn't. In addition, she wanted to tear the corset off her person and stomp on it with her pointed ankle boots.

The only portion of the ensemble that she didn't itch to destroy was her brand-new spoon bonnet. And not because it perched comfortably on her demurely coiffed head, but rather the colorful flowers upon the brim drew curious eyes away from her face.

It had taken her all of two minutes after leaving the Rock River sheriff's office to decide that her next stop was St. Louis. If Alexi hadn't sold knowledge of her whereabouts to the highest bidder—and she still wasn't certain of that—she thought he might know who had. If she was lucky, he might even know why. Alexi, as he often told her, did his best to know everything.

When the conductor called, "Next stop, St. Lou-eee!" Cat slipped into the washroom. There, after much tugging and cursing and one accidental knock of her elbow against the basin —followed by more cursing—she stuffed the damnable crinoline through the window. She watched it fly backward and out of her life with immense satisfaction.

She exited the train dressed as a boy. In the city, on the streets alone, a woman drew too much attention.

St. Louis was a river town. Old by American standards. Settled in the late 1600s by the French. More urbane than Wichita or Abilene, St. Louis smelled of water instead of dust, fish instead of cattle. Not that one was much better than the other.

She found what she was looking for on a vacant slice of land near the river. A kaleidoscope of people—male and female, short and tall, fat and skinny, young and old, blondes, brunettes, redheads—crowded around the covered wagon, awaiting the show.

And a show it would be. Sleight of hand. Glib of tongue. Promise the world. Deliver much less. Then disappear.

Everyone's attention remained on the curtain draped across the back of the wagon. A heavy board jutted out to provide a stage. Not an ordinary Conestoga, this one had been fashioned, as the sign attached to the canvas proclaimed, for *Count Sukhorukov! Famed Healer of Balshika!*

Cat snorted. Another of Alexi's tricks. The more confusing the name, the less likely folks were to remember it. They wouldn't even be able to pronounce this one. She wondered if anyone besides Alexi could. Not that it mattered. The name Sukhorukov wasn't any more real than he was.

Her snort had drawn a curious glance from the man in front

of her. She coughed, then sneezed and wiped the back of her hand across her nose, producing the wet noises made by the soon-to-be dying. Not only did the fellow face front, but he moved away, as did several others nearby. Cat hid her smirk beneath the shadow of her hat.

The curtain shivered once, then stilled. The audience, who had caught their breath in anticipation, let that breath out on a collective sigh of disappointment.

Cat knew better than to get excited over the first hint of his arrival. He would make them wait. Anticipation increased his allure. The continued presence of a crowd would only cause the crowd to swell. The chatter of a few would become the cacophony of many. Those who had not planned to stop would be unable to help themselves, and when they least expected him, he would—

"Ladies and gentlemen, boys and girls," intoned a pleasing though slightly foreign voice. "May I introduce . . ." A muffled bang, smoke trailed upward. "Me."

He glided free of the cloud, and people gasped. One blink and you missed him. The platform was empty, and then it was not.

Taller than most, elegant and slim, Alexi's hair shone like ebony tossed in the sunlight; his sapphire eyes glittered as brightly as the jewels that dotted his long, slim fingers. He was an exotic jungle predator set loose amid the barn cats.

"Today," he continued, his accent so light he could be easily understood. Yet the unusual cadence of his voice, the peculiar twist he put on some words—not too many, only a few—contributed to his air of mystery.

This man had been places; he knew things. And soon those who watched would know too.

"Today, my *droo-ziya.*" He paused, high, perfect brow wrinkling as he pursed full, supple lips. Then, seemingly to himself, he muttered what sounded like curses but could just as easily have been gibberish—no one here would know—before curving those lips upward.

"My *friends.*" His voice deepened with triumph, the lower register causing everyone who heard it to feel as if they were, indeed, his friends. "I will share with you an elixir created by my ancestors—the Sukhorukovs of Balshika—a village south of the Crimea within view of the great Black Sea."

Cat doubted any of them knew the location of Balshika. She had her doubts it even existed. But enough had heard of the Crimea—the British had fought a war there against the Russians not fifteen years past—to give his tale an air of truth.

"This tonic contains water taken from that legendary sea." Seemingly from nowhere, he produced a bottle, the inky liquid within swirling, drawing every eye in the crowd and holding it captive.

"This sea is enchanted, my friends, and I will tell you why. Once upon a time a man named Bogatyr possessed a magic arm. I know"—he lifted his own and smiled a rueful smile —"such a thing is not possible but listen."

He waited and, when no one raised a single word in protest, continued. "They say his arm was an arrow of great power and precision." His silky dark hair caressed the collar of his equally black shirt as he studied them. "And to have such a legend told in his name, Bogatyr must have been an incredible warrior. My belief is that he was so accurate with this weapon that his enemies began to see it as an extension of him. Thus Bogatyr's arm *became* an arrow."

"Ah" rose from the crowd and many nodded in agreement, their faces rapt with interest for the story and respect for the insight of the man telling it.

"People began to view the arrow as magic, and maybe it was." Alexi spread his hands; the jewels caught the light and flashed. "I know for certain that what happened later"—he shook the bottle again, and the liquid whirled—"was a miracle."

Cat's lips curved as Alexi moved in for the kill. "Though Bogatyr was a good and just man, using his gift only to keep his village safe, he was but a man, and eventually his time upon the earth drew to a close. Rather than allow his charmed *arrow . . .*" Alexi tilted an eyebrow, and the crowd chuckled at their shared joke. Was it an arrow or was it an arm?

"Rather than allow that arrow, which always flew straight and true, to fall into the hands of one who might not be as righteous as himself, Bogatyr threw it into the sea."

Now a murmur rolled from the audience. If his arrow were an arm, how did he throw it? Did he cut off his arm, or did he hurl himself into the depths?

Alexi remained silent while the questions simmered. Only when the crowd was on the edge of shouting aloud their curiosity did he continue. "The arrow plunged through the water, sinking firmly into the bottom. The sea began to boil, and then . . ."

Again he waited, his compelling gaze touching that of several others in the crowd. Cat tilted her head so that her hat shaded her face. Not that she'd fool Alexi. He already knew she was here.

"Then?" blurted a voice from the crowd, and Alexi allowed the small smile he'd been nurturing to bloom.

"Then," he continued, "the roiling waves turned black, bestowing upon the sea its name and hiding forever the location of Bogatyr's arrow. However . . ." He lifted a finger upon which a jewel the shade of that sea shone. "From that moment forward, anyone who drank of those waters beneath a moonless sky was healed."

Silence settled over the crowd. Alexi remained motionless, gaze upon the bottle, which caught the afternoon light and turned the liquid that swirled within to smoke.

"How much?" someone shouted.

A giant appeared next to the wagon. Though Alexi stood upon a platform several feet off the ground, the newcomer's dark head nearly reached his shoulder. The man had to weigh three hundred pounds. His arms and legs were as thick as oak stumps, his hands and feet the size of cannonballs. A collective gasp of surprise and shock rippled through the crowd.

"My associate will assist you." Alexi set his hand on the newcomer's back. "Mikhail's English is not so good as mine, but he counts much better."

Alexi ducked behind the curtain, and Mikhail motioned for anyone who was interested, and there were many, to join him at a nearby table full of bottles where a placard announced: *Black Sea Solution! The ancient Russian cure. Drink only on a moonless night. One dollar a bottle.*

Trust Alexi to build into the legend a block, confidence jargon for a ruse that would keep the buyer from discovering the truth too soon. In this case, the requirement of drinking the potion on a moonless night would ascertain that Alexi would be long gone before anyone pulled out the cork.

The horde crowded to the table. When they began to jostle for position, one glare from Mikhail ended it.

Mikhail was the heavy, the muscle. He prevented any marks from causing trouble. Usually just by being there.

The colossus calmly and competently took their money as he handed out the cure. Ignoring all questions, he never uttered a word.

Alexi's excuse that Mikhail's English was poor was just that. Mikhail's English was fine; it was his Russian that needed work. The big man was as incapable of subterfuge as his boss was of telling the truth.

No one paid Cat any mind as she inched toward the wagon and pushed aside the curtain. As expected, Alexi Romanov was gone.

She found him easily enough. Cat had traveled with the man for months; she knew the kind of place that he liked. One that provided liquor and women, his two favorite things.

After money.

Cat had success in the third saloon she stepped into. "You got a furener stayin' here?" she asked.

"Frenchie," the barkeep agreed, and jerked his chin toward the ceiling.

Frenchie. That figured. Cat headed for the stairs.

Though no one had ever discovered one of his ruses—at least while he was still in town—Alexi made certain to leave not a trace of Count Sukhorukov after he disappeared into the wagon. By the time he exited the other side, he'd already become someone else.

"Where ya think yer goin'?" the barkeep asked.

"He told me to come and get paid after I tended his horse."

As Cat appeared to be a thin, harmless boy, the man returned to his customers, who, considering the ailments they were discussing and the bottles of black water they clutched like the Holy Grail, had recently been the count's customers. That they hadn't recognized the Frenchie was yet another testament to the masquerade of Alexi Romanov.

"I's got the bloody flux," declared an old-timer, who also appeared to have something that caused pustules upon his bald head. "Been crappin' red fer a month."

"The missus has the King's Evil," shared another, much younger, much hairier gent. "Her neck's done swole up the size of a tree stump."

Cat cut around the newel post, grimacing at the continued litany of disease.

"Young'uns done sprouted trench mouth." A short, dumpy fellow dashed back his whiskey, his hiss of pain making Cat think he had a bit of the trench mouth too.

"I've got a strangery. Right-chere." The barkeep rubbed his crotch, and everyone laughed.

Cat bit her lip and averted her eyes. Men were such . . . men.

As she reached the landing. Cat contemplated a line of doors, then waited for a break in the chatter below. When it came, she caught a low, throaty woman's chuckle followed by a man's voice. *His* voice.

Cat tossed her pack against the wall, then strode forward and pushed open door number two. A gorgeous redhead sat before the mirror, brushing her hair.

Naked.

Alexi sprawled on the tousled mattress, watching Cat through half-lidded eyes. He did not appear surprised; he appeared bored.

The duster and slouch hat he'd worn in Abilene, along with a gun belt, had been discarded atop a nearby table. Not very original, but combined with a French accent it had obviously done what he'd meant it to do.

Made the count disappear.

He still wore the black trousers of the Russian aristocrat, but he'd removed the silky black shirt and lay bare-chested and bare-foot, a glass of amber liquid in his long-fingered, magical hands.

Those hands. She still thought of them some nights when she couldn't sleep.

Alexi's gaze flicked from the woman's pale peach breasts to her face. "*Sortez,,*" he ordered, which, when she didn't move, he followed with a heavily accented, "Get out."

She tossed the brush onto the dresser with such force it bounced off the mirror and onto the floor. "Since when d' ya like boys?"

"Go." His eyes returned to Cat.

The woman stomped her foot. "This is my room!"

Alexi slid his attention to the redhead. She gulped, grabbed a robe, and fled.

He made no move to rise, just sipped his drink, then set the glass on the flat plane of his belly. A droplet of water rolled onto his skin, leaving a glistening trail along the curve of his waist. "You see something you would like, *ma chere?*"

He dropped the accent, but his return to foreign endearments reminded Cat exactly what type of man Alexi was. She yanked her gaze from his stomach and cleared her throat. "We need to talk."

He sat up, the movement languid yet quick, the uncoiling of an annoyed snake, prepared to strike but too warmed by the sun to actually bother. "Have you at last given up searching for your outlaw needle in the midst of the great American haystack?"

"No."

As Alexi stood, then moved past her. Cat caught a hint of his scent. No matter how far they traveled, no matter the mud or the heat or the filth, Alexi always managed to smell as if he'd just danced in a rainstorm.

Glass clinked as he poured another drink. The shade of the liquid hinted at brandy, but it could be anything. Alexi drank whatever could be had for free.

"Why do you insist on spending your life on the back of a horse, dressed like a peasant boy when, with very little effort, you could be one of the wealthiest women west of the Mississippi? No." He lifted his glass to the ceiling. "In the entire country."

"Don't bother," Cat said. "I'm not coming back."

Alexi considered her as he sipped, his throat flexing, then releasing as he swallowed. "Even if I can give you what you've been searching years to find?"

Her skin prickled, and she said again what she seemed to say a lot whenever she came near Alexi Romanov. "Say what you mean."

"Why do you think I came to Abilene?"

"Because you regretted selling me out?"

He lifted a set of dark, slim eyebrows. "You know I never waste time with regrets."

Did that mean he'd sold her out or didn't it?

"I sold nothing to no one. Least of all a woman I'd prefer in my—" He paused at her sharp glance, and the corner of his mouth quirked. "Life. If you were dead, whatever would I do?"

"The same thing you've been doing since I left," Cat said, thoughts on the redhead who'd recently fled the room.

"Nothing could entice me to hurt you."

Cat didn't believe him. For a price, Alexi would do anything.

He sighed, obviously reading her eyes, her face, her mind. "I came to you because there's a bounty."

Now they were getting somewhere. "On who and how much?"

"On you, *Liebchen*. For more money than even I can count."

"Me?" Cat laughed, but the sound held no humor. When did it anymore? "What did I do?"

"I told you in Abilene. You've become a legend."

"Half of those stories aren't even about me."

"It doesn't matter. Someone wants you dead. Or at least unavailable."

"I haven't broken the law." *Not really.* "No one's going to pay a huge bounty on me."

"The law has nothing to do with it." He took a deep breath, letting it out slowly. "I misspoke. Not a bounty per se. More of an . . . incentive."

"To kill me?"

"The bounty is dead or alive. But you know what happens in those cases."

Most bounty hunters, when given the choice, chose dead. Less trouble that way.

"You need to ask yourself, *mi corazon,* who might wish to see you in the grave?"

Cat considered and came to the disturbing conclusion that a better question might be, *Who didn't?*

CHAPTER 4

*A*s usual, Alexi could divine none of Cat's thoughts from her expression. She'd learned from him well. Too well, he often thought, when he had occasion to think of such things. Perhaps she would have been better served to scream and cry for all she had lost. Maybe then she wouldn't have become this.

But Alexi didn't believe crying changed anything, and raving against death . . . What good did that do?

When she'd come to him and asked that he teach her all that he knew, Alexi had believed Cat merely wanted to get away from her past. Didn't everyone? He'd never suspected what she was really up to.

The creation of Cat O'Banyon. Would he have refused to help if he'd guessed the truth?

Alexi released a short, amused puff of air. There'd never been any question of leaving her behind. From the first instant he'd seen her, he'd yearned.

Standing in the rain, which traced like tears down her agonizingly pale face, the pain she had not yet learned to conceal stark in her brilliant green eyes. He'd wanted to make that pain go away, and he'd gone about it the only way he knew how.

Alexi shook off the memory. "*Mo chridhe,* is the list so very long?"

She glanced up. He was captured anew by her eyes—no longer sad, no longer *anything* thanks to him—which were still brilliant green and so lovely. One day, he vowed, those eyes would again reveal her soul.

"I can think of quite a few." Her lips tightened. "But most of them are in jail or—"

"Dead. Thanks to you." *Which might be why.*

"No," Cat said as if he'd actually spoken. He really had taught her too well to read faces if she could read his. "Their loved ones are either outlaws themselves and too damn selfish to care about anyone else or regular folk who are horrified at what their flesh and blood has done. None of them are going to waste a cent on me."

Which left one other option. Alexi waited for her to catch up. It didn't take long.

"Oh," she whispered.

"Yes," he agreed.

"How wonderful."

Alexi blinked. "Pardon?"

"If he's nervous enough to put a price on my head, then I'm getting close."

Alexi smacked himself in the temple with the heel of his hand. "You'll be getting *dead* very soon."

"They'll have to catch me first."

"I caught you."

Cat scoffed. "I knew it was you."

"No, *vida mia.* You did not." Something flickered in her eyes— fear, doubt, anger; he'd never been certain with her—and he pressed on, hoping that maybe this time she'd listen. "Those men in Abilene were good. They followed me for thirty miles after I left you, and they nearly caught me."

Her brow creased. "Did you kill them?"

Alexi managed to cover his wince by taking a healthy swig of his watered-down wine. Then he gave her a bland look, and her mouth tightened.

"Foolish question. *You* never kill anyone."

He didn't. Not anymore.

"How did you get away?"

"They did not pay attention and . . . ." Alexi waved his hand.

"You were gone."

"*Oui.*" He drank again.

"Then we have no problem. They'll never find you here, and they won't find me anywhere."

Alexi's temper snapped, and he set the glass down on the dressing table too hard. It cracked up the side. At least it was empty. "You are not invisible. And it's a simple matter to bribe a lawman. The next time you bring in a bounty, Lord knows who might be waiting for you."

"I don't think—"

"You don't," he interrupted, "and you need to start. The truth may be hard to come by, yet every truth has a price."

She remained silent but only for a moment. "What do you suggest?"

"Travel with me." She opened her mouth to refuse—he could see it in her face—but he kept right on talking. "It's the best way to keep you safe."

She stiffened. "I don't need any help."

"Of course not, *cherie.* You have never needed anyone or anything."

Her eyes narrowed. She sensed the sarcasm even though his voice had held nothing of the kind. When it came to hiding things, Alexi was as good as she was.

"You cannot continue the way you have been," he said softly. "Not until this threat is past."

Cat bit her lip. He was right. But would she admit it?

"If I hide," she said, "I'll never find him."

That scenario would be quite all right with Alexi. "Isn't it better to confront this fellow on your own terms, with the upper hand, rather than allow him, or those he's hired, to back you into a corner?"

"No one backs me into a corner."

Alexi lifted his eyebrows. He had.

She looked away, the slight flush across her cheeks telling him that she remembered. "I assume you have a plan."

"I could send Mikhail—"

"No!" Her frantic gaze met his; her hands clenched and unclenched. "*I* have to kill him. *Me.* No one else."

"Does it really matter who kills him, *il mio cuore*, as long as he's dead?"

"It does. Promise me you won't send Mikhail."

Promises, for Alexi, often begged to be broken, so he shrugged. "As you wish."

She stared at him. Would she leave right now, refusing his protection and help? It wouldn't be the first time.

Then her shoulders slumped, her hands unfurled, and she turned away. "The plan?"

"You will travel with me. We will make our way to Denver City." He had been there as a child; he knew the place well.

"Why Denver City?"

"Because that is where your dead-or-alive body must be delivered and where the incentive will be paid." He tapped his forehead. "We will be smart. No one will search for Cat O'Banyon in my wagons. No one who matters will pay us any mind. We will discover the identity of the one who wants you dead—"

"Then I'll kill him."

* * *

THE REDHEAD, whose name was Hazel, proved to be quite the shrew. When she returned and discovered Alexi in the process of leaving—even though he'd promised to take her along—she threw a screaming, stomping, cursing fit.

"Take her," Cat said. He was going to need a bed-mate and it wasn't going to be Cat. Just because she had been once didn't mean she would be again. She didn't think she could be. Alexi was too—

Cat broke off the thought before it could form—complete with imagery—in her head. Alexi was a lot of things, most of them *too* something. She didn't need to get specific, even with herself.

Cat watched the argument in amusement until Hazel snatched up Alexi's empty glass and threw it at Cat's head.

"I'll meet you at the wagon." She left Alexi to tell Hazel she would not be joining them.

Alexi didn't care for theatrics. Unless they were his own.

* * *

THE MISSISSIPPI RIVER, dotted with barges and boats of all shapes and sizes, flowed briskly beneath the moon. Alexi's wagon had not only been moved but also refashioned into a plain covered wagon once more. No one who had seen it earlier would recognize it now as the count's conveyance.

Cat approached warily. She knew better than to sneak up on—

"Miss Cathy." The low, slow voice came out of the darkness an instant before he did.

"Mikhail." Alexi's right hand. She'd heard them refer to each other as brothers. She'd never been sure if they were truly of the same blood or merely lifelong friends. Alexi's explanation of the relationship changed with the direction of the wind. According to Mikhail they'd been together since childhood.

Cat had her doubts that Alexi had ever been a child.

Mikhail, on the other hand, was a little boy in a giant's body.

He could break thick tree limbs in two as easily as he broke legs; he could crush a head with as little effort as he crushed an egg. Whatever task Alexi asked of him, Mikhail performed.

"How have you been?" Cat asked.

"I missed you when you went away."

People weren't nice to Mikhail, something Cat had never understood. Why would you poke a stick at a man of his size? Unless you wanted to die.

But Mikhail had a calm disposition; in truth, he never lost his temper, which to Cat only made the violence he committed in Alexi's name more frightening.

"I missed you too. But I had to go."

Mikhail's clear gray eyes met hers. "Why?"

She had never told him about her past; she'd never really told anyone. Not everything.

"There are bad men. I catch them . . ." *Or kill them.* "So they don't hurt anyone else."

"Oh." He nodded. "I remember."

Unease trickled down Cat's back. "What do you remember?"

"Some folks gotta be punished. You and I are the same."

Cat opened her mouth to deny this, then snapped it closed. Justice was justice, especially out here. Just because Cat brought the bad men to meet a fate decided by a court—unless, of course, they forced her to decide their fate herself—and Mikhail meted out justice decided by Alexi didn't mean she was right and he was wrong. Sure, Alexi was playing God, but then . . . Wasn't she?

Cat removed what remained of Clyde's bounty from her pocket and handed it to Mikhail. "Can you fetch me a wagon of my own and some horses?"

Mikhail frowned. "He won't like it none."

"There isn't room for all of us, Mikhail." There was. The three of them had ridden in it before and managed. Back then Mikhail had slept under the stars while she and Alexi had . . .

Well, she and Alexi weren't going to anymore, so Cat required her own conveyance.

"It's good cover," she said. "No one will be looking for two wagons."

Mikhail gave her a glance that very clearly said: *No one had better be looking for us at all.* But he went.

Mikhail still saw Cat as Alexi's woman. He probably always would. Which meant he'd do what she asked. As long as Alexi didn't tell him not to. And by the time Mikhail returned with the wagon—which she had no doubt he could find despite the hour; Mikhail could find anything—it would be far too late for Alexi to tell him not to.

She was somewhat surprised that Alexi didn't arrive before Mikhail. How long could it take to extricate oneself from a woman? Apparently a lot longer than Cat thought because she was making her bed inside the new wagon when he asked, "What is this?"

He was furious.

Cat wasn't scared of Alexi—he'd never given her reason to be —but she didn't like it when he was angry. He was unpredictable enough when he wasn't.

There was always something in Alexi's voice that made folks wonder: Would he kiss you or kill you? Would you see it coming or would it be a complete surprise? Would it hurt or would you like it? Would it happen at midnight or perhaps with the dawn?

The scent of danger rose from him like smoke from a fire. With a word or a glance or a lift of one eyebrow, he could compel anyone to believe anything, even that he might shoot you. Quite a feat for a man she'd never once seen draw his gun on another.

"Why did you waste your money? You could have ridden with me."

"I've ridden you enough."

Silence descended, followed by a short bark of laughter, and the tension that had crept over her disappeared. There was nothing she couldn't say to him. Which was not only liberating but disturbing.

"We'll roll out at noon," he said.

"Why not daybreak?"

Alexi swept his arm toward the east. "It's nearly daybreak now, *mi dulce*. I need sleep."

Easy for him to say. Whenever Alexi closed his eyes, he saw dancing girls, money, brandy, the next city, the next dodge, the next woman.

When Cat closed her eyes . . .

Well, she certainly didn't see dancing girls.

"Fine. Noon. Go away."

He went. Alexi had no need to remain where he wasn't wanted. There were plenty of places where he was.

Cat fell asleep quickly; as expected, the dancing girls did not await. Instead, there was Billy.

They met at a church picnic back home in Georgia. Cathleen was sixteen, Billy eighteen. Just one look and they knew there would never be anyone else in the world for them but each other.

Her parents—Henry and Fiona Cartwright—had their doubts. The Chase family was English, the Cartwrights, Irish. Though the New World was supposed to soothe past hatreds, it hadn't. Still, Cathleen was adamant. She would have Billy or she would have no one.

Her parents, indulgent of their only, late-in-life child, worried about the war clouds roiling on the horizon. Who would take care of their daughter if they could not? So they relented.

Billy and Cathleen married in the spring. Billy marched off in his uniform long before the honeymoon ended. Her parents had been right to worry. Neither one survived the conflict.

Fiona died first of the bloody flux. Henry followed three weeks later of the same. Not long afterward, Sherman and his men stopped by. When they left, Cathleen wasn't any worse off than a thousand other women in the South. She had her land—scorched as it was—she had

Billy's. What she didn't have was money, food, horses, cattle, seeds, parents, or a husband.

Then Billy returned. The joy Cat felt upon seeing him walk down the lane was short-lived. He was thin and pale. He woke in the night screaming.

Billy knew how to farm. However, he couldn't produce money from nothing any more than she could. Then the letter arrived from his brother.

Ben had left home before the war. There'd been trouble with his father over the wrong friends, too much gambling. But he'd recently become a lawman in Kansas. According to him, the land was fine and a soldier could acquire the title to 160 acres just by living on it for a year. If they sold what they had in Georgia, they'd have enough money to get started in Kansas. So Billy and Cathleen packed up what was left, parted with everything they could, and headed for the setting sun.

Life got better. They had their own place. The promise of a future. Billy stopped screaming every night. He started talking more every day. They were working toward something together.

And then—

You or her?

The gunshot made Cat start up; the shriek remained trapped in her throat. She was in the wagon, outside St. Louis, not on a Kansas prairie.

Billy was still dead. Damn him.

Though the sun was up and the air around her already sultry with heat. Cat shivered. Knowing Mikhail rested lightly—nothing and no one got by him—had allowed her to fall asleep quickly after Alexi left. Unfortunately, not even Mikhail could ward off dreams. She was beginning to think nothing could.

Cat peered through the opening in the canvas and frowned at the obscenely large tent that hadn't been there the night before. Obviously, Alexi no longer retired to the wagon when he didn't have to.

Cat closed her eyes, but her mind whirled. As Alexi wouldn't wake for hours, she threw on her boy's disguise, set her finger to her lips when Mikhail's head peeked from Alexi's wagon as she clambered from her own, then began to walk.

Though the hour was early for those who made their livings in the dark, the rest of St. Louis had begun to stir. Shopkeepers swept the dust from their doorways, nodding when Cat tugged on the brim of her hat. Carriages and wagons rumbled; in the distance beat the steady pulse of a train.

She headed for a bakeshop owned by a war widow of her acquaintance who would be happy to sell Cat the first hot loaf from her ovens along with a cup of the best coffee north of Louisiana.

As she turned into an alley, planning to make her way between one street and the next, Cat stopped. The narrow passage wasn't empty. A man bent over a scantily dressed woman, face buried in her décolleté. One hand captured her at the waist; the other was busy lifting her skirts.

Not wanting to interrupt. Cat inched backward. Then the woman made a soft sound—not of pleasure, not even of encouragement—and Cat paused.

A closer look revealed the woman's struggles. Pinned against several old barrels, there was nowhere for her to go. She could have screamed for help; she could have bit and scratched. But from the bright, tight nature of her attire—which Cat had worn often enough herself to recognize—she was a working girl, and no one would believe she didn't have this coming.

Cat cleared her throat. The girl lifted her head; their eyes met, the younger woman's widening first with shock, then with hope. Cat considered drawing her gun, but she didn't want the audience a gunshot would bring. Instead she retrieved her knife from the long, thin pocket she'd sewn into the right leg of her trousers.

The man kept rooting at the girl's bosom like a starving piglet even as his fingers crept ever upward beneath the skirts.

"Hey, mister." Cat tilted the Arkansas toothpick so the sun flashed off the surface, making it appear shiny and new.

He lifted his mouth from the woman's skin long enough to growl, "Go 'way."

"No."

That got his attention. He began to turn. Too fast—nothing good ever came of that. So Cat kicked him in the knee. He went down, the gun he'd been reaching for flying beneath a pile of Lord knows what as he sprawled. The girl scooted behind Cat.

"What the hell, boy!" The man rolled around like a turtle flipped onto his shell, his belly so big he appeared grotesquely with child.

"I don't think the lady welcomed your attention." Cat glanced at the girl. "Am I right?"

She nodded, the frantic movement causing her blond curls to bob wildly. She was a lot younger than Cat had first thought; they always were.

"I was going back to Sally's. He grabbed me and—" Her voice faltered.

"She's a whore." The fellow managed to twist from his back to his knees, wincing as he got to his feet. "What's the difference?"

"Consent," Cat snapped. "You know what that means?" From the crease in his brow, he didn't. "She agrees, you pay her. It's a business arrangement. Forcing her in an alley . . . They call that rape."

"But she's a whore," he repeated.

He'd never understand, and most lawmen wouldn't either. There was no point hauling his ass into jail. Not that she'd planned to. Alexi had his rules and Cat . . . well. Cat had hers.

She pressed the long, sharp blade to the soft, fleshy corner of the man's neck. "Say *you or her?*"

"Wh-what?"

"Say it!" A thin trickle of blood trailed over a roll of fat. "You. Or. Her."

"Y-y-you or her?"

Cat couldn't be sure, not with the stutter and the high-pitched wail of fear in his voice, but she doubted this was her quarry. He might be able to force a woman he thought no one would defend, but to ride about practicing murderous outlawry . . .

He was too gutless for that.

"Wait a minute " he began, and Cat thumped the butt of her knife into his temple. He crumpled to the scum-strewn ground. She glanced at the girl, hoping she wouldn't start to scream. Instead she stared at Cat with speculation.

"You can kick him if you want," Cat said. "Sometimes it helps."

"You're Cat O'Banyon."

"No, ma'am."

The young woman shrugged. "Have it your way, but you'd best be goin'. There's a bounty on you."

Word certainly did get around fast.

"Everyone's talkin' about it. Reward's so big even farmer folk are thinkin' to hunt you down. You need to disappear."

Cat brushed the brim of her hat and backed toward the street again. "Obliged."

"*I'm* obliged." Then the girl hauled back and kicked the unconscious man in the ass before lifting her chin, turning on her heel, and vanishing into the steadily increasing crowd in the other direction.

As soon as she was gone. Cat took a roundabout path to the river. She did not need anyone seeing a "boy" emerge from the alley and head directly for the Mississippi. The fool on the ground would eventually wake and raise the alarm. She probably should have slit his throat and been done with it, but she hadn't stooped to cold-blooded murder yet and she wasn't going to start now. If she was lucky, by the time the man woke up, they'd be too far away to bother with.

a half hour later, Cat reached Alexi's tent, which was large enough to serve as a Rebel hospital. Mikhail stood outside.

"Hitch the horses," Cat said, and he moved off without argument.

Cat drew aside the flap and ducked in. Alexi was sprawled on a feather tick, one arm around a blonde and another around a brunette. The women were naked and fast asleep.

Alexi lay naked and wide-awake. "Care to join us?"

"We need to be on the road."

His lips flattened. "What did you do?"

"Now, Alexi."

He came to his feet, tumbling the blonde onto the ground and the brunette into the dip where his body had been. Both awoke with a jolt and a gasp.

"Leave." He flicked one hand as if shooing a fly.

The girls were obviously familiar with Alexi because they snatched their scattered clothes and fled.

"Should we expect a posse or merely the sheriff?"

"Hard to say." Depended on whom she'd knocked out—citizen or visitor—and what kind of friends he had.

"I need to know, *cara*," Alexi said softly.

Cat quickly told him what had happened.

Alexi didn't say she shouldn't have gotten involved. He knew she couldn't turn away. He also knew she'd been right.

Alexi might have more bed partners than hairs on his head, but they were always willing. He would consider it a terrible breach of his principles to take what wasn't given freely. Women offered their bodies; men offered coins, horses, jewels. After a few hours, sometimes even moments, with Alexi, they just couldn't help themselves.

Alexi struck the tent—folding it over and over, then shoving it onto the floor of the wagon and placing the feather tick that had been his bed on top. Mikhail hitched the horses, the two of them performing their tasks so smoothly it was obvious they'd done so many times before. In less than an hour they left St. Louis.

They traveled five miles that day without incident, setting up camp near a thin stream of creek as the sun set. Cat was exhausted, but camp had to be made, horses watered, fed, and hobbled, fires started, food prepared.

She'd just sat down with a plate of rice and ham, along with the coffee she'd wanted so badly that morning, when Alexi strode up. The tent rose behind him, a white cloud against the ebony night. The dancing flames of her fire threw shadows across his face, making the fine bones even more pronounced.

His dark blue eyes swept over her. "You have to change."

"Don't you like me just the way I am?"

"No time, *querida*." Reaching down, he hauled her up by the arm. "They're here."

Cat didn't bother to ask how he knew. Alexi always knew, because Mikhail, whose large ears seemed to hear better than anyone else's, always told him.

She still wore her boy's clothes. Driving a wagon in a skirt was a mistake, but she should have thought ahead, realized that dressing like this—a woman in pants—was an even bigger one after the events of that morning.

She shoved her plate and cup at Alexi. He nearly dropped them, sloshing coffee over his hand and dumping the plate onto the ground. He cursed, several languages all mixed together so that they sounded so pretty, then called after her, "Costume, *bebe*. You know what to do."

Cat stripped out of her boy's clothes and shoved those at Alexi too. He'd dispose of the evidence, probably in her own fire. Then, wearing only her underthings, she ran to the tent and ducked inside. Not an instant too soon. Seconds later the steady beat of horses' hooves drifted on the night and someone hailed the camp.

Cat's gaze swept the interior, lighting on the valise where she'd once stored her costumes sitting atop Alexi's bed. She couldn't believe he'd kept it for over a year. She tore through, pulling out a brightly colored skirt with many flounces that ended well above the ankle. Cat found an equally bright blouse that dipped low enough to distract just about anyone.

Add large Gypsy earrings that would sparkle and twirl and capture every gaze, then scrub some water through her hair until it appeared tousled by lustful hands and slap on a bit of makeup to darken the skin. Her light green eyes were a problem. But if she kept them cast down and let her hair fall over them, maybe in the dusky light—only one lantern burned within the tent—they'd mistake her for someone Alexi had picked up south of the Rio Grande.

Thanks to him, her Spanish was quite good, and what she didn't know, she'd invent. She doubted anyone in a Missouri posse would notice.

"Everyone out of the wagons and tent!" The man sounded like he meant business. Whoever the fool in the alley had been, he seemed to have good friends indeed.

Cat peered into a hand mirror. The woman gazing back

smiled seductively. She shoved her blouse off one shoulder, tugged the waist of the skirt higher to reveal more of her calf. She just might do.

"Exactly who are you searching *for*, gentlemen?" Alexi sounded half asleep, as if he could care less who invaded his camp or rifled his property.

"Cat O'Banyon."

Cat recognized the voice. Obviously she hadn't hit the man in the alley hard enough.

Alexi began to laugh. "The bounty hunter? Why would he be here?"

"Word is that O'Banyon's a woman who likes to dress as a boy."

"You think a woman could get the drop on all those desperate characters?" Alexi's voice dripped with scorn. "I heard that in Abilene three men caught Cat O'Banyon red-handed, chased *him* for thirty miles. Although . . ."

He drew the word out, and even Cat, who knew Alexi's tricks, found herself leaning forward in expectation of what he might say next.

"The man is quite clever. What better way to throw everyone off the trail than to pretend to be a woman?"

Silence descended. Cat held her breath, hoping that Alexi's talent at lies had saved them again. She should never have made the idiot in the alley say the words. That must have been what gave her away. But she hadn't been able to help herself.

"Doesn't matter," the leader said at last. "Even if the woman we want ain't O'Banyon, she assaulted a citizen. We gotta take her in."

"Why would you think she's here?" Alexi asked.

"Folks along the river said you left in an awful hurry."

"Is that a crime?"

"In my experience, a quick exit usually means something's fishy."

"I assure you we've done nothing wrong." Alexi's voice held just the right amount of sincerity and outrage. He was so damn good at this.

"Then you won't mind if we look around."

"Be my guest." The statement was followed by clangs and thumps as they searched the wagons. They wouldn't find any elixir; Mikhail always sold every last bottle before leaving, which made it easier to deny ever selling it in the first place.

A short while later, the tent flap parted and several big, rough, dusty men strode in. The leader was easily distinguishable by the big tin star on his burly chest, the man in the alley equally recognizable by both the huge knot on his forehead and the sway of his enormous belly.

Cat had been peering into the hand mirror so she could see them enter without staring at the doorway as if she were expecting them. When they crowded into the tent, she spun, gibbering Spanish, berating them for invading her domicile, demanding to know who they were, calling them every name and every curse word she remembered.

None of them paid any attention to her words, her face, or anything else but the slow slide of the brightly colored material as it cascaded downward, catching on the swell of one breast.

Cat stroked her collarbone, making everyone who watched wonder how her skin would feel right there, stretched taut over such a fragile bone. While they considered that, she used the other, unwatched hand, to tug on the hem of the blouse so that the neckline dipped low enough to tantalize. Perhaps they might catch a hint of nipple if the garment would only slip just . . . a . . . bit . . . more.

Every man in the place, except Alexi, who'd already seen this show, held his breath and prayed.

Cat sauntered across the room, chattering in *espanol*. Speaking it brought back memories of the sudden spring snowstorm in South Dakota, the deserted cabin with more holes in the walls than boards. They'd huddled around a fire, and to pass the time Alexi had shared every word and phrase that he knew.

She was very good at learning languages, and she made up for her lack of vocabulary with a flair for invention, adding a few words that sounded like Spanish but weren't anything.

Her skirt twirled, revealing more leg than was proper. Her feet were bare; she'd tied a piece of red string around one ankle. Several of the men couldn't take their eyes off it.

Another thing Alexi had taught her—some men liked legs, some breasts, so it was best to give everyone a peek at everything. If they were to survive, people such as Alexi—and Cat—needed to use each gift they'd been given.

Though few could drag their eyes above her neck, she'd let her hair fall over her too-light-for-a-Mexican-peasant eyes, and she kept her distance from the fat man with the knot on his head.

Cat glanced at Alexi, gibbered louder, waved her hands, which served the dual purpose of distracting attention from her face even more and making her breasts jiggle enticingly beneath the thin cotton blouse.

One of the men choked; another muttered, "Holy hell."

Alexi managed, just barely, not to smile.

The lawman shook his head hard and dragged his gaze from Cat's chest. "Why didn't you come out when we called?"

Alexi pushed his way through the crowd until he stood at Cat's side. "I'm afraid she doesn't speak English."

"None?" The leader of the posse sounded skeptical.

Alexi grabbed Cat by one wrist and yanked her close. "No need." He ran his palm across her bare shoulder.

Cat shivered. Good Lord, those hands.

Alexi brushed his thumb along the soft skin at the crook of her elbow, and Cat planted that elbow in his stomach. She proceeded to give him a piece of her furious Spanish mind. If they weren't careful, she'd end up in jail or worse.

Alexi, who had turned his back to the others, rolled his eyes and smirked, but he let her rant on. They both understood that the more Spanish she spoke, the less Cat O'Banyon she appeared.

"What's she sayin'?" whispered a heretofore silent man. Considering his high-pitched voice, Cat understood his reticence to speak.

"How should I know?" the lawman asked. "This is Missouri, not Texas."

Alexi winked at Cat, then turned. "I doubt very much you'd want to hear the translation."

The leader's gaze narrowed. "I say we do."

Alexi shrugged. "She says you are the sons of swine to barge into a lady's tent. She believes your mothers were . . ." Pausing, he tilted his head. "Well, I should not repeat that in the presence of a lady."

"*She* said it," one of the others pointed out.

"Nevertheless," Alexi continued. "Something about how you will die. Blood, sweat, pain, your intestines in a fire." He waved one hand. "It all blends together after a while."

The men shuffled and murmured.

Cat was certain she heard one of them say, "Witch," and she tensed. Being accused of witchcraft didn't happen often these days, but it happened. And it always ended badly.

For the witch.

"What good is she if she can't speak English?" the lawman asked.

"Ah, but gentlemen." Alexi glided in behind her, then dipped one hand down the front of Cat's blouse, boldly cupping a breast and thumbing the nipple until it peaked and drew every eye, every thought, in the room. "She is so very good at everything else."

Cat gritted her teeth and waited for the men to leave. Unfortunately, Alexi was giving them a performance for free that they couldn't find outside a raree-show for several dollars.

He kept his hand down her shirt, palm around her breast,

thumb just brushing the nipple. She wanted both to elbow him again and to lean back against his shoulder and sigh. It had been so long.

However, it hadn't been long enough that she could overlook an audience.

"*Detener,*" she said.

Alexi put his mouth to her ear, as if he were nuzzling her. "Patience, *Chiquita.*" He licked the lobe.

The moan that escaped her was low and full of promise. A couple of the men watching answered in kind.

Alexi lifted his head, but he kept his hand right where it was. "Pardon me. I had forgotten you were there."

Cat couldn't see his smile, but she heard it in his voice. Felt it in his—

He pulled her more firmly against him. Yes. He was definitely smiling with more than his mouth.

"You will understand if I ask my associate to show you out."

Cat risked a quick glance through the curtain of her hair. Mikhail stood in the opening, and she hadn't even heard him arrive.

"Hold on, now," the lawman began, and turned. When he had to lift his head, then lift it some more, for his gaze to reach Mikhail's, the remainder of what he'd been about to say faded to a gurgle.

Everyone else appeared frozen, staring as well. Obviously none of them had seen Alexi's show or purchased his elixir. Which was probably for the best.

Mikhail cracked his knuckles—the sound like gunfire in the sudden silence—then swept aside the tent flap.

The posse filed out, though each one could not resist throwing a final glance over his shoulder. Perhaps to make sure the big man was not going to break their necks as soon as they turned their backs. Or, more likely, to discover if Alexi would be unable to wait until they were gone to toss her onto the mattress, throw up her skirt, and—

He pulled his hand free of her shirt, and Cat had to stop herself from snatching it back. She spun, clapping a palm to either side of Alexi's head, narrowly missing the boxing of his ears—she was out of practice at the art of grabbing a man with anything other than violence—and yanked his mouth to hers.

One of Alexi's first rules: If you give an audience what they want, they don't look beneath the surface for the how or the why or the what. Therefore, Cat hoped if she gave the posse what they wanted now—a peek at what they thought would be happening later—they could quit dragging their feet and *vete!*—

Go!

She also wanted them to leave with the picture of Alexi and his Mexican peasant woman foremost in their mind. They would imagine what occurred after the lowering of the curtain—or in this case the tent flap—and they would forget about Cat O'Banyon. If not forever, at least for the time it would take the three of them to disappear. However, as Alexi's lips touched hers, Cat was the one who forgot things. Or perhaps she merely remembered.

The taste of his tongue—iced whiskey, maybe wine. Its texture worn satin—smooth, familiar—both comfortable and infinitely exotic. Her hands gentled, her fingers sliding into his hair, one lock curling about the base of her thumb, then fluttering against her wrist, causing gooseflesh to race up her arms, across her chest, down her back.

His tongue withdrew, and she nipped his lip in case he was thinking of following it. Instead, he trailed kisses to her neck, her shoulder, the warmth of that clever mouth burning every last shiver away. He'd always known exactly what she needed. Alexi knew what everyone needed before they knew it themselves.

His lips brushed the tops of her breasts; his hands skated the backs of her legs, pausing when they encountered nothing but skin.

"You were short on Mexican peasant woman drawers," she murmured into his hair.

"Do Mexican peasant women wear drawers?" His breath casted along the damp trail left by his mouth.

"You would know."

"Perhaps."

Her lips curved against the top of his head like a caress. Typical Alexi, to agree but never to answer. She thought back on the times she'd asked him questions about himself. Had he ever told her anything worth knowing?

His tongue slipped beneath the bodice of the blouse, sliding over a nipple, and for just an instant her mind went blank.

She fought her way free. She could not afford to let her body cloud her thoughts. Better if Alexi's body clouded his. Best to keep him off balance.

It was the only way to remain in control.

CHAPTER 6

"They're gone." Cat stepped free of his arms, and Alexi nearly grabbed her hand and yanked her back.

However, he'd learned the hard way that grabbing and yanking Cat led to bruises, cuts, and black eyes. The only time she permitted such behavior was when they were in the middle of a "show." The only time she permitted a lot of these things was when they were pretending.

He couldn't believe he'd become so involved in the ruse that he'd forgotten the danger, their audience, himself. But when she'd pressed her lips to his hair as he'd tasted her, he'd actually started to think this was real. He, who should always know better.

Alexi counted to ten in Russian and willed his erection to wither. It didn't take long. All he had to do was look at Cat and remember how she'd said, *They're gone,* then walked away. As if she'd been covertly watching the posse the entire time and not paying attention to Alexi in the least.

She pulled the peasant blouse over her head and shoved it into the case without seeming to care that she'd just bared herself to him as if he were her ancient, half-blind grandmother.

"Hell," Cat muttered.

"Problem?" he asked, thrilled when his voice came out sounding as bored as she'd just appeared.

She cast him a quick, irritated glance. *Good.* Why should only one of them want to punch something?

"What did you do with my clothes?"

"Tossed them into the flames."

"Thought so."

She shifted and every movement made her breasts shake, causing the erection he'd just tamed to whisper. When she presented him with her back, the ripples of muscle beneath skin caused it to snarl.

"Here." He rooted through the case, then tossed the costume he'd worn in Abilene in her direction.

The clothes fell across her bare feet. She bent, her hair nearly touching the ground, then sliding up her body, the ends caressing her nipples as he had.

Alexi moved to the decanter of wine and poured himself more than usual, drank it, then poured more than usual again. Why was she undressing in front of him as if he were a relative and not her . . . what? He'd once been her lover.

No. Alexi sipped from the glass, staring at the canvas in front of him and trying to ignore the rustles of cloth and the scent of her that drifted from the other side of the room. Love had had nothing to do with it. He'd been her teacher, her partner, her savior. But the only man she would ever love was dead.

Alexi knew very little about Cat's past. She revealed as much of herself to others as he did. Of course, he was adept at reading people, at taking each word or one tiny, accidental phrase and piecing them into something more.

He still didn't know much. Both her names. That she had loved and lost. That she would have her vengeance. Or die trying.

They worked well together. Neither one of them had any problem taking what was freely offered and moving on. They were easily able to slip into the skin of others. Probably because their own skin was not something they enjoyed wearing for long. However, because Alexi had been too close to dying too many times, he had decided that all he wanted was to live. Apparently, Cat's dance with death had made her long for it.

He turned. The sight of her wearing his pants and his hat, feet still bare and impossibly white against the dirt floor of the tent, with his shirt hanging open to reveal the creamy weight of her breasts made every curse word he'd learned in a dozen different languages flutter through his head.

She lifted a length of moss-green cloth. He vaguely recalled buying it for some woman—what had been her name?—then tossing it into a bag when he had to leave town in a hurry without ever seeing her again.

"May I use this?"

He nodded, unable to speak as she took off the shirt, then wrapped the material around and around her breasts, crushing them, hiding them from both him and the world.

Alexi lifted his glass and drained what was left.

"Boots." She stared at her dust-covered toes. "You didn't burn those, did you?"

"Of course not." Boots were expensive and hard to come by. Besides . . . she could roll up the cuffs of his pants, use a rope around the waist, cover the billowing shirt with an equally billowing coat, but his boots would fall right off her feet.

"I'm not going to sleep with you, Alexi."

His lifted his gaze from her breasts, or where her breasts lay flattened beneath the shirt and the green cotton and allowed his lips to curve in mockery. "No?"

Cat cursed. She knew him so well. By saying that, she'd only made certain he'd stop at nothing until she did.

"No," she said firmly.

He nodded, considering the decanter of wine, turning the glass in his hand and wondering how it had gotten so empty.

"Did something happen after I left?"

The concern in her voice made him set down the glass. "My heart broke, *mon ami.*"

"You don't have a heart."

He placed a palm against his chest. "You wound me."

"Your heart's on the other side."

He dropped his hand. "You left, and we moved on. Now you are back, and we must do the same."

Mikhail loomed in the doorway. Cat, obviously not hearing his approach, started. Despite his size, very few heard Mikhail coming before he was already there.

"Gotta pack the tent," Mikhail said.

"Everything else is ready?"

Mikhail nodded.

"The posse?"

"Gone."

Talking with Mikhail could give anyone a headache. He answered only the question that was posed and nothing more. A good habit, in truth, less trouble that way. But it could be maddening.

"Gone where?"

"Away."

Alexi rubbed his forehead, and Cat stepped in. "They didn't ride off, then follow their back trail, did they?"

Understanding spread over the big man's face like the sun spreading over the earth at dawn. "No, Miss Cathy. They were tryin' to figger out how you . . . I mean, she . . . I mean—" His mouth kept working, but no more words came out.

"I understand. They believed our charade."

Alexi snorted. *Who wouldn't?* He'd once pretended to be an eighty-year-old Frenchwoman, and everyone had offered their seats and called him *Madame.* Cat was almost that good. She was definitely accomplished enough to fool the posse.

"They did. I followed 'em a piece and listened. They kept a-goin'. Ain't gonna sneak up on us and make me—" He stopped, clamping his lips together before glancing at Alexi.

"Bring Cat's boots. I tossed them into her wagon."

Mikhail disappeared much faster than a man of his size should have been able to.

"Why do you make him?" Cat asked.

"*They* make him."

"The only person who can convince Mikhail to do something is you."

"You're mistaken."

"You don't tell Mikhail who to get rid of and how?"

"Why would I?"

Cat gave a muffled half shriek, half gurgle and pulled on her hair as if she would go mad.

Alexi stifled a smirk. He could be as annoying as Mikhail when he wanted to be.

"Why don't you do your own dirty work?" Cat asked.

Alexi's smile faded. "If I could, *mio dolce,* I would."

He walked out of the tent as memories of the dirty work that had once been his specialty flickered.

The report of a gun made him flinch. But the sound was only in his mind; it probably always would be.

Mikhail approached with Cat's boots and held them out. Alexi shook his head. He wasn't going back in.

"I'll meet you in Brooks." A town so close to the Missouri/Kansas border Alexi wasn't sure to which state it belonged.

They had passed through not long ago, and Alexi had thought it would be a good place to perform a particular dodge. Right now, he really needed one. Only when he was pretending to be someone else could Alexi forget who he had been.

"Brooks." Mikhail's face brightened. "I remember."

"Good." Alexi mounted his horse, saddled and waiting as promised, and galloped from camp.

* * *

When the thunder of hooves rose from outside. Cat cursed and bolted for the exit. She emerged just in time to watch the dust kicked up by the horse fade away on the evening wind.

"Where's he going?"

"We'll catch up." Mikhail patted her with a huge yet gentle hand. "I can follow a field mouse 'cross the prairie in a cyclone. Even Alexi can't get away from me."

Cat considered climbing into her wagon and striking out on her own. But that would mean leaving Mikhail alone. She wasn't sure she could do that. And Alexi—damn him—knew it.

"Here's your boots. I cleaned 'em." Mikhail's face crumpled. "But they wouldn't shine up nohow."

She accepted the footwear. "The shine went out of these long ago, Mikhail."

The shine had gone out of a lot of things a long time ago.

Cat shoved her feet into the boots, then crossed to the wagon, but her horses weren't in the traces. Instead, they stood saddled and packed a few feet away.

"What's going on?" she asked just as Mikhail pulled the center pole of the tent. The canvas descended through the night like the wings of a great white bird.

Mikhail stepped free an instant before he would have been trapped beneath, then began to yank up the stakes.

Cat followed, collecting them. "We're leaving the wagons?"

"Have to. Alexi took a horse."

"You'd already saddled and packed them before he took one."

Mikhail grinned. "You're so smart, Miss Cathy."

Cat narrowed her eyes. Alexi had obviously told him to saddle the horses, leave the wagons, and tell her as little as possible. What was he up to?

"We can't travel with wagons now that the law knows about 'em." Mikhail handed her the last stake.

"You said the posse wasn't coming back."

"Not now." He began to fold the tent into smaller and smaller lengths. "But later . . ." He stood, lifting the thick canvas into his arms as if it were no heavier than the swaddled child it resembled. "Who knows? Might not be that posse who comes. Could be another from a town we can't hardly recall. You know Alexi."

She did. He changed modes of travel as often as he changed clothes. It was why he was still alive, free, and plying his trade. When people went looking for him, he was no longer the man they had seen.

"'Sides . . ." Mikhail strode toward the pack animal. "For the dodge we're gonna do next, we need to split up."

"Dodge?" She hurried after him. "What dodge?"

He secured the tent to the horse. "Alexi's doin' the advance."

"Advance." Cat got a very bad feeling.

Mikhail cast her an indulgent glance. "You ain't been gone that long that ye fergot, did ya?" He patted her hand. "'S okay. I kin explain. Alexi goes into town afore us. Finds out what we need to know so's we can do the dodge."

"I never agreed to that."

Confusion flickered in his gray eyes. "You said you'd travel with us."

"That's right. *Travel.* To Denver City."

"But . . . but . . . the dodge is what we do."

Cat tilted her head. "How long have you been doing it?"

"Long's I can recall."

"Just you and Alexi?"

"Well . . ." He blinked at her. "Sometimes we had you."

"Anyone else?"

Mikhail turned away, hunched his shoulders, and began to rub his head. "Mebe."

Cat had never heard this before. Of course, she'd never asked. Before, she'd just been trying to find a reason to keep breathing.

"How long have you known Alexi?"

"Long's I can recall," Mikhail repeated.

"Is his name really Alexi?"

"Sometimes."

Did it matter how long they'd known each other? Who they'd traveled with? Even what they'd done? All that mattered was that they could help her find *him*. If she had to run a few double crosses along the way, so be it. She'd done worse.

Two days later, Cat and Mikhail approached a midsized Western town.

She'd never been here before. She wasn't sure if that was good or bad. No one should recognize her—not that anyone ever had —but she was also walking in blind. One thing Alexi had been adamant about was reconnaissance. Always know the layout. Always have an escape route. Lack of preparation led to discovery. Or worse.

She was certain Alexi had a plan. According to Mikhail, the two of them had passed through before, and Alexi had told Mikhail the town would be perfect for one of their favorite performances. However, in this dodge she wouldn't hear the details until she was already there.

She didn't like it. But then Alexi hadn't asked her what she liked before he'd taken off in the night like—

Cat's lips tightened.

Like she had.

Cat flicked a glance at the sign posted on the outskirts of town. *Brooks, Missouri—Founded 1845* had been carved into the wooden plank.

Cat just wanted to ride hard for Denver City and finish what she'd started. That she was riding into Brooks, Missouri, on a Tuesday afternoon in July, made her mad as a hornet and ready to sting. However, any emotions but the ones necessary to her masquerade could get them caught.

Since Katriona Capezzi, the greatest medium in all of Italy, knew what would happen before it did, she had no reason for anger, for fear, for anything but calm. Cat enjoyed playing Katriona; she'd done it several times before.

Trust Alexi to pick a well-worn and familiar dodge to get Cat back in the game. What she wasn't quite sure of was why he wanted her back in.

She'd dressed for the part, donning the peasant skirt she'd worn for the posse, but instead of the low-necked blouse, she wore a black shirtwaist and a black hat with a veil. Signora Capezzi communed with the spirits while behind that veil. Only if she remained hidden from the eyes of the world would they continue to speak.

Alexi's idea—and a good one. The more mystery surrounding the signora, the better.

Cat entered town slowly at the busiest time of the day so everyone could scrutinize her, become curious, begin to talk among themselves. She would take a room at the hotel, and she would wait. If Alexi had done his job right—and when hadn't he? —telling his tale of the medium he'd seen in the last settlement, a woman who knew so much, who would tell them all about it . . . for a price, then people would come to her.

Cat rode through Brooks, but no one seemed to care. No one whispered. No one pointed. No one followed her. Instead, they all stared toward the east end of town.

Their behavior made Cat uneasy, but now that she was here, she had little choice but to follow the plan. So she sat in her room throughout the stifling afternoon, with Mikhail parked in the hall. He would inform every arrival that the signora was conversing with the spirits and would be unavailable for readings until the following day. This not only increased her prestige, but gave Alexi time to slip in and tell her everything he'd learned about everyone.

However, no one came to call. No men, no women, no children. No Alexi. Considering the way everyone had acted earlier, Cat shouldn't be surprised. But she was.

For the dozenth time over the long, hot afternoon. Cat opened the door. Mikhail's increasingly long countenance turned her way, and he shook his head.

"Something's wrong," she whispered from beneath the black veil. "You need to search for him."

"Can't, Miss Cath—"

Cat shushed him, and Mikhail flinched. She would have felt badly if she wasn't already so on edge she was dizzy with it.

"Signora." He bowed. "I won't leave you."

She crooked her finger, and he bent until his ear was next to her mouth. "You know who I really am, right?"

He nodded.

"No one's gonna sneak up on me. I'll be safe."

"That's right." He straightened. "'Cause I ain't leavin'."

"Fine. I'll just go mys—"

The dull, steady thud of a hammer against boards started up outside. Both Cat and Mikhail listened for a moment; then they crossed the room and peered out the window. At the end of the street, where the townsfolk's attention had been drawn earlier and where most of them appeared to have gathered now, several men were building something. The structure had not yet taken shape, but Cat knew.

"Gallows."

And this time, when Cat attempted to leave the room, Mikhail didn't try to stop her.

* * *

WHAT WERE the odds that Alexi would meet someone he knew in Brooks, Missouri? And that he would be recognizable to that someone when he did?

Alexi was very good with odds, and he thought they were quite high in his favor. Why else had he succeeded in avoiding a jail cell for this long?

The chances that someone Alexi had conned would appear in a town Alexi had never worked before while Alexi was wearing the same disguise he'd worn when they'd met the first time were so low he hadn't bothered to count them. Besides, he'd heard Pardy Langston had been hung in California around '67.

Alexi's gaze flicked to the overly thin man on the other side of the bars. Apparently he'd heard wrong.

Of course, the longer Alexi practiced his trade, the more towns he rode into, the more people he met, the more money he was given—

Alexi's head began to ache. Gently, he probed his nose. He thought it might be broken. And wouldn't that be just his luck? He'd survived a brutal childhood, then years on the road and hundreds of dodges, only to receive his first broken nose from a riverboat gambler—and a very bad one at that.

"He stole the life savings of a war widder in Tupelo," Pardy was saying. "Convinced her to bet everything on one single turn of the cards. Poor woman had no choice but to sell 'erself after that. She jumped into the river instead."

The town marshal cast a revolted glance in Alexi's direction. However, his disgust wasn't strong enough to keep him from asking: "What else?"

Pardy was happy to fill the lawman's ears with a litany of Alexi's crimes, most involving gambling of some sort. Because Alexi did not much care for games of chance, and Pardy did, Alexi began to suspect each offense the man recited, in truth, belonged on Pardy's dance card. Like the war widow.

The marshal gazed at Alexi consideringly. "What'd he have planned here?"

"Don't rightly know." Pardy's long, thin nose wrinkled. "When I found him, he was just talkin' to folks."

Pardy no longer dressed like a dandy; instead his clothes appeared quite frayed. Apparently, since Pardy had last come into contact with Alexi, things had not gone all that well.

"Now that I recollect, talkin' to folks is how he figgers out who's got enough money to steal. Natters their ear off until they can't help but tell him secrets he's got no bizness knowin'. Always did have the gift of gab, did Josiah Farmington from Chicago."

"That true?" The marshal lifted an eyebrow in Alexi's direction.

"N'sir," Alexi insisted. "Name's Jed Nelson, from down San Antone way. Me and the wife were thinkin' about movin' to yer town. Business is pitiful in Texas 'bout now."

"Ya seen that wife?" Pardy asked.

"Have not."

Pardy's bulbous lips curved, and his dark rat eyes bored into Alexi's. "Didn't think so."

Ironic that Alexi would hang for gambling when gambling was what he did the least. Gambling depended on luck, and in his opinion the lady was fickle. Unless she was dealing with him— then she was downright vicious. Luck had rarely been kind to Alexi Romanov.

From outside came the *thud-thud-thud* of hammers on wood.

Right now she was being an incredible bitch.

The practice of stringing up gamblers had been more popular several decades back. Most towns wanted to discourage the repeated fleecing of their citizens, and nothing did that like a good lynching. However, the old favorites had a way of *hanging* about.

Alexi stifled a spurt of laughter. If he wasn't careful, he might laugh himself to death on the way to the gallows.

Pardy's small eyes went smaller. "What's so funny?"

Alexi met his gaze. "Not one damn thing."

Despite the iron bars between them, Pardy took a step back.

"Got any proof that what you say is true?" the marshal asked.

Alexi switched his attention to the lawman. "Got any proof that what *he* says is?"

The marshal stared at the ceiling. "It's yer word against his, I know. Problem is . . ." He lowered his eyes, and Alexi knew, even before the man spoke, that nothing he could say would stop this. "Crafty cardsharp come through last month. Folks lost a lot of money. Someone's gotta pay for that." His gaze shifted to the growing gallows. "People are all het up for a hanging. We don't get much entertainment 'round here."

Alexi had never understood the frontier fondness for a necktie party. Those west of the Mississippi, and a few east as well, made a celebration of them—brought the family, packed a picnic. It was downright ghoulish.

He spared a moment to be grateful that Pardy hadn't mentioned Mikhail. Which must mean he and Cat hadn't yet appeared. Once Mikhail entered a town, he was fairly difficult to miss.

"Let's get this over with," Alexi said.

"What's your hurry, Farmington?" Pardy asked.

"I'm not Farmington."

"We'll get to it." The marshal peered with infuriating serenity through the open doorway. "Soon as the gallows are done."

Hell.

Alexi needed to speed this up, make sure his show was over before Cat and Mikhail arrived to begin theirs. There wasn't a thing they could do to help him now and—

"Sweetheart!"

A woman stood in the doorway. The sun at her back threw her into silhouette, but Alexi would know her anywhere.

CHAPTER 7

$\mathcal{C}$at stepped inside and flew across the cramped space toward the cell. The thin, ugly man moved in front of her, and she bounced off his chest. He tried to grab her arm before she fell, and Cat cradled the swaddle of clothing she'd stuffed beneath her dress to imitate a baby.

Alexi growled.

Cat ignored him, dodging the man's groping hands. She couldn't afford for him to pull her *too* close. If the front of her brushed the front of him, he'd know the truth, and then they'd be in trouble.

Cat reached through the bars and cupped Alexi's poor face. The sight of his swollen nose and two black eyes infuriated her. She wanted to punch someone and, for a change, it wasn't him.

His gaze wandered from the top of her sunbonneted head, past her worn calico dress, to her same old dusty boots—they worked with almost any costume—before he lifted one eyebrow.

She stuck out her tongue, then patted her chest and waved at her face as if she might faint. "I was so worried."

"Who *are* you?" the man who had grabbed her demanded.

Cat leaned close and brushed her lips over Alexi's.

"Shh," she whispered against his mouth; his tongue snaked out and touched hers. She jerked back. Would he ever be serious?

The marshal cleared his throat. "Uh, ma'am?"

She turned. "I'm his wife."

"She's some whore," the other man snapped.

Alexi growled again. She gave him an elbow, and the growl puffed away on a soft "urgh."

"Hey, now." The marshal stepped up. Had he seen murder in her eyes? Sometimes it was hard to tamp down.

"If she's his wife, then ask her name; ask his. Where ya from? Why ya in Brooks?" the shorter fellow asked.

This fool was dumber than he looked, and that was saying something.

Cat lifted her chin and he smirked. He thought he had her. Because if she was just *some whore* she wouldn't know her *husband's* name, where they were from, or why they were here. Although why *some whore* would bother to save Alexi was beyond even Cat's powers of invention.

Lucky for them, everyone in town was milling about the building, eavesdropping on what was being said in here, then repeating it out there. The situation was the most excitement they'd had in years.

"I'm Meg Nelson. From San Antonio. And you are?"

Manners made him answer "Pardy Langston" before he scowled and continued. "Your name's no more Nelson than his is."

"I don't understand." She turned wide, innocent eyes toward the marshal. "Why's he saying that?" She rubbed at her stomach. "I think I know my own name and the name of my husband."

Cat considered asking if they often hung people without benefit of a trial in these parts. But she knew better. Judges traveled a circuit, and by the time they arrived at one town or another, the local sense of justice—or boredom—sometimes prevailed ahead of any arguments by the lawyers.

The marshal's cheeks flushed. "Of course, ma'am."

"Ma'am," Langston muttered. "Sheesh."

The marshal cast him a glare, and he shut up. For now. Langston didn't seem the type to shut up for long. Which was no doubt why they were here.

Cat planned to shut him up. But first she needed Alexi out of that cell.

"What happened to his face?"

"He did." Alexi flicked a finger through the bars to indicate Langston. "He seems to think I'm someone else." Alexi lifted that hand to his nose and probed gingerly. "Someone he doesn't much care for."

"*He* hit you; then the town marshal locked *you* up? Is that common in Brooks? Folks are assaulted and you put *them* in jail?"

The marshal's color deepened, and Cat pressed her lips together to keep her smile from blooming. She'd have Alexi free in no time.

"Well, there's some confusion."

"I know." Cat motioned to the cell. "Why is my husband with the broken nose and two black eyes in there? While the man who gave them to him is . . ." She narrowed her gaze on Langston.

"Because he's—" Langston began, and the marshal interrupted.

"I'll take care of this." The lawman glanced at the gallows, then at Cat, his gaze catching on her stomach again before returning to her face. "What brings you to Missouri, ma'am?"

Cat blinked, opened her mouth, closed it, then glanced at Alexi, who shrugged. She tilted her head, staring at the marshal with an expression that very clearly said: *Why are you questioning me? A solid, upright, married woman?*

When the fellow didn't apologize or withdraw the question, she released an exasperated sigh. "We heard Brooks was a town we might like to settle in." She eyed her husband behind the bars. "I don't think we will."

Cat was convincing. Not only because she was very, very good at this, but because *this* was who she was. Or at least who she'd been.

The calico dress was hers, as was the bonnet. Even the accent —pure Georgia—belonged to her. If you considered Cat was still Cathleen Chase somewhere deep inside.

Cat hadn't been certain how much of Cathleen remained. She thought now it might be just enough to save Alexi. It had to be.

"Is anyone going to explain to me why he's in there?" She considered stomping her foot, but discovered she couldn't manage it. Stomping, unless it was upon Pardy's head, was not something Cat, Cathleen, or even Meg would ever do.

"'Cause he's a two-bit thief," Langston snapped.

"He is not!"

Again, the truth shone through, making her words sound as believable as the sworn testimony of a nun with her hand upon the Good Book. Because Alexi wasn't a *two-bit* anything. Perhaps a silver dollar or a gold eagle, but two bits . . .?

How common.

"Jed," she began. "What—?"

"His name's not Jed," Langston interrupted. "It's Josiah. Josiah *Farmington.*"

"You have him confused with someone else."

"It's him all right. 'Cept. . ." Langston scowled at her middle. "Last time I saw him he was travelin' with a huge hulk of a brute."

Cat hoped the marshal hadn't seen Mikhail and the signora ride into town. He wouldn't recognize her, but Mikhail was another story. How many huge, hulking brutes were there?

She took a moment to be glad she'd sent Mikhail on his way before she'd come. If they went looking, they would not find him.

Langston had gone silent, thinking. The process was obviously painful, involving much squinting and scowling, even a little squeezing, if the sounds he made were any indication. "I bet he's here somewhere. Farmington was awful attached to the idjut. If ya jest ask around—"

Cat gasped, laying both hands on her protruding belly. She swayed and everyone—except Alexi, who snorted—leaped into action. Luckily the others were too worried the baby might drop onto the floor to notice her *husband's* reaction.

A chair was produced. She was helped into it. A dipper of water was pressed to her lips. When she asked for a cool cloth, Pardy Langston provided it—after the marshal swatted him on the back of the head. Cat had a hard time containing her smirk. The tide had begun to turn.

She dabbed at her brow, then returned the unpleasantly stained bandana to Langston. "I should lie down." Cat glanced pointedly at the cell.

"Of course." He reached for his keys.

"What the fuck!" Langston shouted.

Cat clapped a palm to her mouth.

The marshal backhanded the offensive bastard in the face. "Watch your language."

"But he—" The man began to hop back and forth as if he had the sudden and nearly uncontrollable urge to pee. "She—They—"

The ring of keys rattled as the marshal shoved one into the door.

"It's *my* word against his," Langston continued. "And I say he's a thief. So his word shouldn't mean nothin'."

"No." The marshal turned, leaving the keys hanging from the lock and the lock yet unturned. Alexi stared at them as if he wanted to turn them himself. He lifted his eyes to Cat's, and she gave a tiny shake of her head.

"It's his word *and* hers. *Two* folks who say he's who he says he is. One who says he ain't. I don't have no choice."

The marshal turned the key; the door swung open; Alexi stepped out. In keeping with the ruse, he rushed to her side, knelt and took her hand, kissing the knuckles before he set his palm on her swollen middle. Something in Cat's chest shifted, and her hand nearly jerked free of his. Alexi's fingers tightened, and he gave her a quick, hard, warning glare.

Langston was watching them.

She leaned forward and brushed her lips over Alexi's brow. Her belly pressed into his chest, and now he was the one who jerked.

"Oh!" She let her hand fall to her waist. "Did you feel that, darling?"

Alexi appeared, for the first time she could ever remember, unable to speak.

"Quite a kick, wasn't it?"

He nodded, swallowed, glanced away. What was wrong with him?

"This has all been so upsetting. I should really lie down."

Alexi leaped to his feet, offering his arm. She made a great show of rocking back and forth, panting, gasping, grunting even, before she stood.

"Sorry 'bout the misunderstanding," the marshal said.

"Don't mention it." Alexi hustled Cat toward the door so fast she could barely keep up.

"Slow down," she whispered. "I'm huge."

Alexi choked, covering the sound with a cough.

"Too bad about the hanging," the lawman mused. "Folks are gonna be disappointed."

Alexi's arm tightened, and Cat dug her nails into his coat. He leaned in and nuzzled her. "Mikhail?"

"Gone."

His exhale of relief blew back the drooping crown of her bonnet. "Langston won't let this go." His voice was lighter than the wind. "He's gonna come after us."

Cat threw a glance over her shoulder. Langston—face beet-red, big lips pressed together until they'd nearly disappeared—

seemed ready to burst. She thought he was going to come after them too. Which was why she'd planned ahead.

Cat stopped. "Oh no!"

"The baby?" Alexi blurted.

She rolled her eyes in his direction. He'd sounded truly panicked; he looked it as well. He was good. Or perhaps she was.

"My ring!" She spun, patting her dress just above her breasts, then stuck her hand into the bodice and felt around.

The marshal and Langston became very interested in the ceiling, which gave her the chance to cross the floor much quicker than a woman as far along as she should be able to, then poke Langston in the chest. "Give it back."

He gaped, his overly ripe lips opening and closing like a beached fish. "I ... Me ... What?"

"When I arrived, you tried to grab me."

"Ya almost fell."

"You stepped in my way. You touched my neck."

"Your neck?" His gaze went to her belly again. It *was* hard to miss.

"I keep my wedding ring on a chain." She held her hands in front of her. "My fingers are too swollen for it to fit."

The lawman frowned. "You think he took it?"

"Who else?"

"Ya lost it 'fore ya come in here!"

Cat gazed down, thought of Billy, let her eyes flood before lifting them again. "I kissed it right before I walked inside." Her lips trembled, and she glanced at Alexi, who was staring at her as if he'd never seen her before. She smiled at him anyway. "For luck."

"Well." The marshal cleared his throat. "It's a simple thing to prove." He jerked his chin at Langston. "Empty yer pockets."

Langston gaped. "Ya believe her?"

"Don't say I do and don't say I don't. But it'll hurry this up if you just empty yer pockets."

"Fine." Langston stuffed his hands into his pockets, began to pull them out, and froze.

"Come on," the other man snapped.

"I ..." Langston glanced at the door.

Alexi, who leaned casually against the casing, smirked.

"He put it there!"

"He?" Cat repeated. "You mean the *he* who was behind bars?"

The marshal yanked Langston's hands free. Clutched in his left was a gold wedding ring on a chain.

"Maybe you won't have to disappoint folks after all," Alexi murmured.

* * *

ALEXI CONSIDERED LIGHTING out while the marshal struggled to get the gambler into a cell, but he doubted that was something Jed, or Josiah, would do.

No, an innocent man would expect an apology. A poor farmer wouldn't leave until he had that gold circlet in his possession. So Alexi played his part and stayed where he was, even though Cat kept trying to tug him out the door.

"Reckon I owe you a sorry 'bout that," the marshal said.

"Reckon you do." Alexi held out his hand, palm up, to receive the ring.

Instead, the fellow grasped his hand, lowering and lifting Alexi's arm like a water pump. "Nice of you to accept."

"I ..." Alexi glanced at Cat, who widened her eyes and jerked her head at the door. "Yes. You're welcome."

The marshal released him but Alexi didn't move. "The ring?"

When Cat muttered, "Jesus," he stepped on her toe.

"Oh, yeah. Sure." The lawman dug into his vest pocket and deposited both ring and chain into it.

Alexi had never seen either one of them before.

Where had she kept it? Did she often take it out and kiss the surface when he wasn't around to see?

The image made his stomach burn. Damn the rotgut he'd drunk in the saloon earlier. He should know better than to swallow such swill; it always came back to haunt him in one way or another.

The slight crease between Cat's eyebrows reminded Alexi that he'd been standing there with the ring in his hand for too long.

When he looped the chain over her head, she smiled at him with what most would believe true affection. But Alexi knew the love in her eyes was as much of a show as the tears of a moment before.

Cat had always been able to cry on cue. It was one of her many exceptional talents, along with an incredible sleight of hand that had allowed her to slip the ring into Pardy's pocket during the instant he'd been distracted. Certainly Alexi had taught her how, but the ability needed to be there in the first place to have any hope of success. He almost felt sorry for the man.

Almost.

"Darling."

Alexi's teeth ground together and Cat's lips twitched. Then she stuck a finger into the neck of her horrible farm-wife gown, pulled it out, and dropped the ring between breasts he could swear were more luscious and ripe than they'd been the last time he'd seen them. He wanted to test them with his hands, taste them with his tongue—

"You need to lie down." He took her arm.

They exited to the shouts of Pardy Langston as he denied stealing the ring, threw more accusations at Alexi's back, called Cat a few more vicious names. Alexi really wanted to put a stop to the latter with his fists, but the quicker they got out of here, the better. Although—

"Walk slowly. As if we haven't a care. Anyone wants to talk to us, do your 'gonna drop that baby right now' act; then we'll hustle."

He patted her arm and spoke more loudly. "Don't you worry none, sweet-ums."

Cat arched an eyebrow.

"Just a silly mistake. Shouldn't have let yourself get so het up." He laid a hand on her belly, ignoring the way his palm hummed. He wasn't touching *her* beneath the horrible dress, he was touching—

His fingers flexed. Cloth. A lot of it. Bundled into a sack so tight it *might* feel like a baby. He had no idea. He'd never felt one. What might that be like?

Alexi's stomach flared. "Rotgut," he said, then stroked what wasn't even her.

Both eyebrows slammed down. She took his hand, squeezed it —hard—then let it go with a near imperceptible shove. "We need to get gone," she said between her teeth.

"No." He patted the hand that still curled around his arm. The fingers clenched; he was going to have more bruises than the ones he'd gotten from Pardy. "Jed and Meg wouldn't race out of town as if they had something to hide, and we can't either."

She uttered several curses a woman like Meg Nelson would never know. Then she smiled at him as if he really was the father of the unborn child beneath her heart, and Alexi stumbled like an untried youth. Something he hadn't been in—

"Forever," he whispered.

Her clear green gaze met his. "What is *wrong* with you?"

He had no idea.

"Why did you come?" he asked, as they strolled along the boardwalk like they had nowhere to go, no place to be, nothing to hide.

Beneath the horrible bonnet, she frowned. "What?"

"You should have taken Mikhail and disappeared. There wasn't anything you could do for me."

"Obviously there was. You're out, and the man who put you there is in." Her frown turned into a smirk. "Ass."

Alexi wasn't certain if she was referring to him or Pardy, and it didn't really matter. "Where is Mikhail?"

"Waiting outside of town." She lifted a hand before he could speak. "Far enough away not to be found. He *has* done this before."

"How did you know what to say to the sheriff?" he asked.

Cat let out an exasperated huff, sounding exactly like a wife great with child should sound—or at least what Alexi imagined one would sound like. "Everyone in town was talking about what had happened. Who Pardy said you were, what you'd done. And what you said in return."

Alexi paused, and Cat tugged him along. "Don't stop! We need to get out of sight."

Since she was right, he continued walking, but his mind was too full of questions to remain silent. "You heard what Pardy said I'd done."

She nodded; the brim of the bonnet flopped into her eyes, and she shoved it out. "Didn't sound like you."

"Doesn't mean it wasn't."

"How true."

"Then why did you risk yourself to get me out?"

"You wouldn't have left me there."

It wasn't a question; she believed he would have done anything to release her if she'd been the one in jail. Was she right?

Probably.

"What if the marshal hadn't believed you?"

"He'd have hung you, and I'd have cried."

"Over Jed? Or Alexi?"

She cast him a quick glance from beneath the limp, ugly bonnet. "Does it matter?"

He thought it did. But he wasn't sure why.

* * *

BY THE TIME they reached the hotel, Alexi was behaving so strangely Cat's skin started to itch. Was someone watching them? Following them? Was that target she felt on her back real?

"How long should we stay?" she asked.

"Until full dark at least."

Cat understood why, but she didn't like it. She wanted out of this town.

Yesterday.

They meandered through the lobby, heads together, murmuring like the lovebirds they weren't. Alexi nodded to the clerk, who'd been here when the signora arrived but obviously hadn't been when Jed had since the man stared at them without recognition.

"Jed and Meg Nelson." Alexi held out a hand. "Room twelve."

The clerk handed over the key after a quick glance at the register. Alexi's scribbled name was so illegible, it could be anything, even Jed and Meg. Another trick of their trade. One never knew when an identity might need to be changed middodge.

Alexi's room was exactly the same as hers, right down to the deck of cards sitting in the center of the table. She crossed to the window, through which a tepid breeze blew. Tossing off her bonnet, she stuck her head out, banging the "baby" against the casing. She wasn't used to having all this extra front.

She reached around to remove her costume, and Alexi snapped, "Leave it."

Cat started. He was closer than she'd thought. "Why?"

"All we need is for someone to knock on the door and you've . . ." He waved vaguely in the area of her midsection.

"Lost the baby?"

He winced, and she heard what she'd said. The words gave her a strange, hollow feeling. But what was his excuse?

Cat couldn't decipher his expression. His face seemed . . . different.

The bruises, she thought. She'd never once seen Alexi with a bruise on his face. It changed him, made him vulnerable. She wasn't sure she liked that any more than he appeared to.

Come to think of it, she'd rarely seen Alexi with a bruise anywhere. And she'd seen everywhere.

The memory of that seeing, the touching, the tasting hit her so hard she swayed.

He cursed. French? Spanish? Italian? She wasn't certain, but whatever language, the words, the tone, the cadence were both beautiful and brutal.

Like Alexi himself.

She brushed her fingertips across his face. "Why did you let him hurt you?"

"Sometimes the hurt just happens."

She didn't think he was talking about Langston anymore and she froze, hand still in the air.

Alexi crossed to the table, where he picked up the deck of cards and began to shuffle. She became entranced, seduced by the grace, the rhythm. How could she have forgotten? In Alexi's hands, cards did whatever he wanted them to. Like women.

"When you say 'knock,'" Cat began, bringing them back to their earlier conversation, happy to pretend the other had never happened, "you mean 'bust in here and drag us back to jail'?"

"No." He didn't look up; he just kept shuffling the cards. "As long as you keep that kid in place and Meg on your face, we'll be fine."

Why was he irritated with her? She'd just saved his life.

Cat paced in front of the window. The urge to peer from it again was nearly overwhelming. What was out there that was bothering her? If there was a rifle, and considering the prickling of her skin, there might be, she should stay *away* from the window.

She sat on the bed. Then on the chair. Then on the bed again.

Alexi ignored her, seemingly captivated with the cards.

Cat went to the door, put her hand on the knob, but Alexi "tsked," and she turned away. Her gaze went again to the window, and from this angle, with the horizon framed like a picture, she saw what was wrong. She couldn't believe she hadn't noticed it before, but she'd been Meg, and Meg wouldn't recognize that vista. Only Cathleen would.

She had not been back to the farm since she had left it nearly two years ago. It took Cat only an instant to decide that she was going back as soon as she could get away from Alexi.

"Deal."

Alexi glanced up, expression curious, hands still shuffling, shuffling, shuffling.

"If we have to stay in here, we can at least make it interesting."

His lips curved. "Faro?"

Cat took a chair at the table. "You know better."

Cat loathed faro, known by many as "Bucking the Tiger." Every saloon between St. Louis and San Francisco offered the game, and most of them cheated. Stacked decks, with many paired cards that allowed the dealer, or banker, to collect half the bets, as well as shaved decks and razored aces were common.

Alexi wouldn't stoop to such tactics; he'd consider mundane cheats beneath him. Besides, he'd already taught her how to spot them, so why bother? Certainly he cheated, but with faro Cat had never been able to discover just how.

He'd swindle her at poker too if she wasn't paying attention, but at least with that game she had a better-than-average chance of catching him.

Alexi laid out five cards for each of them. "Stakes?"

"We can't play just to pass the time?"

He didn't bother to dignify that foolishness with an answer.

Cat considered forgoing the wayward nature of the cards and, instead, getting him drunk. But she'd attempted that before. Alexi had remained annoyingly sober, and she had been rewarded with a three-day headache, which Alexi had found beyond amusing.

She had more tolerance now—Cat O'Banyon had drunk many a bounty beneath the table—but she still doubted she could drink this man into a stupor. Sometimes she wondered if he sipped on watered wine daily just to ascertain no one ever could.

Which meant her only other choice was the cards.

Cat gave away nothing; neither did Alexi. After pulling her purse from her pocket, she tossed a few coins onto the table. With a lift of his eyebrow, he did the same. They played in silence as the day waned.

The room grew hot. In the way of cards, first Alexi was ahead, then Cat. She watched him as closely as he watched her. Neither one of them cheated.

Much.

Cat arched, rubbing absently at the ache in the small of her back with her free hand.

"Stop that." Alexi flicked a glance from his cards to her face, then back again.

"What?"

"You're not expecting." He set two cards onto the table, then took two more with stiff yet fussy movements. "Stop acting like it."

There was something in his face she'd never seen before. Was he scared? Had coming a hair from a hanging frightened him at last? Or was she merely seeing in Alexi a reflection of herself?

An hour later, a commotion ensued on the stairs. Many booted feet, loud voices. A door was banged upon. "Open up in there!"

Cat put down her cards. "Two of a kind."

Wood splintered. More thumps and curses, then footsteps descended once again.

Both Cat and Alexi exhaled.

He set his cards on the table. "Three of a kind."

Cat didn't bother to frown; she merely swept up the cards and dealt.

Alexi peered at his new hand. "The signora's room?"

"*Sì.*"

He muttered a few words in who the hell knew what language and played a card. Somehow Langston had convinced the marshal to ask around about the big, hulking brute; then *voila,* someone had seen a big, hulking brute, and the lawman had been forced to investigate.

However, with no big, hulking brute—and no signora—the entire tale fell apart. Langston's fate was sealed.

Cat would have felt badly about that if she hadn't been of the opinion that the litany of crimes Pardy had attributed to Alexi had, in fact, been a recitation of his own.

When the sun slanted toward dusk and the pile of coins on both sides of the table lay about even, Cat lifted her eyes. "Wanna make this interesting?"

"*Khriso mou,* when you say things like that . . ." Alexi moved a card from the right side of his hand to the left. "I get excited."

"How about we raise the stakes to . . ." She drew out the moment, and even though he knew exactly what she was doing, as he was the one who had taught her to do it, eventually his anticipation caused him to lean forward. Only then did Cat give him what he sought. "Anything."

"Anything?"

"*Oui.*"

He cast her an exasperated glance as she purposely mangled one of his favorite words.

"I win this hand, you give me anything I ask. You win—"

"I get anything I ask."

"You've played this before," she said.

"Not with you."

She doubted he'd played it with anyone. What idiot would promise anything?

Only someone with little left to lose or . . . Cat considered her cards without so much as a flicker of an eyelash. Someone with a hand like hers.

"All right. Who am I to turn down *anything?*"

Not the man she knew and—

Cat brought herself up short. Not the man she knew and what?

Well, not the man she knew.

Alexi turned his cards faceup.

Cat kept her face blank as she placed hers facedown. "You win."

CHAPTER 8

*C*at crossed to the window and, again, peered out. She was behaving like her namesake.

In a room full of rocking chairs.

Alexi didn't think his winning the bet had anything to do with her behavior, as she'd been behaving that way since they walked into the room.

Alexi followed, leaning so close his cheek nearly brushed her shoulder, trying to discover what could be so fascinating on a dusty Missouri street.

Nothing that he could see.

Cat straightened, nearly knocking into his poor, maligned nose, and turned. For an instant he looked at her and saw someone else. That horrible dress, her hair drawn back in an atrocious bun, she even smelled of dust and dirt and despair. He could swear he spotted a bit of grime in her hair.

Alexi shook his head and the world, along with Cat O'Banyon, swirled into focus. He set his hands on her hips. "How do you do it?"

She didn't pull away. How could she? He'd just won anything.

"How did you feel Meg Nelson so deeply you became her?"

How did she walk and talk and move like a woman heavy with child when she'd never *been* with child?

Cat merely stared at him—confused, captivated, a little concerned. Why should she be any different?

His palms slid up her body, pausing just short of her breasts. Beneath the faded calico she seemed on fire, and his belly burned.

"Back there, I could have sworn these were fuller." His thumbnail traced the base of one. "Your face seemed rounder. Your skin goddamn glowed." His voice roughened. "How do you do that?"

"I—" she began. "What?"

"In the old country," he whispered, "they'd burn you for a witch."

"Lucky then"—she took a deep breath, lifting, then lowering those fabulous globes so that they brushed his knuckles and made him yearn—"that we're in a new one."

"Lucky." He ran his thumbs along the underside of her breasts —*definitely* fuller—teasing, taunting, tormenting.

Her eyes—those glorious Cat eyes—met his, then she was in his arms, kissing him. The "baby" was now crushed into his stomach, and that stomach no longer burned. But everything else did.

Her mouth opened; she welcomed him in. She tasted of memories—him, her, them. One other.

No. She'd turned to *him*. She'd kissed *him*. He wasn't going to ruin that with thoughts of . . . What *was* his name?

Alexi cursed against her lips. Too slow. Needed fast. Before she changed her mind. Or he did.

Cat must have felt the same, because she didn't ask why he cursed; she didn't lift her mouth from his.

That should have been his first clue, but he was a man. When she yanked open his shirt, spraying buttons all over the floor, he yanked her dress right back. Then he was captured by the silky texture of her skin. She felt like . . .

A full house—queens and aces—his favorite. The faces of the

ladies promising the world, the spike of the aces delivering it. The cards were as dewy and smooth as her breasts beneath his fingertips.

Her nails scraped his nipples, first a mere hint, enough to make him hold his breath, waiting for her to—

She flicked her thumb—back and forth, back and forth—the movement a promise of tongue, the scrape like teeth. Just thinking of her clever mouth made his ravenous, and he shoved the dress from her shoulders, capturing her at the elbows, lifting her breasts.

He let his gaze touch them as he wanted to, as he would. Her breath came as harshly as his own, every inhale an offering, each exhale pure temptation. Though he wanted to dive, to delve, to devour, instead he lowered his head, inch by desperate inch, drawing out the moment, licking his lips, tasting her there, knowing that soon he would taste her everywhere. His breath wafted over her, and she shivered. Fascinated, he watched the gooseflesh race across her ribs, flow over a breast, then—

He stopped breathing as her nipples swelled right before his eyes. One actually brushed his lower lip. He had to bite his tongue to hold it back. His mouth flooded with saliva, as if the juiciest, ripest, most tasty—

"Do it." An order, not a plea. Nothing new. She'd never begged. Then again, she'd never ordered him before either.

His gaze lifted. Her eyes blazed emerald against the nearly russet flush of her cheeks. Something was different. With her? With him?

With us? his mind whispered.

"You think too much." Her hands, trapped at her sides, nevertheless found him and stroked. "You always did."

"Someone has to."

"No." Cat stepped back and shifted; the dress fell to the floor. Reaching around, the movement causing muscles to ripple beneath her skin, which in turn caused muscles to ripple beneath his, she tugged the tie on the *baby*.

He discovered he no longer cared what it had been made of—amazing what the sight of a naked woman could do for one's curiosity—and it fell too, tumbling away, unraveling into a pile of faded, wrinkled cloth atop that horrible dress.

She stood there in nothing but her stockings and boots. "Someone doesn't."

His gaze on her hips, slim and perfect, her legs, just the same, her breasts—oh, those breasts, sonnets he could write to them, if he were capable of writing sonnets. He had to rummage through his brain to remember what she was talking about.

Ah, yes. She was right. No one needed to think. Him least of all.

He reached for her. She was looking out the window again, and he frowned, looked out there himself. What was so—

She went to her knees. He forgot all about the window. It was only later that he remembered. Later was when he always remembered.

She pressed her mouth to his stomach, her tongue chasing the ripples, dipping beneath the waistband of his trousers, brushing across his tip. She inched back, he thought to remove his clothing, so he released the button at his waist. Instead she mouthed him through the material, lips running his length; she used her teeth down low at the root.

Where in hell had she learned that?

He stepped away. She stayed where she was. The sight of her on her knees with the dying rays of the sun slanting across her, hair tumbling over her breasts, boots and stockings still on, eyes wide and green, both aware and aroused, made him realize something.

He didn't care.

He shrugged off his shirt, dropped his pants, lost his own

boots and socks. She watched, the gaze that brushed his body gentle as a caress.

Coming to her feet, she slid her palms up his thighs. "Shh," she murmured when he tensed. "Let me see."

Then she closed her eyes and traced those palms over him, as if she were learning his curves and dips, the hard and soft places. Or maybe she merely remembered. Her fingers curled over his shoulders, thumb trailing the insides of his arms. Her belly brushed his cock, and it leaped. Her lips curved, one hand dropping lower, coiling around him, tightening, testing.

"Shh," she said again. "Just . . . shh."

He didn't point out that he hadn't said anything. Instead, he watched her as she touched him, and he fought not to lose control. He who had always been completely in control, especially of situations like these. He'd had so many women so many ways. He'd had her. But he'd never *had* her. He'd discovered that when she disappeared from his life without a single word of farewell.

Her supple fingers still around him, he grasped her wrist and her eyes opened. The sudden urge to make her his as she'd never been his consumed him. Problem was . . .

He didn't know how.

If she hadn't been dazzled by his prowess before, she certainly wasn't going to be now. Then again . . .

She stood with one hand still on his chest; the other he held clasped in his own.

If at first you don't succeed—

Alexi twirled her around in a quick two-step, then released her so that she fell onto the bed. "Try, try again."

She was breathless—smiling, almost laughing. But the mirth died when he removed her boots, then drew her stockings down her legs, trailing kisses in their wake before he stood. He let his gaze wander over her as she'd let hers wander over him. Then he touched her—eyes, fingertips, lips, tongue—in places he'd never touched her before.

The inside of the right knee.

The outside of one thigh, where leg ripened into the sloping swell of a buttock.

A rib. The hip. Her wrist.

Her fingers fluttered over his hair. Neck. Shoulders. Back. Eventually she began to tug. He ignored her.

Belly button. Left ear—high up where her hair lay. Crook of the elbow.

Low, desperate gasps broke from her throat. She began to whisper suggestions in his ear.

Now. Hard. Fast.

But never *please.*

When he nibbled her jaw, right at the tip, the part she led with whenever she was desperate, the hands on his arms clenched and she shoved. He tumbled, landing on his back with a bounce that was interrupted when she straddled him. He tried not to smirk, but it was hard.

She took him within and began to move.

Very hard.

Her eyes slid closed; her breasts shimmied, then shimmered in the dusky light through the window. He began to reach for them and without even opening her eyes she caught his hands, wrapping her fingers between his, then pinning them to the bed —palm to palm. "Let me."

"*Sicherlich,*" he said, and she opened one eye. "Certainly," he translated.

Sometimes the words he'd learned during the most trying period of his life slipped out when he least expected them to. He couldn't help it. Learning other languages was how he'd once kept himself from going mad. As she was attempting to drive him mad now, it was understandable that the expressions trembled on the tip of his tongue, where he wanted her to be.

She held his hands motionless. He held himself in check by reciting in his head all the ways that he knew to say her name.

Goto.

Katze.

Chat.

Kot.

Macska.

She opened her eyes, and a crease appeared between them as if she didn't quite know where she was.

"Cat."

She stilled, gaze gone wide—trapped, or perhaps captured. He was. Then she shifted, and he feared she meant to leave—lift herself from his body, roll away, run away—and he caught his breath. What would he do? Stop her? Force her to stay? He thought not, even though by all rights, she was his. He had won.

Anything.

Anyway, anyhow, any why and where and what. But he didn't want her like that; he wanted her . . .

Well, he just wanted her.

She was fire, burning around and within him, pain and passion, need. When he closed his eyes all he saw was her; when he opened them, there she was—no longer a dream but reality. He hadn't understood how very much he'd missed her. How that hollow feeling inside had been the lack of her and not the lack of success, money, danger, women. He had gorged himself on all four, but he hadn't felt like this since the last time he'd gorged himself on her.

Alexi let his gaze wander up the slim curves of the woman still riding him as if her life depended on the journey. No man could resist that, especially not a man like him.

She took him deeper, rocking slower, the bud within her sliding over his head and making him bite his lip to keep from finishing before she did. She knew exactly how to make him come. But then he knew the same about her.

Though she still held his hands, she did not hold his mouth, and those breasts, ah, they were so close. He captured one rose-hued tip, and she gasped, biting her own lip, though she kept shifting, rocking, arousing him. As he kept arousing her.

Suckling, pushing her against the roof of his mouth, first slowly, gently, then faster, harder, the movements of her body echoing his.

She stiffened, clenching around him, forgetting to breathe, releasing his hands. He lifted up, gathering her against him, holding her as she came, coming himself, unable to keep from joining her one second longer.

When he fell back upon the mattress, she followed, pressing her cheek to his chest. Cat had never been one to remain entangled afterward. Usually she turned away, not leaving his bed, but leaving just the same. This time she cuddled against his side like a—

"*Koshka.*" He ran his palm over her hair.

When she sighed, then slept, he did the same. As he drifted off, he had one final thought.

Perhaps he did know how to make her his after all.

* * *

CAT WAITED until Alexi's breathing evened out; it didn't take long. After that performance, it shouldn't.

She glanced again at the window, but the sun had gone down and the angle was wrong. She could no longer see the familiar hillside in the distance and that was good. Because the sight of it had nearly sent her over the edge.

Cat slid from beneath the sheets. Alexi didn't move; his breathing continued with exactly the same rhythm it had held before. That of a deeply satisfied male. Exactly what she'd been aiming for when she touched him.

Not that she hadn't enjoyed herself. Alexi Romanov was a

connoisseur—of the fine art of confidence, of women, of languages, but especially of sex. He'd taught her that the act could be about something other than love. More important, he'd taught her that it could be about something other than hate.

As she dressed in his discarded clothing, it occurred to her that there was one thing she didn't think Alexi had meant to teach her, but she was nothing if not a good mimic.

The body could be used as a weapon. By a woman as well as a man. The lesson had served her well over the time they'd been apart. There were times when that lesson had saved her life.

She mouthed a silent curse when she slid into his shirt, realized she'd yanked off the buttons and had to root around in his bag for another. As she put it on, she caught the scent of rain and glanced again at the bed, expecting to glimpse his blue eyes shining against the darkness, perhaps even a pistol pointed in her direction. But he was still asleep, gun belt slung over the bedpost, hair stark against the creamy sheets, skin both smooth—across his chest—and rough—across his jaw.

He was quite possibly the most beautiful man she'd ever seen. She enjoyed looking at him. She also enjoyed talking to him, traveling with him, working next to him, and sleeping with him.

Which meant she had to go. Enjoyment had no place in life. Enjoyment made you soft. Liking someone made you vulnerable. Loving him could get you dead.

Worse, it could get *him* dead.

The only reason she'd gone anywhere near Alexi was because he could take care of himself. No one got the better of that man. If they tried, Mikhail made sure they never did so on a second occasion. However, because she felt safe with Alexi, with Mikhail, she hadn't been paying attention. She hadn't been watching where they were going, hadn't realized where they were. And now . . .

She would have to go there again.

Cat lifted the gun belt, careful not to rattle the bed. She'd left her six-shooters in the signora's room, and Mikhail had no doubt moved them when he'd moved himself and their horses out of town.

She hadn't wanted to leave the weapons behind, but Meg Nelson would never carry a worn pair of Navy Colts. She wouldn't be able to fit them over her pregnant belly.

Cat's hand was reaching for her own flat stomach before she realized it. She clenched her fingers and forced her arm back to her side. She'd liked being Meg, feeling that weight against her, imagining it move, dreaming of a child with her green eyes, his dark hair. Or maybe his blue eyes and—

Suddenly Cat couldn't breathe. Blue eyes? Billy's had been brown.

She rubbed her face. Foolish dreams, foolish thoughts. She'd never have a baby. And not just because riding across the prairie searching for someone—*the* one—to kill would be damn difficult if she were expecting, but because she wasn't capable of it.

She and Billy had tried. Her eyes burned as she remembered how very much they had wanted a child, but she had never quickened.

Not. Once.

As she'd told Alexi the single time he'd asked, she was barren. And nothing since then had proved her wrong. Why did that make her sad? Would it have been better to have Billy's baby or worse? What would she have done with a child?

More important . . .

What would *they* have done?

CHAPTER 9

The instant Alexi's eyes opened, he knew she was gone. He'd been here before, and just like that time, he hadn't seen it coming.

He considered the window she'd been obsessed with, or perhaps with something she'd seen through it. She'd been nervous. She'd made him nervous, and then—

His gaze switched to the table. The cards still lay where they'd placed them.

Alexi got a very bad feeling. Sliding from the bed, he stalked naked across the floor, let his fingertips drift over his two beautiful ladies dancing with his two solemn gents. Then he flipped her hand faceup.

Full house.

"What are you up to?"

But he thought he knew . . . at least the first part. She'd wanted to slip away, and he wasn't going to let her. Not alone. Not anymore. So she'd concocted a plan. First suggest cards. Once he was hooked, up the ante. Promise him anything. He wouldn't be able to resist.

Alexi lifted what was left in the deck and bent them with one hand, then released them, flinging the cards in a glorious water-fall. They splayed onto the floor with a soft whoosh.

"But she won." *She* could have had anything, and if what she'd wanted was to go, he would have let her. He didn't welsh on bets. Ever.

However, did Cat know that? What if she believed that the instant she asked to leave he would tie her up, toss her on a horse, and take her away from here to prevent her from . . . what?

He had no idea. But it had been important enough to let him win. Important enough to touch him without pretending to be someone else for the first time he could remember. Unless, of course, she had been pretending.

Alexi had been touching Cat, but perhaps, in her mind, Meg had been touching Jed and vice versa. In the past, they'd always come together in the guise of the parts they had played. It was easier that way. Safer. Both more exciting and less upsetting. For both of them.

If such had been the case in the past, then why should now be any different? And why had he thought it was?

Cat had swindled him with her body, voice, and eyes the same way she'd swindled him with the cards. She'd known what his choice would be. From the moment she'd told him he couldn't have her, she was all that he'd wanted.

She'd known that, being a man, once his pecker was involved he would not be able to think with anything else. Then, once he was done "thinking," he'd sleep through her escape, as any satisfied man would. Considering the enthusiasm of their encounter, he was surprised he wasn't still snoring.

She hadn't even waited for him to voice his decision, because there had been no decision. She'd lifted her lips, and he'd been lost.

Alexi contemplated the window again. Should he go after her? "*Oui?*" he asked the darkness. Or . . . "*Nein?*"

He couldn't decide. Then his gaze fell on the empty bedpost.

"*Zur Holle mit ihr!*" He searched for his clothes, found only hers. "*Zur Holle mit mir.*"

She'd taken his only pair of pants and his last clean shirt—everything else he owned was with Mikhail—leaving behind his socks, boots, and the garment she'd torn apart.

He eyed Meg Nelson's dress and stifled a laugh. Cat might be able to don Alexi's apparel, but there was no way he had a prayer of squeezing into hers.

Alexi took a childish pleasure in stepping on the gown and bonnet as he crossed to the door. A quick glance into the hall—empty—then a few strides to the next room. When his knock went unanswered, he assumed it was empty too. A quick session with the lock picks from his bag—at least Cat had left him that—and he was soon donning new clothes.

Well, not new, not even washed recently. He left puffs of dust behind when he moved. However, double-crossed, half-naked confidence men couldn't be choosers, so Alexi scowled and finished dressing.

At the livery, the stable boy blinked, mouth opening and closing as he pointed at an empty stall. "But . . . but . . . ya already took yer horse."

Alexi rubbed his forehead, the movement causing the scent of a long day's ride to billow across his face and nearly choke him.

"You came and you paid me; then you said . . ." The boy's forehead creased beneath hair the color of straw. Or perhaps there was merely so much straw *in* his hair Alexi could not see anything else. "*Blag-da* somethin'. And *re-be* or *re-ba*." The kid shrugged. "I don't know."

"*Blagodarya rebenkom.*"

Basically, *Thanks, kid.* He'd said it a dozen times in a dozen different towns. And, of course, Cat had absorbed the words, the tone, the usage probably without even realizing it.

"That's it!" The boy slapped his knee. "Real purdy. Sounded just like you. But you kept your hat pulled low. Couldn't see your face." The kid narrowed his gaze. "Didn't have no broken nose. Then neither did you when you come in here afore. How was I supposed to know he weren't you?"

"How indeed?" Alexi stared into the relentless indigo night.

As he headed out of town on foot and alone—no point in buying another horse when Mikhail waited close by with more—he ran through a string of curses in his head that weren't at all purdy.

An hour later, Mikhail materialized from the gloom.

"Which way?" Alexi asked.

Mikhail lifted a massive hand and pointed northwest. Alexi peered in that direction but didn't see even a puff of dust. He hadn't expected to.

"Told me to wait for you. Said she'd meet us in Denver City." Alexi blew a derisive bit of air between his lips, and Mikhail's big face crumpled. "She won't?"

"Maybe yes, maybe no."

Alexi pulled the satchel that held his clothes from the packhorse, stripping off the offensive borrowed garments and letting them fall to the ground. He dressed in his own much-sweeter-smelling things. He kicked the discarded clothes into a pile and caught the last trace of another man's sweat.

Memories flickered. Scents brought back the past most vividly. Which was why Alexi made certain he was always well bathed and his clothes were clean. It was one of the best ways he'd found to keep those memories at bay. Yet still, sometimes, they insisted on coming out to dance.

"You need whiskey?"

Though Mikhail remembered little of their shared past, he was familiar with the signs that indicated Alexi was close to dredging up everything.

"No." Alexi dropped his fingers from his temple. "I'm all right."

"Sure?" Mikhail glanced at the stolen clothes and wrinkled his nose. "Makes me think of—"

Alexi tossed a match in the center of the pile and flames licked upward.

Mikhail blinked, and the flicker of pain, fear, betrayal disappeared. With Mikhail it was easy. Remove what had brought forth the memory and the memory was gone. But for Alexi the memories never truly went away.

His gaze returned to the northwest. Was that how it was for Cat? The past always hovering, whispering, waiting. Something simple like a scent or a place or a phrase—*you or her*—and *bam,* you remembered again what you would do most anything to forget?

For Alexi, the only things that made the past fade were whiskey and women and a really good dodge. Becoming someone else meant who he was, who he'd been, what he'd done were no longer his problems. For the short time he lived in another's skin he forgot his own. If he hadn't been able to do that, he wasn't sure he would have survived.

CAT HAD SWORN NEVER to go back. What good would it do? The house was gone. Even if it had been standing, there was nothing left for her there but the memories she was trying to forget.

"Liar," she whispered to herself. If she were truly trying to forget, she wouldn't bring them out every time she asked: *You or her?*

Still, the instant she'd seen that hill in a place where very few hills existed, she'd known she would have to go there. In order to do that, she needed to leave Alexi behind.

Her plan had been simple. When Alexi devised a swindle, he did so based on the laws of human nature. Folks wanted something for nothing. They were greedy. They would buy into a dodge because the idea of cheating the cheater was irresistible. While Alexi might be different in many ways from any other person she had ever met, at heart he was human. He'd agreed to her game because he wanted something from her. He'd believed he could get it with ease. When he'd won, he'd taken his prize, never suspecting that he'd been manipulated from the beginning.

Underhanded? Yes. But Cat had learned from the master. Alexi might be annoyed when he awoke and she was gone—again—but people like him knew better than to throw stones. How many women had woken in Alexi Romanov's bed well satisfied?

And alone.

Cat approached the burned-out homestead cautiously, though she could easily see in the gray light of dawn that the place was deserted. The wind whistled through the few standing boards; the chimney had collapsed; the barn was completely gone. Amazing what two years could do. Only the outhouse remained, and the door hung open to reveal an empty interior.

Cat climbed off the horse and let him graze while she moved through the ruins of the house. Grass had begun to push up between the ashes. Was that supposed to give her hope? Proof that life went on, even in the midst of death?

Cat fell to her knees, yanking out the few green tufts and tossing them into a corner. Life didn't go on. Not for—

She turned her head. The marker still sat on top of that hill. High up so she could see him. And so he could see her.

Back then she'd still believed Billy was watching over her. Back then she'd even believed she could stay on the farm and not go mad.

It was the little things that did it. Getting up in the morning, making breakfast, setting the table for two, sitting down and staring at the extra plate, the empty chair.

Hearing her name on the wind, running to the doorway, looking toward the field, seeing the headstone, and collapsing in grief—again.

Losing hours. Maybe days. Who knew? Starting up in the night— just as she had that night—believing it all a dream—it had to be—then reaching for him, encountering a cold, gaping space in the bed and remembering the truth.

When she woke atop his grave on the fourth morning in a row, Cathleen had decided: Enough. She had to do something. So she'd packed a bag, then set fire to the only thing she'd ever wanted—that home with Billy.

She headed west—didn't everyone?—riding their horse, leading the cow, which she easily sold to the first farmer she found. She'd spoken to lawmen—hell, she'd spoken to her brother-in-law—but no one could help her. She hadn't seen the face of the man who'd ruined her world. She'd only heard his voice. And as Ben had asked, "You gonna go around forcing every outlaw type you see to say the words until you find the one who actually did?"

That had sounded like a fine idea to her. But she'd needed a strategy. Coming up with one had occupied her mind, taken her away from the memories, begun to soothe the madness. Still, it hadn't all come together until Omaha.

Cat made her way up the hill as the sun threatened the eastern horizon. She sat in the grass and pulled away the weeds that had begun to obscure the marker.

The first time she'd seen Alexi Romanov, he'd been an ancient, hunchbacked, one-eyed Indian fighter named Horace Redstone. He'd come to Omaha to raise funds to train an elite unit of cavalry that would protect the construction of a new arm of the Union Pacific.

As the residents of the city were familiar with the problems caused by the Indians during the original construction of the railroad, they were easily persuaded of the necessity to protect any additions. That the Union Pacific had no plans to add to their already extensive amount of track and that the Indians were occupied much farther west than Nebraska at the time did not appear to occur to anyone but Cathleen.

Alexi was too convincing. He knew exactly what to say to get folks to remember what had happened before. He knew what would be necessary to keep it from happening again. People handed over their money with not only a smile but a pat on his pathetically humped shoulder. What gave him away were his hands.

He wore gloves. He wasn't stupid. He could alter his face with makeup. He could create a hump. He could walk, talk, breathe old man. But when it came to his hands, even gloves couldn't disguise their innate grace.

Certainly, he shook with palsy. He'd even slathered God knew what on his wrist to make it look as if he had a bad case of something no one wanted to catch.

"But he made one mistake." Cat touched her fingertip to the W carved into the marker. Wind and rain—it was fading already. She pulled out her long, sharp knife and set to work on the letters, cutting them more deeply into the wood.

"Then again," she continued, "maybe it was two."

She would never have given the fellow another thought after she tossed him a coin, but as she'd walked by, the wind chased over him, then swirled past her.

He didn't smell like ancient, dirty man. He smelled like dew at dawn, the sun at dusk, the rain just as it began to tumble down.

Cathleen's neck prickled, and she turned her head as "Captain Redstone" palmed her coin with a dexterity that should have been beyond such sadly shaking fingers.

She continued on with no indication that she'd seen anything out of the ordinary. Then she'd lurked about the rest of the day, watching him. She'd never witnessed a single other hint that he wasn't exactly who he said he was.

"Even when I knocked on his door"—Cat dug the sharp edge into the curve of the C—"I still wasn't sure." She paused, knife in the air, eyes on the violet sky, mind on the past.

She'd tracked him to a shed around back of the saloon. The bartender, a veteran of Sheridan's cavalry, had offered the shack when he'd discovered the war hero sleeping on the plank boardwalk early one morning.

Cathleen had stared at the door as her plan clicked into place. She didn't notice when it began to rain; she didn't care that she was soaked.

The captain answered her knock still wearing his eye patch, his hump, his disgusting cavalry hat, and those gloves. They'd considered each other as the rain trickled down her face like tears.

"I know what you are," she said.

His eyebrow lifted; he didn't say a word.

"You're not old. You're not an Indian fighter. You're not going to teach soldiers anything."

He contemplated her for so long Cathleen began to wonder if he might do something rash and what it would be. Eventually he lifted one shoulder—the one without the hump—the movement full of the grace she'd already witnessed in his hands. "You are telling me what I'm not. I thought you knew what I was."

"A cheat, a liar, a confidence man."

His lips curved, and she found herself fascinated by them. Not because they were attractive in any way. His lips were as dried up and ancient as he appeared to be. The lower one even cracked and began to bleed in response to the upward movement. "How do you plan to prove that?"

She yanked her gaze from his mouth to his eye. "I don't."

He blinked. She'd surprised him, and she doubted he was surprised often. Probably one of the reasons he was still alive.

"What do you plan to do?" he asked in the same rough, fading whisper of a man who'd shouted in battle until his voice had been ruined forever.

Yet below that voice, Cathleen heard another. One that made her shiver. And not because rain had begun to slide down her back and pool at her spine, but because the voice beneath this one was the hiss of a snake in the grass—one you couldn't quite see yet knew was not only very much there, but deadly and coming for you.

She lifted her chin. "I want to learn everything you know."

He peered at her with his one visible eye, and she resisted the urge to *yank off the patch and stare defiantly into the other. What if it really was an empty socket?*

"You want me to teach you how to fight Injuns?"

She laughed. Again, he looked surprised, and just a bit intrigued.

"I want to learn how to fool people. How to make them think you're someone else. How to be someone else."

His gaze flicked behind her, as if he'd just realized this was not a conversation he wanted anyone in Omaha to hear. Then the captain yanked her inside and shut the door.

The place was what one might expect to find behind a saloon. Boxes everywhere. He appeared to be using them both for chairs and tables. Upon one lay a set of Colt Dragoons that could easily have belonged to Captain Redstone. Had he stolen them? From whom?

"What if I say nyet?*"*

The final word—hard and foreign—was another chink in his Captain Redstone armor. It was the first foreign word Cathleen had ever heard, but, thanks to him, it was not the last. She understood its meaning easily enough.

"I'll visit the sheriff. Suggest he telegraph the Union Pacific and see if they've ever heard of you."

He appeared unconcerned with her threat, which concerned her. Could he reach those guns before she did? Would he shoot her? Did she care?

She stepped between him and the weapons. He rolled his eye. The movement, when performed by just one of them, left the impression of dizziness rather than derision.

"If I wanted you dead, then dead you would be."

Cathleen snorted.

He moved quickly, proving, if he hadn't already, that he wasn't who he pretended. He had her by the throat before she could think, let alone move or scream. His nimble fingers squeezed, and the whole world shimmered.

"I do not like threats." He released her as quickly as he'd captured her.

She rubbed at the dull-edged throb in her throat. "Who does?"

Silence fell over them like a cool gray mist. Then he began to laugh, and the sound of it was even rustier than her own.

"Who does?" he repeated. "Blestyashchiy."

Blest—?" she began, but could not get her tongue around the rest. "What?"

"Never mind. You wish to learn the fine art of confidence?"

"You seem to have enough to spare."

"Clever." His voice still bubbled with laughter. "That will help."

The weight that had pressed upon Cathleen's chest since her whole world died lifted just a little. He was going to agree.

"I have only one question."

She waited, expecting a request for her reasons, her origins, her name.

"What's in it for me?"

She opened her mouth, shut it again. She'd told him what was in it for him. "I won't—"

"I know." He no longer spoke in the gruff captain's voice but instead in a smooth, slightly foreign one that she didn't think was his either. "You won't."

And while he hadn't removed his hump or revealed his other eye, or taken a wet cloth and washed off the makeup that he must be wearing, even if she couldn't see it, he no longer limped or hitched. His hand hadn't trembled since he'd touched her.

And he was right. She wouldn't tell what she knew. Not only would this man throttle her if she tried, but she'd seen how quickly he could move, and in his eye there'd been something . . . ominous.

She rubbed her arms. He was not someone who appreciated, or forgot, betrayal. If he let her leave this room alive and she decided to tell what she knew to the law, he'd not only be gone before she ever reached the sheriff but she would spend the rest of her life looking over her shoulder more often than she already did.

If she didn't have the threat of exposing him, she had nothing. The weight returned to Cathleen's chest, making it hard for her to breathe.

"Calm down," he snapped, and she realized she'd been gasping like a fish. "I didn't say I wouldn't teach you."

A deep breath filled her lungs. She let it out, then took another. "But—"

"I said, 'What's in it for me if I do?' "

He was so close she had to tilt back her head to see into his face. His laughter had died; his eye was both as empty and as watchful as the snake she'd already compared him to.

"What do you want?" she asked.

"You."

CHAPTER 10

*T*he silhouette on the hill continued to converse with a tombstone.

Alexi couldn't hear what she was saying; he probably didn't want to. He had a pretty good idea whose tombstone that was.

His gaze wandered over what remained of the cabin and outbuildings. The fields were fallow; she'd been gone a while.

He'd never figured her for a farm wife.

"Should I fetch her?" Mikhail asked.

Alexi considered, then shook his head. If all she'd wanted was to visit with the dead, she could have done so and returned. That she'd said she would meet them in Denver City meant she was up to something. He wanted to know what.

By the time the sun washed over her, she'd taken care of business—pulled weeds, then carved something into the marker, which meant it must be wood and not a stone. She'd chatted up a storm, ran her fingers over the letters, then gotten on *his* horse, and moved on. What he hadn't seen her do was cry. Alexi couldn't remember when he had.

No, that wasn't true. She'd cried on cue every time that he'd asked. But real tears . . . Not a one.

When she disappeared over a very flat ridge, Alexi flicked a finger and Mikhail followed.

Then Alexi headed for the grave.

* * *

CAT HEADED FOR ROCK RIVER.

"Be truthful."

The horse flicked back his ear. He seemed a practiced listener, and she appreciated that, even though she wasn't talking to him but herself.

"You knew from the moment you left Brooks where you'd end up."

Rock River—or someplace like it—had been inevitable.

She took her time; she didn't rush. As before, Cat didn't want to arrive with the daylight.

If Ben was surprised to see her so soon after the last visit, he didn't show it.

"Got anything?"

He handed her a sheet of paper. One glance and she smiled. Her brother-in-law might disapprove of what she was doing, but he still saved the most likely culprits for her.

Frank Walters. Wanted—dead or alive. Crimes: horse theft, murder, rape; appeared he'd even shot someone's dog.

"Last seen?"

Ben frowned at her costume. Or maybe just at her. He didn't comment on the obvious—the clothes weren't hers. They were too big. They were too new. Alexi didn't wear anything old unless he had to.

Lifting her eyebrows, Cat waited.

Ben just shook his head and answered her question. "Indian Territory."

"Damn."

In the years before the war, many tribes had been granted

land in the West to compensate them for the land they'd been pushed from in the East. The Territory had once encompassed Kansas, Nebraska, and part of Iowa. However, when white folks spread past the Mississippi, saw the ripe farmland and coveted it, the Indians were again relocated.

Indian Territory now lay south of Kansas, and it was a mess. The Five Civilized Tribes—Cherokee, Chickasaw, Choctaw, Creek, and Seminole—had been dragged west long ago. They'd established governments and laws; they'd enjoyed a relative peace. Then the United States had not only started shoving other tribes onto their land, but they'd pretty much ignored that it *was* their land and let anyone that wanted to traipse over it on their way to California and Oregon.

Indian courts and lawmen held no reign over the white intruders. Once the outlaws discovered this, Indian Territory became their favorite place to hide. Cat had gone there before to retrieve bounties. She didn't much like it. Didn't mean she wasn't going back. Right now she needed to.

Alexi believed the man she'd been searching for was in Denver City. Maybe he was; maybe he wasn't. Maybe he'd just put the bounty on her head to distract her so she'd stop looking elsewhere.

And maybe she was just making excuses. In truth, she needed to hunt. Every time she removed another outlaw from this earth —by sending him to hell on her own, or taking him in so the law could do it—she felt like she retrieved another splintered shred of herself.

Although she wasn't quite certain anymore just how much of Cathleen was left. What really disturbed her was that she wasn't certain how much she wanted there to be.

"You takin' that bounty?" Ben asked.

Cat nodded, then glanced at the window. She couldn't see past the night pressing against the panes, but he was out there. She could feel him.

"Ruby still bring your supper every night?"

Ben's brow furrowed. "How else would I get anything to eat?"

Cat didn't bother to point out that he had a stove in his room. He wouldn't know how to use it any more than Billy had.

"When?"

Ben pulled his granddad's timepiece from his pocket, and Cat flinched before she could stop herself. He did that exactly the same way Billy always had.

"Twenty minutes."

"Good." Cat didn't want to be near Ben any longer than she had to. "Here's what we're gonna do."

* * *

ALEXI KEPT to the alley between a haberdashery and an apothecary, directly across the street from the sheriff's office. His hat shaded his two black eyes, while doing little to disguise the unfortunate size of his broken nose. He'd received a few too many curious glances already.

"You're sure she went in there?" Alexi rubbed his thumb over the small, smooth object in his pocket like a talisman.

Mikhail, standing even farther back so as not to be seen and remembered by the citizenry, or seen and recognized by Cat, merely grunted. If there was one thing Mikhail excelled at, it was tracking. Therefore, if he said Cat had gone into the sheriff's office an hour ago, then she had gone into the sheriff's office an hour ago. Alexi would bet his life on Mikhail's abilities and often had.

Though he wasn't certain of the specifics involved in bounty hunting, Alexi didn't think it would take anywhere near an hour to complete bounty hunter business. Therefore, the longer Cat remained within, the more uncomfortable Alexi became.

They'd watched a woman enter carrying a covered plate, then leave again a short while later without it. Since that occurrence there had been no one in, no one out. It was maddening. But maddening pretty much summed up Alexi's life since Cat had come back into it.

"His name was William," Alexi said.

"Whose name?"

"No one." At least not anymore.

Mikhail gave Alexi a look that very clearly said he needed to stop talking to himself.

Alexi had wanted to learn the man's name, but now that he had, he wasn't sure why he'd thought it important. What did it matter if he knew the name of her dead husband? The point was that Cat knew.

And she would never, ever forget.

Alexi inserted his thumb into the gold circlet of her ring. She'd left the chain looped over the tombstone. He still hadn't figured out why.

Alexi squinted at the window, but as had been the case the dozen or so times he'd squinted at it before, he could see nothing through the glass but the edge of a desk and the far corner of the room.

"You're sure—"

"No back door," Mikhail interrupted. "I'm sure."

Alexi could see where a back door on a jail would be a mistake. One way in, one way out was best. Of course, Alexi always preferred multiple exits, but he had good reason to.

He should just stroll across the street and walk in. As far as he knew, he wasn't wanted for anything.

In Rock River.

And every other town that might be searching for him was not searching for *him*. Still, to set foot inside a jail voluntarily for no reason other than to—

The door opened; the sheriff stepped out. Cat followed, hat tipped low, the trousers she'd stolen from Alexi seeming to hang on her less loosely than they should. She laid her hand on the sheriff's arm. He patted it fondly; then the two of them strolled around the back side of the building. Before they disappeared, Alexi could have sworn the man's other hand also patted her behind.

"He lives up the stairs," Mikhail said.

"What stairs?"

"In the back."

"You didn't tell me about any stairs."

"You asked if there was another door. There ain't."

What possible reason could Cat have for going upstairs with the sheriff? Alexi could think of only one.

He was across the street and around the corner the next instant. The stairs were easy to climb, the lock even easier to pick. He entered the room so quietly the couple embracing in the center wasn't aware of anything but each other. Alexi doubted they'd have noticed if he'd slammed the door and sung "hallelujah."

The man's hands were on Cat's ass, his mouth on her lips. His tongue was no doubt caressing her teeth, tasting the flavor that was uniquely hers—spiced apples in midwinter, wine cooled in a mountain stream long about August.

When the fellow lifted his blond head, his expression followed by the sound of her voice murmuring "Ben" in a way she'd never murmured "Alexi" caused an explosion of fury in his chest.

He was across the room, shoving her aside, fisting his hands in the sheriff's shirt, and yanking him onto his toes before he really heard her. Then he snatched the gun out of Sheriff Ben's hand and spun to face Cat O'Banyon.

Who *wasn't* Cat O'Banyon.

* * *

CAT HAD no trouble retrieving another set of clothes from Ben's room, leaving Ruby's behind, then returning to what she now considered her horse and galloping south. If Ben did as she asked, Alexi wouldn't know he'd been duped until she was so far away even he couldn't catch up.

Oh, he'd find her. Eventually. Or rather, Mikhail would. But by then she'd have done what she needed to do. Maybe then she'd be able to breathe.

Finding Frank Walters wasn't hard. Not only was the man painfully short, but he possessed a nose the size of Texas and a knife scar across one cheek. The physical description aside, he couldn't seem to stop stealing things and shooting people. He cut a trail through Indian Territory it would have taken an imbecile to miss.

She caught up to him in Tennyville, which wasn't much more than a circle of smaller tents surrounding a larger one. Considering that men went into the center construction walking straight and came out weaving, stumbling, and falling, Cat labeled it the saloon.

She considered strolling in and removing her quarry by force. But as most of the residents had the rough appearance of the men she usually hunted and she hadn't brought along a Gatling gun to back up that kind of volume, Cat decided to wait until Frank rode out alone, then follow. It didn't take long. Less than two hours later, Walters saddled his horse and headed south.

She should have figured he was up to something, considering what he'd been up to so far, but she was trying to keep enough distance between them so Walters wouldn't see her, while at the same time searching for a grove of trees to duck into or a dip in the land that would allow her to catch up, then catch him.

But the Territory wasn't known for its forests and hills. The few trees this area might have once possessed had been yanked from their roots and whirled away to parts unknown by both recent and long-ago twisters, leaving great gaping holes in the ground but no cover. Which meant by the time she reached where Frank was going, a small Cherokee village more villagelike than Tennyville would ever be, she was already too late.

The first shot exploded as Cat passed the outskirts of the settlement. The second sounded as she urged the horse to gallop toward the one building from which light poured. The third and fourth cracks came as she leaped to the ground and ran, pulling Alexi's guns from the holsters as she did.

She had a moment to wish she'd retrieved her own weapons from Mikhail—Alexi's were both bigger and strangely lighter than those she was used to—before she glanced inside and saw Frank taking a bead on another victim.

"Frank Walters, drop your weapons," she ordered, pulling breath from her belly, expanding through the chest, her shout that of a man, just as Alexi had taught her.

In the middle of a nasty game of Shoot the Cherokee, one he appeared to be winning four to nothing considering the dead men on the floor, Frank was so surprised at her command he didn't pull the trigger.

"Who's that?" He squinted at the door.

Cat hugged the wall next to the open hole in the plank that served as a window. "There's a bounty on you. I've come to take you in."

Frank guffawed. "You and what army?"

He sighted on another Indian, and Cat stepped from cover. At least he stopped what he was doing.

"How about you just repeat *you or her,* and I won't make this painful?" If he moved, she'd wing him. She needed the man to say the words, after all.

Frank's eyes widened; he swung the gun in her direction. "Yer Ca—" was all he got out before Cat pulled the trigger.

The gun made a sick, clicking, empty sound.

CHAPTER 11

*W*ho the hell are you?" Alexi demanded of the woman wearing Cat's—no, his—clothes.

She stared in horrified fascination at the gun in his hand. He felt equal horror, combined with a sharp bite of nausea. The weapon seemed to weigh a hundred pounds, and Alexi had to fight to keep it leveled in their direction.

But he did. He had to. Sheriff Ben looked like he wanted nothing more than to snatch the gun back and blow off Alexi's head.

Why hadn't he sent Mikhail up here? The big man would have had the truth out of these two in an instant with no squeamishness about the gun. Or anything else.

But Alexi hadn't thought; he hadn't planned. He'd seen Sheriff Ben's hand on Cat's ass and he'd run.

And it hadn't even been Cat's ass.

"Where is she?" He glanced around the room as if Cat might be hidden behind the sparse furnishings.

The dress on the floor tweaked his memory, and he cursed, long and low and—from the expression of the woman who was not Cat—obviously in English.

"Hey, now. Not in front of the lady."

"Where?" Alexi repeated.

The lawman glanced away. Alexi cocked the weapon, and Sheriff Ben stepped in front of the woman. "She's got nothin' to do with this."

Alexi swallowed back bile, bit the inside of his lip, gave himself a mental pat on the head for keeping his hand—and therefore the pistol—steady. "What do *you* have to do with it?"

Ben's forehead creased. "I'm the sheriff."

"The star gave it away." Alexi waved the gun to indicate the badge. "But why would you go along with her charade? Why would you risk your life to keep her whereabouts secret?"

"She said you wouldn't hurt me."

"I won't."

The sheriff took one step forward. Alexi snapped the fingers of his free hand, and Mikhail entered the room. The other man froze.

"He, on the other hand—"

"Indian Territory," the woman blurted.

"Ruby Dean!"

"Ben Chase!"

"Chase?" Alexi repeated. "How interesting."

Ben stilled. "Why would that be interesting?"

"I knew a woman once." Alexi held Ben's gaze. "Cathleen Chase."

"She died," Ruby said. "Or at least everyone thinks so. Had a place 'bout thirty miles from here. It done burned to the ground, and by the time anyone got out there, the animals had—" She winced. "You know."

Alexi considered asking why, if Cathleen was dead, there was only one grave on that hill and the marker hadn't read *Cathleen Chase.* Then decided that question would only lead to answers he either didn't want to hear or things Cat didn't want discovered.

Ruby patted Ben's shoulder. "She was Ben's sister-in-law. Both she and Ben's brother, Billy, died in that fire. Was real sad."

Alexi hadn't realized he'd been holding his breath until he let it out on the words "sister-in-law." His overactive imagination had fashioned Cat and Sheriff Ben as man and wife, the grave at the farm that of their child. The two of them on a path of vengeance—Ben as a lawman, Cat as a bounty hunter.

Considering that Cat had told him she was barren, his leap to those circumstances was large, even for him. Then again . . . Cat O'Banyon wasn't a legend because of her truthfulness.

However, the strange and unreasoning fury that had flowed through Alexi at the idea of Cat, even when she'd been Cathleen, carrying another man's child both chilled and fascinated him.

"Indeed." Alexi kept his gaze steady on Ben. "Sad."

The man flushed, taking Alexi's meaning. The sad part was how Cathleen had become Cat and taken to hunting her husband's killer while his brother sat in Rock River and let her.

Alexi considered having Mikhail remove Ruby so he and Ben could have a private talk. He'd like to know the details of Cathleen's "death."

"This man Cat went after," Ruby said. "He's a bad'un."

"Aren't they all?" Alexi continued to contemplate Sheriff Chase, wondering how much he knew, how long it would take to get him to tell.

Mikhail tugged on Alexi's arm. Alexi shrugged him off.

"But Al—"

Alexi shot him a look that stopped Mikhail instantly.

The big man licked his lips, glanced at the window, then back at Alexi. "She doesn't have a gun."

"Don't be foolish. Of course she does."

"She did," Ben said. "Though she wasn't toting her usual Navy Colts."

Alexi's gaze fell on Ruby's clothes. *His* clothes. The ones Cat had stolen—along with his guns.

Then he felt very sick.

* * *

CAT TRIED to throw herself to the side; maybe Frank would miss. But at this range Frank would have had to be half blind not to hit something.

Frank was not half blind.

Fire erupted just below her shoulder. The useless gun dropped from her suddenly useless hand. She followed it to the ground, the lighter clatter of the weapon followed by the heavier thud of her body next to it.

The gun had been empty. Why would Alexi carry an empty gun?

A shadow fell over her; Cat glanced up. The end of the barrel, when pointed at your face, seemed to loom as big as a cavern.

"Yer her. Cat O'Banyon."

"Nope." Cat tried to answer using her manly voice, but all that came out was a whisper.

Frank pulled her hat from her head, and Cat's hair tumbled down.

"Hell," she muttered.

"Huge bounty on Cat O'Banyon. Dead or alive." He glanced toward the door. "Too bad that shot didn't kill you. Guess I'll have to truss you up and drag you all the way to Denver City." He pursed his mouth, thought a while. Finally he cocked his head, then the weapon. "Too much trouble."

The explosion was deafening.

* * *

ALEXI AND MIKHAIL approached the Cherokee village around midmorning. The place had a deserted air that made Alexi's skin prickle.

They'd followed the trail left by Frank Walters. It wasn't hard. The man left dead bodies behind like breadcrumbs.

Unfortunately, they'd gotten caught on the far side of a raging creek after a driving rainstorm and lost that trail for the better part of a day. Alexi had feared they might never find Frank, or Cat, again. He should have known better. Mikhail could find anyone.

"Why is it so quiet?" Alexi asked as they walked their horses through the far-too-silent settlement. Didn't Indians keep dogs? Perhaps a screaming child or two?

Mikhail pointed to a near ridge where several men stood. They moved about, bending, straightening, tossing the earth.

Alexi kicked his horse into a gallop.

The Cherokee had dug shallow trenches next to several large boulders. Some continued to dig near other boulders; some had begun to build knee-high walls of smaller stones around each trench.

They lifted their heads as Alexi and Mikhail arrived. Chests bare, skin gleaming, breechclouts hung to their knees. A few had tattoos; some wore woven arm or ankle bands. Every neck supported a thong off which hung a claw or a tooth or a shell, some all three. Their ears had been distorted by metal inserted into the lobe, a type of adornment that stretched the supple skin to abominable lengths. From their belts hung deerskin purses to the front, a knife to the right. Nearby lay several rifles.

When the Cherokee saw neither man meant them harm, they went back to what they were doing.

Alexi slid from his horse, crossed to the nearest trench, glanced inside. As expected, a dead Cherokee lay within. He couldn't tell from the body how the man had died, as he had been cleaned and dressed in his best breechclout and deerskin shirt. But considering there were several bodies, Alexi had a feeling Frank had been here. What he needed to know was if Cat had been here as well.

"What happened?"

The Cherokee continued to build, stone upon stone, over and over. No one gave any indication they'd understood.

Alexi glanced helplessly at Mikhail, who spread his big hands. Alexi was the one who knew languages. So many, but not one of them Cherokee.

"Was there a—?"

The Indians paused and waited for him to continue. He had no idea how, so he began to act out the words. He patted his belt where a gun might be, made an angry face, used his finger and thumb to point, squinted down the "barrel," then pulled the "trigger."

All but one of the Cherokee went back to building. The other let his dark gaze pass over Alexi's fading bruises and crooked nose, then pointed behind Alexi's shoulder and said in perfect English, "The man hunter is over there."

Alexi spun, hope lifting the heavy weight that had pressed on him since he'd awoken in bed alone. He blinked at the empty vista, then frowned at the other man, who made a shooing motion with his large work-roughened hands.

Alexi's frown deepened, but he shooed, first striding in the indicated direction, then stopping so fast his boots slid in the loose dirt when he saw the edge of another open hole.

This one had been dug away from the others—no boulder to mark it, no lovingly placed stones surrounding it. Just a hole big enough for a much smaller body.

He approached, light heart now thundering so fiercely, his chest had begun to ache. He didn't want to look inside, but he had to. Even so, he stopped a foot away, closed his eyes, fought for control, waited as long as he could before moving closer, then opening first one eye—slowly—then the other quite fast.

The sight of what lay in the grave caused his already wobbling legs to give out completely. He went to his knees—head bent, shoulders slumped.

It wasn't her. From what was left, he thought this must be Frank.

"Where is she?" he whispered.

"The woman who dresses as a man?"

The Cherokee who'd sent him here stood at his side.

"You saw her?"

"A woman both brave and foolish."

Alexi sighed. He'd seen her. "Which way did she go?"

"Go?" The Cherokee's forehead creased. "She did not go."

Alexi's hope came back. "She's . . ."

"Dying."

"Dying," Alexi repeated stupidly.

"Durga." One of the Cherokee beckoned to the fellow at Alexi's side, but the man shook his head, rattled off a few sentences in Cherokee, then beckoned to Alexi.

"I will show you." He indicated Mikhail should remain near the graves, then he headed down the ridge.

"Alexi." Mikhail's big shoulders hunched. "Don't leave."

"It's all right." Alexi patted the massive hand that plucked at his sleeve. "They won't hurt you."

Mikhail laughed with the clear, sweet innocence of a child. "'Course not." Then his laughter faded, and his brow creased. "But I'm supposed to take care of you."

"I'll be fine." Alexi removed Mikhail's hand from his arm, and as always, Mikhail believed whatever Alexi told him.

Alexi followed Durga down the ridge, through the town, over an embankment, and across a dusty, crusty hillside to a stream where a humped structure of mud and grass covered with blankets sat near the gurgling water. A fire burned outside the door, the smoke obscuring what lay within, although the chant of "Caaaat" gave a good indication.

"They are calling her back from the spirit world."

"I'll call her back." He'd drag her back. And then he'd shake her until her teeth came loose for being so damn . . .

"You must let our women complete the healing ceremony. If you don't, she will be lost forever between this world and the next."

Alexi hesitated. Sometimes the Indian medicines worked the best. They'd been here longer; they knew the land and what grew in it. Alexi certainly had no idea what to do for—

"What happened to her?"

"Shot."

Of course shot. What else?

"Can your women help?" Alexi asked.

Durga indicated the structure. "The sacred turtle shields her."

The domed building did look like the back of a turtle.

The Indian pointed to the fire at the entrance, which sent up herb and tobacco-scented smoke. "The head."

A woman came out then used a thick cloth to remove a stone from the fire. As she carried it within, she laid a trail of herbs along the ground, connecting the "head" to the "shell" by a "neck." Seconds later, a hiss rose; then steam puffed from the opening. Low-voiced chanting began, no longer Cat's name but words Alexi did not understand.

"They pray. For her health, her life, her strength, and her soul."

Alexi hadn't prayed since the war. He was surprised to discover the sound of it could still bring comfort.

"She has gone back to the womb."

Was that good or bad?

"Unclothed we come into this world. Back to the earth we will return. If she emerges, she will be reborn. Cleansed. New. She will leave behind the troubles that brought her to this point." Alexi's expression must have been dubious, for the man's lips curved. "Death has a way of changing one's life."

Alexi figured Cat knew that better than anyone.

"How long?" At the Indian's raised eyebrows, he lifted his chin to indicate the lodge. "Until we know?"

"Do you have children?"

Alexi's mind flashed on Cat with the bulge of clothes beneath her skirt. Longing hit him so hard, he went breathless with it. He could do nothing but shake his head.

"Birth takes a very long time. Rebirth just a bit longer."

The day grew hot. The sun beat on the turtle's back and Alexi's head. Steam rolled out the door. The women continued to chant.

"As long as they keep praying, that's good, right?"

Durga nodded.

Alexi knew without asking that if they began to again call her name, he had lost her. He wasn't sure what he would do if that happened. And then . . .

It did.

CHAPTER 12

From the darkness rose a low, wordless hum.

No. Not wordless. One word.

Caaaaaaaat.

Silence descended, and she nearly fell back where she'd been —a cool, painless place where memory did not exist—until the hum, the chant, the name pulled her out.

Caaaaaat.

Cat opened one eye. She lay in the center of a domed structure surrounded by Indian women. All wore loose-fitting sleeveless dresses, similar to a shift but fashioned of soft hides. Beneath that, a woven skirt, beads and feathers dancing with the fringe, brushed the tops of their moccasins. Necklaces of shells and bones circled their throats; earrings swayed in their ears, and their hair gleamed with grease; red and yellow dust sparkled in the dark strands.

One woman took a breath so deep, she rattled the necklaces that lay upon her chest. Then, as the breath streamed out, she chanted, "Caaaaaaat."

Cat hurt all over, but especially her head and shoulder. She was so hot, her skin seemed both on fire and incredibly damp. The very air around her seeped with steam. From what she could tell, she wore not a stitch of clothing. Considering the number of furs and blankets, she didn't need any.

"Caaaat!"

A man's voice this time. Strange. She saw no man within the circle. Her eyes slid closed and she returned to the cool, dark world.

Suddenly there was light. Intrigued, she went toward that light and inside it she felt . . . Billy.

She rushed forward.

No.

The word blew her back. Pain erupted—shoulder, head, belly —she was so hot. She clawed at the night, trying to get away from the pain and the heat and the darkness. Trying to get to him.

No.

Again she flew in the other direction. Again the pain, the heat, intensified. She was so tired, so weak. Not herself. Or at least not the self she had become.

"Billy. Please."

Begging. Something she'd sworn never to do again. Begging never helped. Begging made them laugh.

One step forward, two steps back. The story of her life. Or at least her life since she'd lost him.

"I want to be with you."

The wind ruffled her hair. *"Not your time."*

Had it been his? She didn't believe that. The man she hunted had cut Billy's time short.

"You or her?"

"Me," Billy had said.

"Me. Please, me," Cat had begged.

Then the gunshot. The blood. The dying.

And the one who was left . . .

There were things worse than death. Much worse.

"I didn't know," whispered the voice from the light.

"If you had, would you have chosen me?"

Silence. The whisper of a wind that felt like him, then an answer. *"I could never watch you die. "*

Instead he'd left her alone. With them.

Words like *cowardly* and *selfish* and *fool* floated through Cat's mind. Words she'd never before thought in regard to Billy.

"You've got a purpose here. "

She had vengeance. For him. For her. For them. *"Don't you hear him calling?"*

Cat glanced behind her, saw nothing. Heard no one. Felt only heat and pain and darkness. Then—

"Cat!"

A man's voice tugged at her. When she thought of that voice words like *strong* and *clever* and *determined* came to mind. Along with several others she shouldn't be thinking anywhere near Billy.

"He'll give you your purpose."

She peered at the light, but it was fading, receding, disappearing, and strangely she didn't mind. Because the voice that came from the dark was one she knew, one she . . .

Trusted.

That voice would never let anyone hurt her. That voice would never leave her alone.

She hovered in the darkness and waited to be drawn once again into the light.

* * *

WHEN THE WOMEN began to call her back from the realm of death, once more Alexi panicked and cried out her name.

Ignoring the murmur of dissent from Durga—he didn't think the man would ever shout—Alexi rushed into the hut.

The place was full of steam, full of women, but all he saw was her.

The blood on her face made his heart lurch, then stutter. He lifted a hand to his chest and rubbed.

"Shot," they'd said, and he'd practically shrugged. Those who lived by the gun, as Cat did, inevitably wound up shot by one. But why did it have to be in the head?

Head shots were difficult. Only the very best could find that target. Most went for the chest. But not him. Men survived chest wounds. Few survived a bullet to the head.

He'd been one of the Union's very best. Sharpshooting had never bothered him; he'd only been doing his job. Until—

Alexi fell to his knees, his own blood pounding in his ears so loudly he didn't hear the women, didn't hear himself; all he heard was—

"Shoot. Now. Do it."

The crack of a whip, the scent of blood. Then a moan.

"I won't hurt you. I promise. Everything will be all right."

A stupid, worthless promise. Why had he made it? He'd been trying to give comfort. Instead he'd given—

The sharp report of a gun. A body dropping to the earth. Blood everywhere. The face beneath it so still.

Nothing was ever right again.

Alexi reached out and brushed Cat's cheek. What if she was never right again?

"Cat."

Her eyelids fluttered. He held his breath, listened for hers, tried to remember how to pray. But the only word that came to mind right now was, "Please."

Her eyes opened. He didn't have time to panic—would she know him? Could she speak?—before she whispered, "Alexi."

The women started singing, joyful and very loud. He had to lean in close so she could hear him. "They called you back."

"No." She set her hand on his face. "You did."

He straightened. The gentle touch, the words she would never utter causing him to fear that her mind was indeed gone. But she'd known him; she'd said his name. The question was. Did she know *her* name?

"Cat?"

Her arm fell back to her side. "What's wrong with you?"

"Me?" He wasn't the one covered in blood.

"You're staring right at me. You just bellered my name like an orphaned calf. But you're looking at me as if you think I'm someone else."

The snappish tone relieved him. *That* was more like her.

"How's your head?" he asked.

"How's yours?"

"Fine, but I wasn't shot in it."

She scowled. "Neither was I."

He tugged something dry, flaky, and rust-colored from her hair. "You're covered in blood."

"Not mine."

Now that he was less terrified, he managed to focus and discovered she was right. There might be blood all over her face, but he could see no wound. Before she could stop him, Alexi yanked the blanket to her waist.

She slapped at his hands, but she was so weak the blows felt no more substantial than the rain. A large, disgusting hole marred the once-perfect flesh between shoulder and breast. The women had packed it with something brown. At least the bleeding had stopped.

"Is the bullet out?"

"No," Durga answered from the doorway.

Alexi caught the Cherokee staring and jerked the blanket up and over Cat's breasts. He couldn't fault the man; they were exquisite.

Cat cast him a wry glance, which he ignored.

"Why not?" It would have been better to do the digging while she was unconscious.

"She hovered between the worlds. Until she chose this one, there was no point."

"Chose?" Alexi's gaze met Cat's, but she glanced away.

She had chosen to live?

"She would not be here otherwise."

Alexi had experienced a lightening in his chest that had felt like . . . he wasn't sure. He couldn't recall having felt it before, but he thought it might have been hope. Might Cat have decided to stop seeking death now that death had come seeking her? Or had she chosen life only so that she could impart the death she'd been waiting so long to accomplish?

She'd never really told him what had happened to her. She hadn't needed to. Alexi was a master at adding parts and seeing a whole.

"Just dig it out, Romanov."

Her words made him start as if someone had poked him in the rear with a stick. "Me? No, thank you."

"Your hands," she said.

Alexi looked down. They were just hands.

"I've seen you do things with them no man should be able to do."

He raised his eyes to hers. What he saw there made his stomach shimmy. She trusted him.

"No."

"Yes. It's you or no one."

"There are at least ten people in this hut. I'm sure any one of them would be happy to—"

"I don't care." She closed her eyes. "I want you."

Alexi swallowed, his throat clicking over the huge lump there. How many times had he dreamed she would say those words? Of course, in his imaginings, she'd been saying them naked.

Not that she wasn't naked now, but . . . His gaze flicked to the

Cherokee women surrounding them. This wasn't what he'd had in mind.

"Cat," he began.

"Alexi," she returned. "Do it."

He winced as her words echoed his past. "Isn't there a doctor?"

"Here?"

"A medicine man? A healer?"

"Yes." Durga appeared at his side.

Alexi nearly fainted in relief. "Where is he? I'll pay him. Whatever he wants."

"He has no need of money where he has gone."

"Shit." Alexi remembered the graves. "Damn Frank Walters's murdering soul to hell."

"I did," Durga said.

"*You* did?" Alexi glanced at Cat, but she still had her eyes closed. Sweat had broken out on her brow; she appeared far too pale.

"She carried empty guns. Why would she do that?"

"Yes." Cat's eyes were bright, feverish, but still aware. "Why would she?"

Alexi wasn't going to explain about his guns. Not now. Probably not ever.

A knife appeared in Durga's hand. The thing seemed far too large to dig out a bullet without making a much bigger hole.

Alexi stared at it for several seconds, then withdrew his own blade, which was a long, thin, sharp weapon he'd won in a card game. If he was going to do this, and it appeared that he was, he was going to do it right.

A hand landed on his wrist as someone attempted to take the weapon from him. He clutched it tightly, his other hand already coming about in a fist as he spun.

The tiny Cherokee woman stared at him impassively, and

Alexi's fist fell away. She tugged on the knife, but he did not let it go.

"She must cleanse the blade in the fire," Durga said.

"Why?"

"It seems to help."

Alexi released the knife. He'd take any advantage he could.

The Cherokee woman stepped outside, bent and shoved the blade into the leaping flames, turning it every which way so that it caught the sun and sparkled, even as the edge seemed to glow. Then she ducked inside and shoved the weapon into a bucket of water. The resulting hiss made Alexi flinch. She handed the knife to him and turned away.

Alexi knelt next to Cat. "You're sure I can't bribe someone else to do this?"

Her lips twitched. "I'm sure."

"It would seem that one of the women—"

"Everyone out."

"All right." Alexi practically leaped to his feet.

"Not you, Romanov. Everyone else."

Durga motioned to the others and they filed through the door.

"If I'm going to snivel," she said, sounding more tired with every word, "I'm going to do it in front of as few people as possible."

The idea that he was going to make her cry when she'd never cried before, except on cue, made Alexi's hand sweat. The knife slid around in his palm like a deer skating across the surface of a frozen pond. He glanced about, hoping for . . . what? Inspiration? Courage? An excuse?

"I don't have enough light."

As if he'd been heard on high, two flaps in the hut rolled away and brilliant sunlight poured in. Alexi cursed.

"Quit being a baby."

"You do realize I'm not a doctor?"

"Haven't you pretended to be at least once or twice?"

He had, but he'd never actually cut into anyone. He was a confidence man, not an idiot. Taking money was one thing. Murder quite another.

"Alexi," she said.

Just that. Nothing else. But in that one word he heard so much. She needed him to do this. She trusted no one else.

So he could watch her die, or he could help her to live.

CHAPTER 13

*W*hen Alexi flicked out whatever the Cherokee had packed in, the wound began to ooze. "It's deep. I don't think—"

"Finish." Cat spoke between clenched teeth.

"Your skin, *ma chere*. I have ruined it."

"It was ruined before you came along." She closed her eyes. "I was ruined before you came along."

She was really starting to frighten him. "Cat—"

Her eyes snapped open, and they glittered like emeralds in the sun. "I haven't asked much of you, Alexi, but I'm asking this. Dig now, as far as you have to, and do it fast."

He sighed like a finicky grandmother and did as she asked. He dug deep; he worked fast. Her fingers clenched on the blanket; her teeth ground together so loudly she might have been chewing rocks. But she did not writhe; she did not cry out.

When the tip of his knife scraped lead, Alexi wanted very badly to do both. Instead, he swallowed back bile and, with a quick twist of his wrist, forced the bullet free of her body. He held it up so she could see. Her lips curved; then her eyes drifted closed.

"Help," Alexi said, not shouting, not whispering either. He could no longer work up any emotion. Not worry, not joy, not fear—he'd spent all he had on her.

Durga must have been standing right outside the turtle because he appeared in the doorway immediately. Alexi liked the man more and more with every passing minute. When Durga waved his hand and several women poured in, shooing Alexi away, Alexi nearly hugged the fellow.

"They will clean and dress her wound. You and I will smoke."

Smoking sounded good to Alexi. Drinking even better.

Alexi was surprised to discover the sun on its way toward the western horizon. Time had seemed to stop while he was digging a knife into Cat's flesh, but apparently it had gone on merrily without him.

Durga indicated the stream with the flick of one dark finger. Alexi washed Cat's blood from his hands. There was little he could do about what had splattered his shirt and pants.

He followed the man to town, then into a house where Mikhail sat at the kitchen table eating a huge bowl of stew. Whoever had made it was nowhere in sight.

Mikhail's gaze narrowed on Alexi's stained clothing. "Miss Cathy all right?"

"For now." When discussing Cat, it paid to be cautious. "Our horses?"

Mikhail pointed at the window, open to the late-afternoon breeze. Their mounts contentedly grazed behind the house, unsaddled and rubbed down. Mikhail would never take his own respite before making sure the horses had theirs.

Three packs sat just inside the door, and as Mikhail returned to slurping his stew, Alexi snatched his bag. He followed Durga's finger to a room, which contained only a neatly made bed and a small chest at the foot that must have contained his possessions. Alexi drew off his blood-dotted garments and drew on his last unmarred set of clothing before returning to the kitchen.

Durga awaited him on the front porch, sitting in one of two well-made wooden chairs. Alexi took the empty one; Durga opened the pouch at his waist and began to roll cigarettes. He handed the first to Alexi, then started a second. His movements were unhurried, deliberate, soothing.

Alexi considered recovering his saddlebag and the whiskey he kept there, but he'd heard Indians should not be given firewater. Then again, he'd heard a lot of things about Indians—they were lazy; they were dirty; they were vicious—and none of them had proved to be true. Still, he might need the whiskey for Cat.

Durga removed a box of matches from his pouch, struck one, and held it to the end of Alexi's cigarette and then his own. They smoked in companionable silence. Once Alexi opened his mouth to ask what, exactly, had happened with Frank, and Durga's dark eyes flicked to his. "We do not talk while we smoke."

Alexi lifted his eyebrows, but he remained silent. He owed this man so much, he could at least adhere to his customs.

By the time they were done with their smokes, Alexi was considering adopting the Cherokee way himself. He had enjoyed this cigarette so much more because he didn't have to inhale jerky puffs between words. A slight headiness spread through him, causing his tense shoulders to loosen; even the knot in his gut eased. He took a deep, easy breath and let it out. One thing at a time; everything at its own pace; listen to your body, your mind, the earth.

Alexi held the stub of cigarette in front of his face. "What is this?"

"Shhh." Durga took a final drag of his own, allowing his eyes to drift closed as the smoke drifted slowly from his lips, then upward.

Alexi thought the man might have fallen asleep, and he was considering it himself, when Durga's eyes popped open and his gaze turned toward the edge of town. "They come."

Alexi opened his mouth to call for Mikhail, and Durga snapped, "Inside."

Why Alexi listened, he wasn't sure. Perhaps because everything Durga had done so far had been the right thing. Perhaps because this was Durga's town and not his. Or perhaps because the approaching line of riders appeared ready to kill, and he knew even before the first man spoke whom they wanted.

"Lookin' for Cat O'Banyon."

Alexi, who was standing to one side of the front window, jerked a thumb for Mikhail to take up a position on the other. Mikhail was a very good shot. Alexi had made sure of it. However, the five men strung out in front of Durga's house were so close together almost anyone would have been able to plug two, maybe even three, before the others cleared leather.

First, they needed Durga out of the line of fire. Alexi wasn't quite sure how to accomplish that without revealing his presence, and he wasn't going to do that unless he had to.

"You will find her there." Durga lifted his arm. Alexi's breath hitched, and he could not catch it again. The betrayal, or perhaps lack of air, caused his chest to ache. Why had Durga saved Cat only to turn her over to these hunters?

Alexi had begun to raise his hand and set Mikhail loose upon them—to hell if Durga was caught in the crossfire—when he saw where the Cherokee's finger pointed.

The graves on the hill.

Genius! Had he mentioned how very much he liked this man?

The leader of the bounty hunter posse frowned, the numerous creases in his face deepening. "Mind if we take a peek?"

When Durga did not answer, the others wheeled their horses and galloped up the slope. The leader kept his gaze on Durga.

Alexi had to give the Cherokee credit; he stared resolutely back, saying nothing. Alexi had learned long ago that further explanation in the face of suspicion only created more suspicion.

Continued silence worked best. Apparently, Durga had learned this long ago as well.

At last the bounty hunter flicked his thumb against the brim of his hat and followed his men. Durga stepped inside.

"What if they dig them up?" Alexi asked.

"Digging up Indian graveyards greatly annoys the Indians," Durga said.

Alexi's lips twitched. "I thought it greatly annoyed the spirits of those who have been dug up."

Durga shrugged. "Such behavior will bring about immediate bad luck."

"How can you be so sure?"

"Because the *Aniyunwiya*"—at Alexi's lift of the eyebrows, he clarified—"the Principal People. The *Cherokee* who hide in the trees with their guns have been told to shoot anyone who disturbs the sleep of the *duhasata*, the dead."

"That could cause problems for the *Aniyunwiya*."

Due to Alexi's gift with mimicry and languages, the word came out exactly as Durga had said it. If Alexi stayed here another week, he'd be speaking Cherokee as well as a five-year-old.

"You should have let me . . . let *us* take care of them."

"Your woman saved me. I will not repay that debt by allowing harm to come to you."

Alexi didn't bother to correct the man's assumption that Cat was his woman. The way Durga spoke of her—with both respect and adoration—if the Cherokee didn't believe she was already taken, he might decide to take her. Alexi didn't want to have to strangle his new best friend.

However, he would correct one assumption. "You don't need to put yourself or your people at risk. No harm will come to me."

Mikhail would not allow it.

"No matter." Durga moved to the doorway. "They are leaving."

Alexi followed, keeping out of sight in case anyone decided to look back. "They didn't seem the type to be convinced by a few overturned plots of earth."

And Alexi made his living, had avoided dying, because of his talent at gauging types.

"What they saw is more than overturned earth." Alexi imagined a witch doctor's spell placed upon the land, one that made everyone who walked there experience an intense need to be far, far away.

"Grave markers," Durga said, causing Alexi's fanciful thoughts to disappear. "One with the name of her quarry, the other with the name of her."

"That wouldn't convince me." Alexi knew better than most how simple illusion could be. "If those hunters are any good at their job, it shouldn't convince them either."

"What they saw fits with what they know. The bounty hunter followed a bad man. The bad man came here. As both the bad man and the hunter are not known for their patience, or the sparing of bullets, they killed each other and were buried. In the end, there is one important question that should convince anyone if they but think to ask."

"What's that?"

"Why would we lie?"

Alexi could always think of a reason to lie. Lies were what you made them. They improved stories, improved lives, improved memories and histories. Sometimes he wondered why on earth anyone would ever want to tell the truth.

However, Durga was not Alexi, and there was no reason for the Cherokee to risk the wrath of five well-armed gunmen to protect a strange white woman.

None at all. Except the honor of the man in front of him.

Alexi held out his hand. "Thank you."

"I did not do it for you," Durga said, but he shook. "Now you must come with me."

Mikhail, who had gone back to his stew, began to stand.

"Not you."

Mikhail sat without argument.

Alexi followed Durga from the house and toward the stream. "He doesn't usually listen to anyone but me."

"He knows I will not hurt you."

"How does he know?"

"What possible purpose could it serve?"

As always, Durga made a solid argument. Unfortunately Alexi knew there were many people in the world who needed no reason to cause pain. Mikhail, if he remembered back further than yesterday, would know the same.

Durga went over the ridge, down the hill, past the turtle, which appeared abandoned. Alexi glanced inside to make sure it was. "Where—?"

Durga had waded through the shallows, then continued several yards along the opposite shore and Alexi had to hurry to catch up, doing so as the man paused in front of what Alexi first thought to be a natural rock outcropping jutting from the ground. When he neared, he discovered another shelter, this one built partway into the earth, domed like a beehive.

"*Asi.*"

"*Asi,*" Alexi repeated, thinking it was a welcome.

"It is what we call our winter dwellings." Durga's expression became nostalgic. "When we still used them. We have become civilized; we live in the town, but some of us still pine for the old ways. And once in a while we must behave as if we are once again *Aniyunwiya.*"

"You'll always be *Aniyunwiya.*"

Durga cast him a thoughtful glance. "You will be comfortable here. Even if one of my people wished to remember the past, it is summer now and there is a summer lodge for such things."

"I'm sure the *asi* would be very comfortable, but we have to leave."

Durga shook his head. "She must rest; so must you. And it

would not do for you to be on the trail so near the hunters who believe that she is dead."

The man had a point. He so often did. Whatever had kept Alexi going so far—first fear, then dread, then joy and then, perhaps, whatever had been in that cigarette—was fading. Exhaustion pulled at him like a wailing March wind.

Durga drew back the skin that hung over the door. "All you desire is within."

* * *

A SHADOW FLICKERED across Cat's face. The sun at someone's back, movement, then darkness. She wanted her gun. She wanted her clothes!

A hand brushed her forehead. She snatched the wrist and squeezed.

"You're awake."

Alexi. If her nose hadn't been full of the scent of her own blood and the herbs the Cherokee women had used to stop its flow, she would have known it was him the instant he came near, although . . .

He didn't smell quite so fresh anymore. She'd inhaled the nervous sweat of those she hunted often enough, but she'd never caught the scent of it on Alexi Romanov. Until now, she hadn't been certain he allowed himself to sweat. She, on the other hand, was drenched.

"Water."

More rustling, he tripped, cursed, and she couldn't help but smile. Alexi never tripped. Even in the dark, he had eyes like a cat.

The slosh of liquid, the scent of it, then the dipper pressed to her lips. Cat drank greedily, enjoying the few drops that slid down her chin and across her neck almost as much as what went down her throat.

"More?" he asked.

"Not now."

He moved back to wherever the bucket was—she couldn't see it, she couldn't see anything—this time without tripping, then returned to her side. "How are you?"

"Alive." She paused. "Right?"

"Yes. And then again no."

She squinted against the darkness but could discern only the dim outline of his head. "I must have lost more blood than I thought. Did you say both yes and no to my being alive?"

"You are alive." His hand on her arm was so deliciously cool, she sighed with pleasure and wished he would leave it right where it was. Alexi, being Alexi, did just that. "Are you disappointed?"

"A little." The darkness, the herbs, the blood loss had apparently loosened her tongue.

"Then you might be happy to know that you are also quite dead."

"Interesting."

He made a choked sound—half laugh, half . . . what? Neither she, nor Alexi, ever sobbed.

His thumb slid along the inside of her elbow. "Your skin is on fire."

If that was the case, then why was she shivering?

"Hold me," she whispered. She had definitely lost too much blood. Along with her mind.

His thumb paused, midstroke; silence filled the enclosure. He didn't move. Why would he? Unless it was to run fast and far away from the need even she heard in her voice.

"Talk to me," she said, thrilled when she managed to sound almost like herself again. "Tell me why I'm dead."

He lifted his hand from her arm. She had to grit her teeth to keep from snatching it back. How could the coolness of his skin feel so delicious even as she shivered so badly she'd begun to ache from it?

Rustles and thumps ensued; then the blanket was lifted—the air outside it felt delightful—and Alexi slipped in next to her.

Naked.

"Hush," he murmured when she stiffened, then pulled her to his chest, running a hand over her hair. "Long ago I learned that the best way to impart warmth is skin to skin."

Cat gave a soft snort. Alexi thought the best way to impart anything was skin to skin. But his body did feel glorious next to hers. It always did.

"And talking is one of my specialties," he continued.

"What about the holding?"

"I will practice."

Cat's eyes stung. She blinked several times. The scent of smoke rose from the blanket. Smoke always stung her eyes.

He began to speak, the rumble of his voice beneath her cheek soothing her as nothing else ever had. "Hunters came for you." She shoved at his chest; he held on tight. "They're gone." He pressed his lips to her brow, then quickly told her what had happened, ending with her name on a grave marker.

"They were looking for me and not Frank?"

"They asked for you."

"Hmm."

"That's all you can say?"

"What am I supposed to say?"

"Shit?"

Cat laughed, then took a sharp intake of breath when the movement jarred her wound.

"Be still." He stroked her hair again. She wanted to ask him not to stop, but she couldn't. "This is the second time hunters have followed you to the exact place where you are. How is that possible?"

"I don't know. It's not like I leave a trail of dead bodies."

"Frank did."

"But they weren't after Frank."

"Who knew that you were?"

"My—" She paused.

"Your brother-in-law."

She should have known that Alexi would have wheedled all he wanted to out of Ben.

"Is there any reason he might want you dead?"

While Ben didn't like what she was doing, he continued to help her do it. He wanted the man who'd killed Billy captured or killed as much as she did.

Well, maybe not as much, which was evidenced by his lack of pursuit. However—

"No," she said. "Besides, the first time the hunters came after me—"

"Abilene?"

She nodded. "I didn't get the information on Clyde from Ben." She *had* turned him over to Ben, but that was after the fact. "Besides, I was Sissy in Abilene."

"Until you made Clyde say *you or her* That's like shooting your rifle toward the sky and screaming, *Come and get me!*"

"By the time I had Clyde repeat after me, those men were already in town."

"True."

"How did *you* find me?"

"Moya krasavitsa, I will always find you. You shine like a beacon in the darkness of my world."

Cat blew a derisive puff of air from her lips. Even Alexi laughed. "Where do you come up with this stuff?"

"Practice," he said, but the laughter in his voice had died.

"How *did* you find me?"

"How do you think?"

"Mikhail." Why did she even bother to ask? "But the bounty hunters didn't have Mikhail, so how did they?"

"How did *you* end up in Abilene?"

"Letty's was one of Clyde's haunts. I got lucky."

"Or unlucky."

"He's in jail, maybe swinging by now. How am I the unlucky one?"

"If I hadn't been there, you would be dead already."

"Maybe," she said. But it disturbed her that those other hunters had known where to find her. They hadn't been after Clyde; they'd been after Cat.

"Being shot makes you feel lucky?"

Right now, here, safe in his arms—despite the pain and the heat—she did feel lucky. "I'm not dead."

"Not for lack of trying."

"You sound like an old woman." No doubt a result of the many times he'd pretended to be one.

"Perhaps this will work out for the best," he said, refusing to acknowledge her jab. "Those men will spread the word that they have seen Cat O'Banyon's grave."

As the truth of his words sank in, she tried to sit up; but she couldn't disentangle herself from Alexi's arms, and she was too weak to do more than struggle for a minute. "Now I can sneak up on the guy. He won't even know I'm coming, because I'm dead."

"I meant"—Alexi sighed—"you could start over."

"Start over?" She was so close; why would she start over?

"Go on. Begin a new life."

Cat stilled. "I can't go on until he's dead."

A silence settled over them much louder than any words.

"You mean you can't go on *because* he's dead."

*a*s soon as the words were out of his mouth Alexi wanted to snatch them back. Why had he said that?

He waited for her to ask what he'd meant, but Cat was as good at disregarding what she didn't want to discuss as he was.

The air inside the *asi* was warm, even though by now the sun had to have gone down. Despite the fiery temperature of her skin, Cat continued to shiver. He'd hoped the reaction was shock over what had happened. But if that were the case, she would have stopped by now.

"Are you all right, *moya zhizn'*?"

She remained silent and still; he thought she might ignore him completely.

"'*Moya zhizn'.*" The words and the accent were as perfect as his own. "What does that mean?"

My life, his mind whispered.

"Silly fool," his mouth said.

He waited for her response—laughter, a punch in the gut, anything. What he got was an increase in her shivering. So much so he feared she might bite off her own tongue between vehement clicks of her teeth. She had a fever. The question was: How bad?

He pulled back and as his eyes had adjusted to the darkness, he could see her face quite well. Her eyes had rolled back, the whites gleaming despite the lack of light.

Not shivers. Violent, uncontrollable, convulsive paroxysms.

He tried to remember what they'd done during the war when this happened, and it had happened a lot. Usually right before the person—

Cat stopped breathing.

Did that.

Her face was so pale, so still. He pressed his mouth to hers.

No response, but her lips were so damn hot. Soon they would be forever cold, unless he did something.

Alexi leaped to his feet, gathered Cat into his arms, and rushed outside. The moon shone like a beacon across the surface of the stream. He ran to the water, uncaring when stones jutted into his feet, slipping on the grass, sliding in the mud, going down on one knee, then hauling himself back up.

On your feet, Yank! Keep walkin'. Know how you blue bellies like the mud, but if you don't stand you'll die there. Hell, if it were up to me. I'd have shot ye already.

Would those voices *ever* go away?

He splashed into the shallows, fighting the current, pushing forward as if he could outrun his past. He knew better. The past continued to creep up on him when he needed it to the least.

He checked her face—still pale, unresponsive—kissed her lips again but found no breath, no life. He could think of nothing to do but tread deeper, which proved a good thing. The soft center of his foot came down upon a stone. He recoiled, lost his balance, and they plunged beneath the surface. His mouth, his nose, his lungs filled with muddy water. He shoved against the sandy bottom and the two of them burst free.

Alexi choked, spat, breathed. His heart thundered in his head so loudly, he nearly didn't notice that she was breathing too.

"*Go raibh maith agat, Dia.*" He pressed his forehead to hers. "*Grazie, Dio.*" Then, as she opened her eyes, "Thank you, God."

Her lips curved, but then her eyes fluttered closed and he panicked, thinking she'd left him again. However, this time her chest rose and fell against his. And he couldn't even enjoy it.

"That's it." He clambered from the water onto the opposite shore, climbed the ridge, and continued into town. Though the sun was down, many of the Cherokee sat on their porches, no doubt avoiding the heat of the day still trapped within their homes.

He strode through Durga's open front door. The man sat at the table with Mikhail. Neither one of them seemed surprised to see him.

"Saddle my horse."

Durga continued to roll a cigarette, movements unhurried.

"But, Alexi—"

"I want you to stay with Durga until I return."

The Cherokee's gaze went first to Cat's face, then to Alexi's before he nodded.

"I'll come back for you." Alexi certainly couldn't take Mikhail where he was going.

Mikhail proceeded through the back door.

"Thank you for your help." Cat's lips were bloodless; Alexi could count each vein in her eyelids. " But she . . . I—" Alexi's voice broke; he was mortified.

"Go. Your friend and I will keep company until you return. All will be well."

Alexi doubted *all* would be well. Because the place he was headed . . .

He shouldn't go there, but he was going to.

Alexi found a blanket in their pile of belongings, wrapped it around Cat, then strode to his horse, saddled and ready. He handed his precious bundle to Mikhail, then vaulted into the saddle and reached for Cat.

Mikhail held back, staring down, shoulders hunched. "Alexi?"

Alexi tried to remain calm even though his arms itched to have Cat back in them, and his entire body tingled with the need to be gone. What could he tell Mikhail that would convince the man he must stay behind?

Something besides the truth.

"'Fore you go . . ." Mikhail lifted wide gray eyes to Alexi's. "You should probably put on some clothes."

* * *

ALEXI RODE THROUGH THE NIGHT. Cat barely stirred despite what had to be constant and painful jostling. He wasn't sure if that was good or bad. All he knew was that by the time he reached the Kansas border they were both drenched in sweat. Whether from the hell-bent nature of their ride, an increase in her fever, or both, he couldn't say. But he knew someone who could.

For the first time, Alexi might actually be in the right place at the right time. Instead of his past haunting him, maybe it could save her.

In the late afternoon of the next day, he galloped into Freedom, Kansas. Folks on the street stopped what they were doing to stare.

Attention wasn't good for a man of his occupation. Certainly, he'd never performed a confidence in Freedom, and he never would. But, as had been proved by the Pardy Langston affair, one never knew when one's past might jump up and bite. Since he'd come here looking for his past, Alexi shouldn't be surprised if he was not only bitten but devoured.

A boy ran out of the livery as Alexi slid to the ground with Cat in his arms. "Doctor," he snapped.

The kid pointed. "Next to the sheriff."

"Of course he is." He shifted Cat, doing his best to keep her face covered. Though no one should recognize her in this state, it was best to remain careful. Finding a coin in his pocket, he tossed it to the boy. "Rub him down; give him—"

"I know how to take care of a horse, mister." The curl of the kid's lips and the narrowing of his eyes on the overworked animal saying without words *Even if you don't.*

As he deserved that, Alexi moved on.

He wanted to run down the boardwalk, knocking folks out of his way, into the mud that swirled in the street if need be, but he'd already made enough of an entrance. People would talk. They would remember when he wanted them to forget him, forget Cat, soon after they left.

Alexi did his best to appear inconspicuous. Unfortunately, it was already too late for that.

A man leaned against a building up ahead. The sun sparking off the star perched upon his narrow chest revealed his identity even before Alexi saw the roughly carved SHERRIF sign nailed above the door.

"Trouble, mister?"

"Wife's taken sick. Heard there was a doctor in Freedom."

The sheriff straightened, and Alexi tensed, managing, barely, not to skitter away like an unbroken horse. His fingers must have clenched too tightly on Cat, because she moaned—the sound both agonized and obviously female. Was she awake and playing her part? The tightness in his chest eased with that hope.

"Let me help." The sheriff stepped past Alexi, covering the short distance to a door labeled DOCTER by the same inept hand that had carved SHERRIF. He walked in, calling, "Doc!"

Alexi would have preferred to do this without an audience, but he didn't have time to argue. He entered just as a man with hair as dark as his own but eyes as gray as the Confederacy shoved aside the curtain that separated the front receiving area from the back doctoring area. His gaze went to Alexi and stayed there.

"Gent's wife is sick."

The doctor's eyes never left Alexi's. He appeared tired and drawn, but these days, who didn't?

"Guess you'd best bring her in."

Alexi forced himself to look at the lawman. "Obliged."

"Hope she's better soon." The sheriff's gaze narrowed.

The blanket had slid free of Cat's face; she was so pale she appeared dead.

"What did you say was wrong with her?"

"Don't know. That's why I'm here."

He held his breath as he waited for the sheriff to accuse him of something or get out. He got out and Alexi released a long, pent-up breath.

"We'd best get at this," the doctor said. "Considering your lie, he's gonna be back."

"Lie?" How could the man know just by the sight of them that Cat was not Alexi's wife?

The doctor reached out, and Alexi flinched. The laughter sliced along Alexi's frayed nerves like the knife in his pocket across Cat's puckered flesh.

But instead of punching Alexi in his already punched nose, the man took the trailing corner of the blanket between his fingers. "You said she was *sick*."

Alexi cursed at the sight of the blood that had seeped through the cloth before glancing at the door, half expecting the sheriff to already be there with reinforcements.

"Fedya."

That single word, filled with scorn, took him straight back to places he did not want to be. But what had he expected when coming here?

"Ethan." Alexi sounded as tired and beaten as he felt.

"Where is Mikey?" A hint of the Irish seeped into Ethan's voice, as it always did when he was exhausted or upset.

"Can we do this later? She's—"

"Where. Is. He?" The scorn was gone; pure hatred had burned it away.

"He's safe."

"Not with you?"

"Not now."

"He's still—?"

"Yes." Sadness caused the word to come out sharper than Alexi wanted it to.

"How did you find me?"

"She needs help."

"You think I'm going to help you?"

"Not me." Alexi took a step forward and Cat's feet bumped against Ethan.

The man refused to move. "Who is she to you?"

"No one." Alexi had hurt the most important person in Ethan's life. He could not let the man know that Cat was the most important person in his. Certainly Ethan was a doctor, but he had also been a soldier. He knew as much about violence and vengeance as Alexi did.

"The sheriff said she was your wife."

"I had to tell him something."

"Heaven forbid it was the truth."

"Didn't you take an oath. Dr. Walsh?"

Ethan gave a long, resigned sigh. "Bring her through."

Alexi followed him beyond the curtain and into the back room, then set Cat on a high, long table. She remained limp, eyes closed. He lowered the blanket past her neck, down her chest and belly; ignoring the travesty of the wound, he set his fingertips against her flushed skin.

"Cover her, Fedya!"

Alexi ground his teeth. He hated that name. But it was the only one that Ethan knew.

He dropped the ragged cloth onto the floor. "She's too hot."

Ethan snatched the covering and placed it over Cat once more. "If she's no one to you, then you don't need to see her naked."

True enough, but the heat of her skin worried him so. He'd never known anyone to be that hot and live.

The doctor slid the blanket down only enough to reveal her injury and no farther. "She's been shot."

"Really?" Alexi asked dryly.

"You said she was nothing to you."

"I said she was no one." His voice had gone quite cool.

"Then why did you shoot her?"

The chill spread through Alexi's chest. "You think that everyone who comes near me winds up with a bullet in them?"

"Yes."

"You're wrong."

"You're telling me you're not responsible for this woman being shot?"

"I didn't say that."

"I knew it!" Triumph punctuated every word.

"Are you going to help her? Or are you going to question me until she expires upon your table?"

Ethan's face tightened. He would like nothing better than to refuse, but at his core Ethan was a healer, and he couldn't. "Tell me everything from when she was injured until this minute."

His tone was now all business with a tinge of concern. Any hint of an Irish accent had disappeared.

"She was shot in Indian Territory. A Cherokee village. The women there packed the wound with something brown."

"I'd like to know what they used."

"Grass. Leaves. Dirt. Take your pick. Whatever it was, it didn't work. When I arrived, she had a fever. She asked me to—" Alexi swallowed, cleared his throat. "Dig the bullet out."

"They left it in?" Before Alexi could respond, the doctor continued: "That explains the fever."

"Explain it to me."

"Foreign objects cause suppuration. Remember?"

How could Alexi ever forget?

"It's my theory the body knows there's something within that should not be and begins to reject it. Removal is imperative."

"So I did something right."

"I'm sure it was an accident. Then what happened?"

"Her fever became worse. She went into paroxysms."

"How did you stop them?"

"Jumped in a stream."

Ethan's mouth pursed. "And then?"

"We came here."

"Did you clean the wound? The instrument?"

"A Cherokee woman purified the blade with fire. I don't know what they did with the wound."

"Obviously not enough." Ethan leaned in close and sniffed—once, twice—before straightening. "Definitely suppuration. Can lead to gangrene."

"But I removed the foreign object."

"Not soon enough."

Alexi's chest ached. "Can you save her?"

The doctor didn't answer at first, and the ache in Alexi's chest burned.

Then Ethan let out a huff of breath. "Your damnable luck holds again."

"Luck." Alexi began to laugh. "You have a strange idea of luck."

"Nearly as strange as your idea of friendship."

Alexi's laughter faded.

With a withering glance in his direction, the doctor continued. "After the war I went to Scotland, trained with Professor

Lister. He believes infections come from miasmas in the air. Impurities. I use carbolic acid to clean wounds, instruments, my hands. I spray it into the air. Because I use this procedure, suppuration rarely occurs in my patients."

"What if it does?"

"Dr. Lister has had great success by washing the injury with the solution."

"You want to put acid in an open wound?"

"No."

"You just said—"

"I don't want to, but I'm going to."

"And if I disagree?"

"I'll give you a few moments to say good-bye."

"*Arschloch*," Alexi muttered.

"*Ag fuck tu*," Ethan returned.

If it weren't for Cat dying in front of him and the fact that Ethan despised him for killing his brother, it would feel just like the good old days.

In prison.

"Do you have any laudanum?" Alexi asked.

"Some. But, as laudanum can *cause* paroxysms, she can't have any until after the procedure. She'll need to remain still."

"If you give her enough of it, she will."

"If I give her enough of it, she won't ever move again." Ethan disappeared through the curtain.

"You can open your eyes now," Alexi said.

*a*lexi leaned against the wall, looking older than Cat had ever seen him look, making her wonder just how old he was. She'd thought he was near her own twenty-six. But the lines around his mouth, the dark circles beneath his eyes—no, those were remnants of his broken nose. Still, he appeared ten years past what she'd believed him to be. He was filthy, unshaven. He didn't look like Alexi Romanov in the least.

"How long have you been awake?"

"Long enough." She considered him. "This wasn't your fault."

"No?"

"As you've been telling me all along, I can't wait to die."

"I didn't need to help you." At her confused frown, he spread his hands. "My guns."

"I stole them, Alexi. I deserved whatever I got."

"*Aingeal mianach*, you did not deserve this."

She wasn't going to argue. She knew what she deserved.

"What does that mean?" she asked. "*Aing—*"

He interrupted before she could finish. "Simpleton and idiot."

Cat's lips twitched

"He lies." The doctor had returned.

Ethan Walsh possessed inky black hair that curled long against his neck, as if he'd forgotten, or perhaps not cared enough, to cut it. He seemed pale, despite his olive skin, and his gray eyes sparkled, though not with humor or happiness. There was something familiar about them, but her head ached too much to decipher what.

"If you've been in his presence for more than a minute"—Dr. Walsh lifted an eyebrow—"conscious, then you know about his forked tongue already."

"I like his tongue just fine."

"Most women do."

She experienced a sudden urge to punch him. If he hadn't been juggling several sharp instruments with a bottle of acid, and if she hadn't feared that sitting up would only cause her to fall down. Cat might have.

"*Aingeal mianach* doesn't mean simpleton or idiot," the doctor continued.

Alexi's lips curved, but his eyes had gone flat and deadly. When he looked at most men like that, they went silent. The doctor kept right on talking.

"It means *angel mine*." He set his instruments and the acid on a nearby empty table, then turned. "He obviously likes your tongue too."

"Alexi," she began, unsure if she meant to tell him to pummel this guy, or ask how many other translations he'd lied about, but the doctor interrupted.

"Alexi? You have the nerve to use that name?"

Cat blinked. Not that she'd ever believed Alexi was his name, but—

"Among others."

"And who's she?" Walsh rearranged his instruments. "Katya?"

Alexi came away from the wall so fast Cat barely saw him move. The doctor, who'd been foolish enough to present Alexi with his back, never saw him. He did feel the blade at his neck.

Considering the trickle of blood that ran down, he couldn't help it.

"She is no one," Alexi said quietly. "As soon as you fix what is wrong, she will leave and you will forget she was ever here. Do you understand?"

"Haven't changed a bit, have you?"

Alexi lifted the knife from the doctor's throat and stepped away. If Cat had any strength left, she would have strangled Walsh for the expression of resignation on Alexi's face alone.

Ethan's gaze narrowed on the weapon. "Fancy knife. Where'd you get it?"

"Where do I get anything? A card game."

"Did you cheat?"

"Don't I always?"

"Could we get this over with?" Cat asked. Obviously they knew each other, and she planned to discover why, where, and how. But not now. Now her skin felt on fire, and her shoulder ached so badly she was dizzy with it.

The two men glanced at her as if they'd forgotten she was there. "You're gonna need to hold her down," the doctor said.

"Doubtful."

"I really think—"

"Do it," Alexi and Cat ordered at the same time.

When the acid touched her shoulder. Cat couldn't breathe. Her gaze, her hand, sought Alexi's. Before she could find him, the darkness found her.

* * *

THE SCENT of Cat's blood made Alexi want to run, to hide, to faint. But he refused to waver; he refused to walk away. She needed him. Or so he wanted to believe.

The first application of acid was followed by the removal of suppurated tissue with a much smaller, sharper knife than

Alexi's. After the cutting came more acid, then bandages bathed in acid. Thank goodness she'd lost consciousness immediately.

When at last Ethan finished his torment, he stared at the wound with a scowl, and Alexi's heart stuttered. "Will she be all right?"

Ethan cast him a suspicious glance, and Alexi wanted to cut out his forked tongue. He'd sounded desperate. If she was no one to him, what did it matter?

If she was no one to him, why had he brought her here?

"Should be." Ethan moved to the bucket in the corner and washed the blood from his hands. "The increase in the number of patients who survive since I've begun using carbolic acid is astounding."

"All of them?"

Ethan cut his eyes to Alexi, then back to the bucket. "No."

That would be too easy.

The doctor crossed the room with a fresh bucket, into which he dumped the remaining carbolic acid.

"No more." Alexi stepped between Ethan and Cat, who continued to lie far too still.

"I need to wash off the blood."

"With acid?"

"It's best to have everything that touches her for the next few days be as free of miasma as possible."

"I'll do it."

Ethan stared at Alexi for several seconds; then he handed him the bucket and disappeared through the curtain.

Alexi stuck his fingers into the water. Several areas, sawed raw by the reins in his hell-bent trip from Indian Territory to Kansas, burned. The thought of a stronger solution poured into an open wound made him ill.

"Courage," he whispered. She had it; he needed some.

He spent the next half hour washing away the blood and dust;

then he wrapped her in a fresh sheet. He'd just laid her on a clean table when Ethan returned.

"Her color is improving. She'll wake soon."

"Promise?"

"I don't make promises I can't keep, Fedya."

"Fedya," Cat repeated, and they both straightened as if coming to attention. "That some sort of Russian insult?"

"In a manner of speaking," Ethan said. "It's his name."

Beyond the pain and fatigue in Cat's expression, Alexi caught a glint of amusement. "Is there anyone, anywhere, who doesn't know you by another name?"

"Hard to say."

Ethan crossed his arms. "He was born Fyodor Kondrashchenko."

"No wonder he changed it."

"Fedya is a nickname."

"Is that true?" Cat lifted an eyebrow.

"My name is Alexi Romanov. I chose it; I will keep it." His gaze cut to Ethan. "And you can go to hell."

"You first."

"No doubt."

"My head's beginning to ache," Cat said.

"Where's that laudanum?" Alexi asked.

Ethan disappeared through the curtain again.

"I thought he'd never leave. Who is he?"

"Dr. Ethan Walsh." Alexi drenched a clean cloth in a bucket of clean water, then laid it on her head.

"Mmm," she murmured, the sound half enjoyment—the water was much cooler than her skin—half suspicion. "He's more than that."

Alexi shrugged. She was far too observant.

"You don't want to tell me. That's all right. There are things I don't want to tell you."

In her eyes, though, he saw every one. Always had. But if she

159

wanted to believe he knew only what she'd shared with him, he'd let her. Perhaps she would do the same for him.

Ethan returned with a small dark bottle. He opened it, then tilted the rim toward a spoon.

"No, thank you."

Ethan paused. "I thought your head ached."

"Because the two of you are hellishly annoying."

Alexi laughed; Ethan scowled. "Sleep helps you heal."

"I'll sleep." Her eyes drifted closed.

Ethan capped the bottle, placed both it and the spoon next to his instruments, then set his palm to her cheek.

"Stop that."

Ethan snatched back his arm.

Cat opened her eyes and met Alexi's. "I meant you."

Only then did Alexi realize he'd been growling like a dog over a bone. *His* bone. Ethan should never touch her.

"The fever's fading." Ethan tucked his hands behind his back. "Let's move her where she can rest."

Alexi lifted Cat into his arms and her head lolled against his shoulder. He followed Ethan up a staircase. At the top stood two doors. Ethan went through the first. By the time Alexi got there, he'd turned down the bed.

His bed.

"No." Alexi stepped into the hall, then continued to the second room. He cursed.

Cat roused herself. "Whas the madder?"

"Shh." He pressed his lips to her brow. "Go back to sleep."

That she did proved her utter exhaustion.

"Get out of there." Ethan's voice had gone as cold as Alexi had ever heard it, which was saying quite a bit.

Alexi got out. Ethan reached past him and slammed shut the door. Didn't help. Alexi could still see the empty crib in the center.

Alexi wanted to ask what had happened to the woman Ethan

had loved. But that empty crib, the empty house . . . it couldn't be good.

Ethan went downstairs without another word. As there were no more rooms on this floor, Alexi carried Cat back into the first and settled her into Ethan's bed. He sat by her until he was certain she was truly asleep and not unconscious; then he followed Ethan once more.

The operating room was clean. The instruments on the table sparkled. The laudanum remained where Ethan had left it.

Alexi picked up the bottle, which seemed very light. How much was left? He lifted the glass to the fading sunlight through the window.

Empty.

He searched the cabinets of both that room and the next, where Ethan had gone to retrieve it, found another, nearly full, and pocketed that one. When he searched for Ethan, however, the man was gone.

As night approached, so did a horse.

Alexi had returned to Cat's bedside. She hadn't stirred, but every time he touched her face, she seemed less hot.

He went down the stairs, stepping into the front office as Mikhail came through the door. Alexi spared a moment to be glad that Ethan had disappeared. "I told you to wait," he said.

Mikhail stared at his feet. "What if I was back there and you needed me here?"

Alexi should have known better than to leave Mikhail behind. He followed orders well, as long as Alexi was there to remind him of them. No Alexi, no reminder, and the order often fell into the abyss. Although there were times Alexi wondered if Mikhail allowed orders he didn't care for to vanish into that great dark hole in his mind on purpose. Was that even possible?

"Ready to go?" Mikhail asked.

"Cat needs a few days' rest."

"Didn't the doctor make her better?" His big shoulders hunched, and his gaze darted around the room.

"He did. She'll be fine." Alexi wouldn't let her be anything else.

"Then let's go." Mikhail sidled toward the door. "Don't like the smell here. Don't like the looks. Don't like it. I don't." His fists clenched and unclenched.

"It's all right."

While Mikhail didn't remember anything that had happened before the war—and a helluva lot during it—certain scents caused memories to flicker for him the same way they did for Alexi. Dirt and sweat brought back prison. The tang of blood brought back the pain.

"Gonna go now." Mikhail turned, then stopped short. Someone stood on the porch.

"Mikey," Ethan said.

Mikhail pushed past Ethan so fast he nearly knocked his brother down.

* * *

CAT WOKE as the sun set beyond a window she'd never seen before. She'd never seen the room before either.

Sparse but lived in, with male belongings scattered across the surface of the dresser, men's clothing strewn across the floor and trailing from the wardrobe. There was obviously not a Mrs. Doctor Walsh.

Something hard and heavy rested at her hip. She glanced down. Alexi Romanov—she doubted she'd ever be able to think of him as Fedya—had pulled a chair next to the bed and fallen asleep with his head brushing against her. He snored lightly, which wasn't like him. She couldn't ever remember Alexi snoring before.

Cat ran her hand over his hair, grimacing at the sweat and dirt that remained. That wasn't like him either.

The snoring stopped; he raised his head. Though he'd just woken from what had appeared to be a very sound sleep, his blue eyes were sharp and alert.

Cat frowned. Something was wrong. "Alexi—"

He lifted her hand and pressed his mouth to the palm. She waited for his tongue to snake out. Then she'd pull away, make a sarcastic comment, he'd return one equally cutting, and the idea that everything had changed while she'd been asleep, that nothing would ever be the same again, would fade.

Instead, he closed his eyes as if gauging something, keeping his lips against her skin until her heart did a strange little stutter. Then he dropped her hand and stood. "Your fever has broken."

"Don't sound so happy about it."

He crossed to the window and peered out.

"You want to tell me what's going on?"

"No."

That was fair. She didn't want to tell him anything either. But the way he stared through the glass made her nervous. "Is someone out there?"

"Many someones."

"Someone we should worry about?"

He hesitated, and she started to get up.

"Stay," he said without even glancing her way.

"No," she returned, but discovered she couldn't lift much beyond her head from the pillow. Her fever might be gone, but she was still weaker than she could ever recall being. However, her mind seemed quite clear.

"Who is it? Are they after you, or me?"

"Darling," he drawled, and she frowned. What had happened to the foreign endearments? "You're dead."

For an instant she wondered if she really was, if this were hell, even purgatory. Definitely not heaven, considering the company. Then she remembered the Cherokee, the graves, her name on one.

"After you, then."

He gave one short, sharp bark of laughter. "Always."

"Who? From where? Why?"

"Why?" he repeated, as if the word were not one he'd ever heard.

"What did you *do*, Alexi?"

"Don't you want to call me Fedya?"

"Not even a little bit."

He took a deep breath, let it out, faced her. There was still something wrong.

"I did nothing." She didn't realize she'd snorted until he cast her a quick glance and muttered, "Lately." Then he added, "Around here."

"So what's the matter?"

"What could be the matter?" he asked in a voice that clearly said: What isn't?

"Alexi—" she began again.

He drew his hand from his pocket. A gold chain unfurled, a gold ring strung upon it. "You forgot this." He contemplated the ring twirling to and fro in the fading light. "I'd hoped maybe you meant to leave it behind. That you were moving on. But we both know you won't." He tossed the band onto the bed.

Cat picked it up, tossed it back. "That isn't mine."

He snatched the circlet from the air before it hit him in the face. "You wore the ring beneath your dress. You kissed it for luck."

"Meg wore it beneath her dress. *Meg* kissed it for luck. What is wrong with you?" She'd had the fever, but he was the one confused.

"I thought—" he began. "You draped the chain over—"

Cat tilted her head. "You followed me?"

He released an impatient huff as he shoved the ring into his pocket. "You know damn well I followed you. Otherwise you wouldn't have pulled that dodge with Ruby and Ben. You're lucky I didn't kill him."

"Kill him? Why?"

"He had his hands all over your ass."

"Wasn't my ass. And since when do you care who has their hands on my anything?"

"Wish I knew," he said.

Cat went silent. She hadn't felt anyone following her until she'd gone *into* Rock River. Of course, she'd been a bit . . .

Crazy.

If Alexi had found the ring, then he'd found Billy. That should upset her more than it did.

"What did Ben tell you?"

"Nothing."

Cat let out a breath.

"However, Ruby was quite chatty."

"She told you?"

"Yes."

Well, that explained what was wrong. Why he seemed different. Why he was looking at her . . . like that.

"She's dead." The words startled her. Cat hadn't meant to say them.

Alexi's brow creased. "Ruby?"

"Cathleen."

Silence descended, so sudden and still she could hear people talking on the street below despite the closed window.

Alexi sat in the chair, took her hand. "If that's what you wanted everyone to believe, they do. Although, in my opinion, to make the story ring completely true, you should have dug another grave and added your name."

"Her name." The more she thought about this, the more she believed it. Cathleen was as dead as Billy.

Alexi frowned. "*Bebe, you* are Cathleen."

"No. I'm Cat." She tried to pull away, but he wouldn't let her go, so she gave up and moved on. "Cat O'Banyon would never allow anyone to kill someone she loved while she just—" Her throat closed. She tried to swallow and choked instead. By the time she stopped, the pain, both inside and out, was excruciating.

Alexi tightened his hand around hers. "She just what?"

"Stood there."

"What should she have done?"

"Cat O'Banyon would have stuck a knife into the belly of anyone who threatened her or hers and twisted."

"Ah."

This time when she pulled her hand from his, he released her. "What does 'ah' mean?"

"I understand better than most the need to become another. To bury the past along with who you were, to create a new life completely different from it, and forget, or try to, the person who came before."

Maybe he did, but—

"You're awake." Dr. Walsh stood in the doorway. As soon as Alexi saw him, he retreated to the window.

Cat was glad to end the conversation. They'd skirted too close to things she didn't want to share. Then again, having Alexi know the truth—or some of it—felt better than it should.

The doctor stepped into the room. Cat didn't like him now any better than she had earlier. But she was beholden to him.

"Thank you for saving my life."

He lifted an eyebrow. "You don't sound very thankful."

"I don't like owing people."

"You don't owe me."

"Because you took an oath?"

"That and—" His gaze went to Alexi, and she knew.

"You owe him."

"Not anymore." The doctor scratched his forearm. From the marks there, he'd been scratching so much he'd nearly torn a hole in himself.

Walsh saw her watching and stopped. He sat in the chair Alexi had vacated and set a hand both clammy and cool to Cat's forehead.

She recoiled. "Are you ill?"

"No." He wiped his palms on his pants. "Your fever's broken. I need to check your wound."

She nodded, and he removed the bandage, leaned in close, then sniffed. The sight of his dark head so near her breast brought the urge to lash out, but he was moving away just as quickly as he'd moved in.

"No smell of suppuration. No pus, no ooze. Slight redness, but that's to be expected. You're going to have quite a scar though."

She shrugged, then wished she hadn't when the pain caused her to see stars. "I've got worse."

"No, you—" He stopped, realizing it wasn't polite to reveal he'd seen her naked and, except for her shoulder, there hadn't been a mark on her. "I'll fetch a fresh bandage." He left the room.

"What's the matter with him?" Cat asked.

Alexi frowned, gaze still on the doorway through which the doctor had disappeared. "Hard to say."

CHAPTER 16

*E*than never returned with the bandage. When Cat drifted off to sleep, Alexi went after him.

He found the doctor tearing apart the surgery. Everything that had once been in the cabinets was now not. Ethan rubbed his arms as if he were freezing, despite the already steamy heat of the day. Both his nose and his eyes wept, and he appeared possessed by a frequent urge to yawn.

"Looking for this?" Alexi held the container of laudanum he'd snatched the night before between two fingers.

Ethan's gaze fastened on the bottle. "Give it back."

"Cat might need it."

"Cat?"

Alexi resisted the urge to curse. *Cat* was supposed to be dead.

"Cathy. The woman upstairs. The one who's actually in pain."

Ethan's eyes flicked to Alexi's, then back to the bottle. "You know nothing about pain."

Considering what he knew of the doctor's past and what he'd seen in that second bedroom, Alexi thought the man was probably right. He still wasn't going to give him the bottle.

"You need to stop." Alexi returned the container to his pocket.

"You need to die," Ethan said.

Alexi shouldn't have come here. But for her . . .

He'd face every demon that he had.

"I'll get more." The doctor began to return things to the cabinets.

Alexi began to help him. "I know."

"I want to die."

"I know that too."

* * *

CAT AWOKE ONLY LONG ENOUGH to determine that Alexi was wrapping her shoulder with carbolic-acid-scented bandages and helping her into a nightdress before falling asleep again.

She surfaced on and off, usually because Alexi was urging her to drink, to eat. Cool cloths bathed her face and neck. She could have sworn the sky went from dark to light and dark again several times. When she was finally able to open her eyes and keep them open, the room was going gray, and someone stood at the window.

"You don't have to stay here every minute," she said.

The figure turned, and the fading sunlight cast across his chest, sparking off the star.

Not Alexi. The sheriff.

Cat tried to sit up and was thrilled when she managed it. Certainly there was pain, but she didn't faint. A definite improvement. "Is there a problem?"

He sat in the chair, gaze far too intent on her face. "That depends."

Cat didn't like this.

"Where's . . . ?" Her voice drifted off. She had no idea who Alexi had said they were. She didn't want to make a mistake.

"Where's . . . ?"

"The doctor." Better to be safe than wrong.

"Rode out to help some other poor soul." The sheriff's gaze remained on hers.

Recognition flickered. "Have we met?"

His mouth curved. "Have we?"

Cat waited. An old lawman's trick—silence made folks want to fill it. They often filled it with information.

The sheriff broke first. Some lawman.

"I shouldn't tease." His smirk broke free. What did he know that she didn't? "I was outside my office when your husband brought you in."

Husband. Right. But what were their *names?* She searched for a memory that contained this man.

Something flickered again. Just out of reach. "Is my husband downstairs?"

"No." The continuation of that smile made Cat long for her guns. "Saw him walkin' to the stable with that big friend of his."

Cat frowned. Mikhail had not only arrived but been seen and noticed.

"Not a soul here but you and me."

Her unease deepened. "Well, it was nice of you to visit, but as you can see. I'm not at my best."

"I see a lot." He leaned closer. "Cat."

Had Alexi given Cat as her name? She couldn't believe he would have. Not that there weren't other women nicknamed Cat in Kansas, but so close to the death of Cat O'Banyon in a shoot-out . . .

"I see you were shot." He licked his lips. "Not sick like he said."

"I am sick."

"What you are . . ." He drew his gun. "*Who* you are is Cat O'Banyon, and there's a great big bounty on you."

"I don't know what you're talking about." She pulled the blanket to her chin.

He yanked it down. "Keep yer hands where I can see 'em."

"I don't know what you want." She tried to make her voice waver, managed it with ease. "I'm not the person you think I am."

He laughed. "You don't remember me, do you?"

"I don't remember much from when I was feverish."

"I don't mean now. I'm talkin' about last year."

"Last year?" She didn't even have to try to sound confused about that.

"In Houston."

Had she been in Houston last year? Maybe. There'd been so many places, so many men.

But that was Cat, and she was dead. What about . . . whoever she was supposed to be? Had that woman been in Houston? Of course not. That woman hadn't existed before this week.

"I've never been in Houston, Sheriff. You have me confused with someone else."

"I never forget a . . ." His gaze lowered to her breasts again. "Face."

What had she *done* in Houston? How could he know about it? She never told lawmen the details of how she landed her bounties. She danced too close to the other side of the law for that.

Then again, none had ever asked. Most—all—didn't care how she captured the outlaws as long as she captured them.

Cat lifted her chin. "You're bordering on insulting, sir."

"Oh, I passed that border long time ago, *ma'am*. Or maybe you passed it back in Houston when you promised to fuck me if I came to your room."

Hmm. That did sound like her. But not with a—

He took off his wide-brimmed, sweat-stained sheriff's hat, revealing a pate as bald as a baby's, and she remembered. He wasn't a lawman; he was a—

"Bastard!"

"And here I thought you'd forgotten me."

"Rufus," she said slowly. "Rufus Owens."

He set his hat back on his head with a nod.

"How did you get a job as a sheriff?" As she recalled, he had a bad habit of killing them.

"You think you're the only one who can change names and become someone else? It's easy enough."

Cat remained silent again. Again he kept talking.

"Ran into a fellow one night. He shared his food and his fire. Told me all about the new job he'd just taken in Freedom. Sounded good to me. Was sick of lookin' over my shoulder."

From the glare he cast at Cat, he'd been looking over his shoulder for her.

Good.

Although if she hadn't gotten sloppy, he would be dead and they wouldn't be having this conversation. Very few men had gotten away from her, but Rufus Owens had been one of them. She had a feeling she was going to be sorrier about that now than she'd been when it had happened.

Once he said You or her? *and proved he was not her man. Cat would have dragged Rufus in and collected his bounty. However, he'd stumbled on the whorehouse stairs and taken her to the bottom with him. By the time she regained her feet, and her bearings, he was gone. She'd intended to recapture him, but there was another promising bounty and then another and then . . .*

She'd forgotten. Served her right that he'd turn up here. Her mama always said: "Clean up your mess or someone's bound to slip in it." Right now. Cat felt as if she'd not only slipped, but also landed on her ass in a large, smelly pile of—

"Shit," she muttered. "So you killed the Freedom sheriff-to-be and stole not only his life, but his name and his job."

"It's not like I'm not doin' the job. I caught you."

"I'm not wanted."

"Tell it to the man with the money. I don't think he'll believe you any more than I do."

Cat didn't think so either.

"Now." Rufus inched close enough she could smell his rancid breath. "How about that poke you promised me in Houston?"

She'd been contemplating poking him in the eyes and making a break for it. His words caused her to stop contemplating and do it.

Alexi had just started up the stairs when gunfire broke out. He drew his own weapon and ran the rest of the way, slamming into Cat as she skidded from the bedroom.

"Ouch!" She reached for her bad shoulder, then as several more bullets smashed into the wall across from the open door—whoever was shooting had to be the worst shot ever—shoved him. "Run."

But Alexi had counted five shots. There might be a sixth bullet in the gun, but most men kept the hammer down on an empty chamber, not only for safety but as a matter of pride. If you couldn't hit what you were shooting at with five shots, you shouldn't be shooting.

He stepped into the room, easily shrugging off Cat's still-weak attempts to stop him. "Drop the gun."

The man, who'd just begun to reload, lifted his gaze. One eye was squeezed shut; the other was watering so badly he could barely focus. No wonder he hadn't been able to hit anything.

"The *sheriff's* shooting at you?" Alexi asked, exasperated.

"He's not the sheriff."

"She's not your wife."

Alexi lifted an eyebrow. "No?"

"She's Cat O'Banyon."

Alexi sighed. "What did you do?"

"Me? I was lying here and he—he—"

It wasn't like Cat to stutter and the hand she pointed at the sheriff, who still hadn't dropped the gun, shook a bit. Alexi cocked his own. The sheriff dropped it.

"Are those . . . ?"

He cast her a quick glance, and she tilted her head to indicate his weapons.

"My guns?" Was she trying to get them killed? "Yes, darling."

He wasn't certain if her eye roll was because of the *darling* or the realization that if the guns were his, then they were empty. He didn't care. As long as the sheriff didn't realize it.

"This is my wife. Her name isn't Cat. You are mistaken."

"She tried to capture me in Houston last year."

"Capture?" Suddenly everything became quite clear. "That would make you an outlaw and not a sheriff."

"Told you so," Cat said.

"Hush."

Amazingly she did. Or maybe not so amazingly since she was pale and trembling, one arm hanging useless. Barefoot and bare-assed, she wore nothing but a borrowed nightgown and a bandage. Her guns still resided in her saddlebags, at the livery with her horse. What else could she do but what he said?

Alexi contemplated the false sheriff. "What happened to your eyes?"

"She poked them like a goddamn girl."

"She is a girl." *My girl.*

He was starting to have a very bad feeling about what had gone on here before he arrived. He could understand Cat escaping by whatever means necessary, even poking someone's eyes. However, merely being threatened with the grave would not cause the quavering voice, the trembling hands. Cat didn't fear death; she courted it. Therefore, there had to be more to this, and he had a fairly good idea what it was.

"Hold this, *moya lyubov'.*" Alexi handed her his gun. "If he moves, shoot him in the head."

She cast him a quick glance. She couldn't shoot anyone anywhere without bullets. But she tightened her lips and took the weapon.

"She ain't gonna be able to shoot me in the head. Even at this distance, that's a helluva shot with her hand shakin' like that."

Alexi crossed the room in two quick strides, grabbing the man by the collar and hauling him close. "I once made my living by shooting anything at which I aimed, and I taught her everything that I know. She will hit you in the head—have no doubt."

"Honey?" Cat said.

"Sweetie?" he returned.

Her impatient huff negated the endearment. "You're in my line of fire."

The sheriff smirked. "You taught her everything you know? I'll have to thank you. She sucked me so hard in Houston, I thought I'd walk bowlegged fer a week." He licked his lips. "Then she fucked me. Just to get close enough to—"

The rest of the sentence was drowned out by the crash of glass as Alexi tossed him through the window.

CHAPTER 17

One moment the sheriff was there, saying vile things; the next he was gone.

Alexi, glass sparkling in his hair like stars in the coming night sky, stared at his palms. "Oops."

Cat crossed the room, setting the useless gun on the bed so that she could reach out with the hand that still worked the way she wanted it to, snatch him by the collar, and yank him away from the window before someone saw him. "We need to go."

It was dusk, not too many folks on the street. No outcry was raised. They might have a chance to escape. But they had to move.

Now.

Alexi continued to stare at his hands. She took one in hers. "Look at me."

He lifted his gaze. "I enjoyed that."

She been afraid he'd gone into shock, but his eyes were clear and aware. "You're an idiot."

"I've been called worse."

So had she. Which was how they'd gotten into this mess.

A door slammed below; footsteps thundered up the stairs. She'd thought they would have more time.

Cat snatched up the discarded weapon, stepped in front of Alexi, and raised the gun.

"Empty, *bebe*," he reminded her.

"Idiot," she reminded him.

Dr. Walsh came through the door. "What did you *do*, Fedya?"

"Wasn't him." Cat lowered the pistol, handed it to Alexi.

"Was too." Alexi took it.

"Shut up," Cat and the doctor said as one, then glared at each other. She had to again resist the urge to punch him; she didn't have the time.

"What's happening outside?" Cat crossed to the wardrobe and selected some clothes.

"Folks are gathering. No one's quite sure what to do. Sheriff's usually the one who handles things like this. But the sheriff's—"

"I know." Cat whipped the nightgown over her head. "We need to get to the horses without anyone seeing us." She stepped into the doctor's trousers, turning as she fastened them.

"Jesus," Walsh muttered, and Cat's head jerked up, her hand slapping against her empty hip as her gaze went to the empty doorway.

She glanced at Alexi, who motioned to her chest as he lifted his exasperated gaze heavenward. The doctor stared at her bare breasts as if he'd never seen any before, as if he hadn't seen *hers* before.

"Thought you were a doctor." Cat presented him with her back as she put on one of Walsh's white cotton shirts.

He cleared his throat. "As you're stealing my clothes for a getaway, I don't think you're a patient anymore."

"So?" She faced him.

"When you're a patient, you're . . ." He shrugged. "Not male. Not female. I don't see anything but the wound."

Cat didn't really care. "How do we reach the livery unnoticed?"

"I don't—"

The door opened and closed again. Footsteps hurried toward them.

Cat jerked her thumb for the doctor to get out of the way. She reached for the gun that Alexi wouldn't use even if it did have bullets, but he shook his head just as Mikhail appeared.

"Mikey," the doctor whispered, face pale, lips stiff and bloodless.

Mikhail sidled away from Walsh as if he were touched. Maybe he was. Or maybe Mikhail reminded him of someone he'd lost.

"We need to get to the horses," Alexi said. "Quick."

At the sight of Alexi, Mikhail's fear and confusion eased. "Soon as I saw the man come out the window, I figgered that. Horses are waitin', saddled and packed, on the next street north."

"As soon as he saw the man come out the window, he figgered," Walsh repeated. "What have you done to him? Besides what you did already."

"What—?" Cat began, but Alexi cast her a glance that froze the question in her throat even before she saw Mikhail wince, then rub his forehead.

The doctor put out his hand. "Mikey."

Mikhail wheeled and pounded down the stairs.

"Go!" Alexi ordered.

Cat hesitated, uncertain what, exactly, was happening.

"Please!" His urgency caused her to follow Mikhail even as her unease deepened.

She reached the first floor as Mikhail disappeared through the door. Cat looked back. Alexi and Ethan stood toe-to-toe.

"We're square now," Walsh said.

"We are."

"Next time I see you—"

"Next time," Alexi agreed.

* * *

ALEXI CAUGHT up to Mikhail and Cat in the alley behind the office. As the three of them hurried toward the next street to the north, the sound of a gathering mob drifted from the south.

"The sheriff done broke his neck!"

"Saw the doc run inside after he fell."

"Someone was up there with 'im. I think they tossed 'im out."

"Who?"

"Let's see."

Cat reached for Alexi's hand. "We need to hurry."

"Don't worry. Ethan lies even better than I do."

"No one lies better than you."

"Merci, ma tres chere."

"English."

"Thank you."

He could tell by the slight clenching of her fingers around his that she suspected there was more to the translation, but she knew better than to ask. If he'd wanted her to know exactly what he'd said, he would have said it in English in the first place.

"It wasn't a compliment," she said.

"And yet I took it as one."

The sun had gone down, and the buildings on either side of them were too close and too high to allow in any light. Alexi was glad. His voice sounded normal; the teasing and the foreign endearments held just the right tone. His palm was clammy, but so was hers. His face, however, might betray him. It had been a very long time since he'd killed anyone, and it had shaken him.

He tried to gather himself. If they were going to get out of this without one of them, or perhaps all, swinging at the end of a rope, Alexi needed to be at his best.

They reached the end of the alley, and Mikhail held up a hand, looked both ways, then motioned them forward. The silent northern street loomed empty except for their horses.

Without the shadow of the buildings, the rising moon cast silver over them all. Alexi's expression must not be as neutral as he'd hoped since Cat took one look at him and cursed. "I should have been the one to throw him out the window."

"With one hand?"

Her lips tightened; her eyes narrowed. She didn't care for being helpless. Alexi couldn't blame her. The last time she'd been so, her entire world had died.

"We'll walk the horses out of town." His voice held not a hint of tension; he was a master at slipping away when no one was paying attention, and by the time anyone knew he was gone he was already someone else. "We don't want folks to hear us and investigate."

As the one in charge of investigating had just been tossed from a window, Alexi didn't think they were in much danger.

They reached the outskirts of Freedom and walked their horses another mile. Even after the three of them mounted, they continued walking. Clouds had rolled in, covering the light of the moon.

Alexi stared at the pitch-black sky. "That might keep them from coming after us. If they're so inclined."

"If Ethan's the big, fat liar you said he was, they shouldn't be inclined."

"He is."

"Where'd he learn that? From you?"

"In truth, *meine Schonheit,* I learned from him."

Cat gave a soft snort, which was echoed by Alexi's horse. "I find that hard to believe."

"Believe. Once upon a time, Ethan Walsh was General Grant's most trusted spy."

Cat said nothing for so long, Alexi wondered if she'd heard him. Then she laughed. "Sure he was."

"I'm telling the truth."

"Truth and Alexi Romanov haven't walked hand in hand since I met him."

Considering he wasn't Alexi Romanov, she had a point. However, on this, at least, he was being truthful. As they had a long night ahead, and he doubted she'd give him a moment's peace until he told the story, he would. But first—

Alexi reined in his horse and Cat did the same. The moon peeked through the clouds now and again, casting the landscape in every hue of gray.

"Mikhail, would you scout ahead, please?"

"Sure thing, Alexi."

"Slowly. Carefully. Stay in sight." But out of earshot.

"Why all the—?" Cat began, and Alexi put a finger to his lips.

The big man and even bigger horse moved off; the clop of hooves and the murmur of Mikhail's voice as he spoke to the beast faded.

"Why all the subterfuge?"

Alexi urged his mount forward, as did she. "You saw how Mikhail was with Ethan. Every time something reminds him of the past, he gets a headache."

"Why did Ethan call him Mikey? Is that a nickname? Or has he confused him with someone else?"

"I need to start from the beginning." Or maybe the middle. He wasn't going to tell her everything if he could help it. "I met Ethan in the war."

"You were in the war?"

Her obvious surprise caused him to snap, "Wasn't everyone?"

"In the South, yes." She took a breath, then spoke more calmly. "Invasion brings the fight to folks' doorsteps, and they tend to get testy. Everyone I knew signed up."

Alexi sometimes forgot Cat was from the South. She was so good at pretending not to be. But sometimes, like now, the accent shone through unbidden. Other times, like when she'd been Meg, she allowed it to.

The image of Cat with that bag of cloth stuffed beneath her dress caused a rash of gooseflesh along the back of Alexi's neck. He swatted at the tickle as if it were a fly.

Neither one of them had ever mentioned the war. Probably because it was something both wanted—and needed—to forget. Such was the way with wars.

"Did you?" she asked.

For an instant he couldn't think what she meant. The memories of the war had begun to whisper. He shook them off, though he knew they would be back. They always came back.

"I'm not a citizen," he said. "I couldn't sign up. I took the bounty."

She stiffened. "Bounty?"

The South had instituted a draft over a year before the North had. The Conscription Act was hugely unpopular as it was considered an infringement upon an individual's rights by the government, one of the reasons that shot was fired at Fort Sumter in the first place.

The Confederacy had allowed substitutes, same as the Union. But if everyone Cat knew had volunteered, she'd probably never heard of the practice.

"A bounty was the term they used for the money paid to a man who would take the place of another in the fight. If that substitute deserted, the hunters sent after him were called bounty hunters because they hunted not a man, but a bounty. A retrieval of *something* that had been bought and paid for."

From the wrinkles in her brow. Cat had not been aware of the origin of her present occupation's name. Few were.

"You fought?" Cat asked, as if she could not get her mind around the concept.

"What did you think I did. Picked daisies?"

"No, I . . ." She glanced at the empty guns strapped to his hips. "Go on. Someone paid you to go to war for them, and you accepted because . . ."

"I needed to escape from my *otets*. My father. He was . . ."

Brutal, Alexi thought.

"Difficult," he said.

Cat's suspicious glance made him wonder, not for the first time, if she could read his mind. "Where were you born?"

"In the streets of a place once called Queen of the Golden Horde."

"You're making that up."

"No." His lips curved. "Although it hasn't been called that for centuries, I still prefer the lyrical name to the new one: Tsaritsyn. The town is located at the mouth of the Volga River."

"That explains the Russian, but what about all the other languages?"

"I'll get to those." Alexi took a breath, let it out, and took another. He was being evasive, but he couldn't help himself. He'd never wanted to speak of his past again. However, when he'd decided to take her to Ethan, he should have known a return to the nightmare was inevitable.

"You said your father was difficult."

He remained silent; he wasn't going to elaborate.

"Your mother?"

"Dead."

He would not elaborate on that either. Not because it was painful but because he did not know any more than that. He remembered a few endearments, but he could not be sure he had learned them from her. Though he certainly hadn't learned them from his father.

"Do you know how the draft worked?" he asked.

"Not yours." She shrugged. "Not ours either, apparently."

Alexi didn't care for those words. Yours. Ours. Us. Them. In his mind, his heart, he and Cat were on the same side. But back then they would have been enemies.

"In the North there was a lottery. Male citizens between the ages of twenty and forty-five were enrolled. If your name was drawn, you could buy your way out by paying a substitute three hundred dollars to march off in your place."

"You sold yourself."

"It was all I had left."

The silence that followed his words loomed loud on a prairie where the only sounds were the muted thud of their horses' hooves and the harsh rasp of his own breath.

"I had to get out. He would have—" He swallowed the bile that threatened to rise. "He would have killed me. I thought it was a bargain." He laughed. "A steal. All that money to do what I'd been trained to do anyway."

"Trained?"

"My father was a soldier. A very good one. The Russians were often fighting the Persians, the Ottomans, as well as the occasional uprisings at home. The country is very large. There is always someone unsatisfied. When he was wounded and could no longer hold a weapon steady, we came to America."

A man who could no longer fulfill his purpose found Russia an unforgiving land.

"He fashioned me in his image. From the moment I could hold a rifle, I learned to use it. I had the eye of an eagle, he said."

When he wasn't shouting that I was a useless dog.

"He taught me well."

Two punches in the gut for a miss. A light tap on the back of the head—a caress in comparison—if Fedya did as he was told.

"We made our living in a traveling show. Fedya, the amazing sharpshooting boy. We went everywhere—New York, Kentucky, Colorado; once I even saw California. I would perform, and my father would make bets with the locals."

If he won, I ate. If he lost, I bled.

"One day we came to a town just after they'd chosen the men who would form a regiment and be sent off to war. We did our show. I was amazing."

"Someone saw you and thought 'He'd be better than me with a gun.'"

"*Oui.*" And, oh, how he was.

"Your father didn't come after you?"

"I didn't say that."

"What happened?"

"My new comrades in arms defended me." It was the first time anyone ever had.

"Mmm."

"What does that mean?"

"They'd seen what you could do. They wanted you with them."

"Most likely." But it had been wonderful.

His father barreling in, shouting, huge fists swinging at Alexi's face. He'd cowered; how could he not? He knew what harm those fists could do.

But no blows had fallen. Alexi had lifted his head and seen that his comrades were holding his father back.

The lieutenant had said, "He's mine now, and there's nothing you can do about it."

They'd tied his father up and left him behind. Fedya never saw the man again.

"I became a sharpshooter. A sniper."

Cat frowned at his guns. Pistols, not a rifle, but he was as good with one as the other. When they were loaded.

"I shot people," he continued when she said nothing more.

"You and the rest of the Union Army."

"I did things differently."

"Why?"

"At the beginning of the war, an entire regiment of snipers was recruited by Hiram Berdan, who was said to be the best rifle marksman in the nation. But no one knew about me yet."

"Don't be so modest."

"Truth is truth, and I was remarkable."

He'd had to be if he wanted to live—both before the war and during it.

"Berdan's Sharpshooters saw action for most of the conflict. They were excellent, but they were a large group and unwieldy. They got noticed."

"You did not."

Ah, she knew him well.

"Secretary of War Stanton decided that snipers, other than Berdan's, should be organized into smaller units and attached to a regiment for special deployment."

"What kind of special deployment?"

"During a battle, if an officer was being foolish"—and many of them were—"shouting orders, riding a horse, standing up as if he were invincible . . . I shot him."

She flinched.

"The loss of a leader often threw the troops into chaos. They'd retreat." Or outright desert. "And the battle was over."

"I find it hard to believe that soldiers would run because their leader went down."

"The majority of men in both armies weren't trained as soldiers. They were handed rifles that were heavy, ammunition just the same. They weren't even told that they had to aim high to hit low. Of course, with the number of men on a field, they could aim at this man"—Alexi pointed—"and hit that one." He moved his hand lower. "Dead was dead; it didn't matter if you were aiming at him. Still, the amount of lead and powder wasted on shots that went into the trees or the sky was embarrassing."

"Then there was you."

"I rarely missed. Which was how I graduated from shooting officers to more difficult missions."

"More dangerous, you mean?"

"The missions weren't that dangerous. I was positioned over eight hundred yards from my target."

"Impossible."

"You've heard of Major General John Sedgwick?"

She shook her head.

"Killed at Spotsylvania Court House by a Confederate sniper. Sedgwick taunted the sharpshooters. Told his men to quit ducking, that 'They couldn't hit an elephant at that distance.'"

"Uh-oh."

"Exactly. A bullet struck him in the face a few seconds later. They say the Rebs were eight hundred yards away. I was better than all of them. And once it became known how very good I was, I was the one they called when the target absolutely had to be eliminated immediately."

With the least possible knowledge of it.

"I began the war with my father's musket. It was heavy and not as accurate as the Whitworth I took off a Confederate sniper."

From her expression, she understood that the only way he could have taken such a prize from another soldier was if he'd killed the man and confiscated it.

"The Confederates bought a handful of Whitworths from the British. Only the best of the best received them. They were accurate to fifteen hundred yards. It was a Whitworth that killed General Sedgwick. Once I had one, I became even more deadly."

"Which led to your dangerous missions?"

Alexi nodded. "We had a man who had infiltrated the Confederacy."

"Ethan Walsh," Cat said. "How did he do it?"

"He was a doctor."

"He spied on the sick and the dying?"

"He *helped* the sick and the dying. Considering the conditions in the rebel camps, they were lucky to have him."

"Lucky to have their delirious ramblings reported to the enemy? You have an odd definition of luck."

True, but that was beside the point.

"Ethan did what he thought was best to end the war more quickly."

"What did you do?"

"I was sent after Jefferson Davis."

"The president?" Her voice carried over the silent prairie like a gunshot.

"Not mine."

"Still. That's . . . that's . . ."

"War," he stated. "No need to be so horrified. I didn't do it."

Although he would have.

"You were caught?"

"I wasn't as good at disappearing then as I am now."

Because of then, he had become what he was now.

"How did it happen?"

"A scout exchanged information between Ethan and myself. Ethan had heard that Davis was going to meet with Lee."

"*Robert E.* Lee?" Cat didn't wait for his response. Who else could it have been? "Were you supposed to kill him too?"

Alexi didn't answer such a foolish, foolish question. Without Lee on the side of the Confederacy, the war wouldn't have lasted half as long as it had.

"The scout led me to where the meeting was supposed to take place."

"He led you into a trap?"

Alexi laughed. "No."

"You're positive?"

"Mikhail was the scout. He would never have betrayed us."

Considering Mikhail's skills, which she was very familiar with, his being a scout made complete sense.

"We were all captured."

Hooves pounding in the dead of night. The shouts. The curses. The blows.

"It *was* a trap," he said. "Lee and Davis were never supposed to be there."

"Who betrayed you?"

"Never found out." Though he *had* tried.

"Why didn't they execute you?"

"I don't know." It was common practice to shoot snipers immediately upon their capture. Many of the men who'd been there that night had wanted to.

Instead they'd uttered two words that had caused Alexi's hands to tremble. He couldn't remember, but he thought he might have begged them to kill him rather than take him to—

"Castle Thunder."

"Hell," Cat muttered.

"Yes," Alexi agreed.

CHAPTER 18

*R*ichmond's Castle Thunder was one of the most notorious prisons of the Confederacy. The majority of the captives were spies, political prisoners, and those accused of treason. As most of those crimes carried the death sentence, the level of brutality at Castle Thunder was high. What difference did it make if you killed someone who was already condemned to die?

Not much, if the survival rates at Castle Thunder were any indication.

The prison was composed of three buildings that had once been tobacco factories and a warehouse. Prisoners were separated between them based on their sex, race, military affiliation, and crime. Castle Thunder held the dubious distinction of housing nearly one hundred female inmates over the course of the war, along with Negroes and deserters from both sides. At one point, over three thousand men and women were crowded into what had once been known as Gleanor's Tobacco Factory, Palmer's Factory, and Whitlock's Warehouse.

"If we didn't die for the amusement of the guards," Alexi said, "we died from dysentery or starvation. Which they also found quite amusing."

"Amusing?"

"Very." He could still hear the laughter. Most often in his dreams. Right before he began to scream.

He had not done so lately. Probably because he had erased the past by re-creating himself as a man without one. He was no longer Fedya but Alexi. Alexi had never been in prison. He had never been in the war. He had never held a loaded gun. Which made it damn hard to shoot someone he cared about in the head.

However, seeing Ethan, who still thought of him as Fedya— why wouldn't he?—had brought everything back. Alexi was surprised he hadn't awoken screaming each night while in Freedom. Though he hadn't managed much sleep. Which might be why he was having a hard time distinguishing now from then, then from now—

"How did you survive?" she asked.

Alexi flinched at the report of a gunshot before he realized the sound had only been in his head.

Again.

"What's wrong?" Cat looked around. "Did you hear something?"

He often heard things. The true question was: Were they real or imagined?

"Are you going to tell me?"

He'd planned to. But suddenly . . . he couldn't.

"Are *you* going to tell *me*?"

"I don't know your story, Alexi. How can I tell it?"

"I wasn't talking about my story." He turned his head so he could see her when he murmured, "Cathleen."

She flinched as badly as he had at the nonexistent gunshot. Then, as he'd known she would, she kicked her horse into a gallop and left him behind.

* * *

BEFORE she even reached Mikhail's side, Cat understood what Alexi had done. He didn't want to tell her any more, so he'd brought up her past, her secrets, her pain, ensuring she would panic; she would run. Concerned with herself, she would forget his past, his secrets, his pain.

And for a while, she did. As they rode west day after day, they spoke only of necessary things.

"I'll pitch the tent."

"I'll make the food."

"I'll water them horses."

She considered asking Mikhail what had happened, but he obviously didn't remember, and she couldn't upset him needlessly. Though she did find herself staring at the scar mostly hidden by his hair, wondering when and where he had gotten it and if it had anything to do with his memories, or lack of them.

Cat would have preferred they skirt Jepsum, continuing on to Denver City immediately, but they were out of supplies, and Denver City wasn't close enough to reach before they needed them. They paused around dusk, far enough from civilization not to be seen, and pawed through their costumes.

They couldn't just ride into town as they were. Who knew what had gone on in Freedom after they left, what people had seen before they'd escaped, what Ethan had said or not said. Besides, entering a new place looking exactly as they had in the last one was just not done when traveling with Alexi Romanov. For good reason.

Alexi tossed Cat a hank of rope, which she caught with her good hand. Her other rested in the sling Mikhail had fashioned from a kerchief the day before. The constant jostling from the movements of the horse had proved too painful.

Cat lifted the rope. "Shall I hang myself?"

"Don't be a fool!" Alexi strode over and began to open the buttons of Ethan's shirt.

She slapped at his hands, then stepped back, throwing a quick glance in Mikhail's direction. But the big man frowned into the makeup case as if all the annoyances of the world lay jumbled inside.

"I'm not going to ravage you."

Her quick intake of breath caused his gaze to lift. She thought: *He knows.*

Then he smirked. "Unless you ask me nicely."

As this was the first he'd behaved like himself in several days, and she was pathetically grateful for that smirk, which plainly said he did *not* know, Cat muttered, "In your dreams, Romanov."

"Ah, yes, my dreams." His gaze darkened, and she had no doubt he dreamed of her. Why that made her cheeks heat, she had no idea. She'd dreamed of him too. It didn't mean anything.

"We must appear to be as far from the people we were in Freedom as we can be." He reached for her slowly, as if she were a wild animal, cornered, captured—perhaps she might bite. He gave her time to flee, but this time she remained.

Alexi untied the kerchief's knot, unbuttoned the shirt, gently laid her injured arm against her stomach. His knuckles brushed her belly, and she had to bite her tongue not to gasp—or snarl. He'd done that on purpose.

Alexi set his palm over her hand. "You can keep it here? Without movement. I could tie it down, but then if you have need of it—"

"If I have need of it, I'm dead. Still doesn't work like it should."

Cat had begun to worry it never would, but as that was a concern to make her toss and turn in the night, she tried to focus on the fact that her good arm was her shooting arm and it still moved just fine.

"Tie it."

Alexi snapped his fingers; Mikhail put another length of rope into it. As Mikhail had so recently been transfixed with the makeup box, Cat jumped when he appeared next to them. But he moved off with equal speed, and Alexi tied her arm to her side, then fastened the first length of rope around the empty sleeve of the shirt.

"You are Joe Enderly. Lost the arm in the war." He rebuttoned the shirt, then shoved her hair beneath his old slouch hat. "The rest . . ." He waved his hand. "You figure it out. But—" He scowled. "Be less pretty." He stalked away to deal with his own transformation.

"I could say the same to you!" she shouted, but he ignored her.

Cat filled her palm with dirt, spit into it, then smoothed the mess across her cheeks and neck, dotted a bit on her hands too.

"Lost the arm at . . . Manassas." She joined Mikhail, who again peered into the makeup case.

"Bull Run," Alexi said.

"It doesn't matter if I call it Manassas in a Georgia drawl"—which she did—"or Bull Run in a rude Yankee tone." She switched to just that. "As long as I don't mix the two."

When Alexi didn't answer, she glanced in his direction and gaped. Alexi Romanov stood before her in the guise of a monk, right down to the tonsure upon his head and a rosary hanging from the belt at his waist.

She took a very large step back; he frowned. "What's the matter?"

"I don't want to be too close when the lightning strikes."

"I've worn this before. No lightning. Not once."

"It's coming. Count on it."

He rolled his eyes; she squinted hers. "How did you do that?" Cat pointed to his half-bald pate. He could not have shaved his head from crown to ears so quickly. He just couldn't have.

"A scalp." He reached up, patted, and the skin waggled a bit.

Cat's lip curled. "Where did you get that?"

"Traded with an Apache."

"What did you give him?"

"Gold."

"Wasn't gold." Mikhail lifted a jar of brownish goo, unscrewed the top, gave it a sniff.

"You're lucky he didn't scalp *you*."

"He wanted the gold." Alexi glanced at Mikhail and lifted his hand before the other man could speak. "Stone. Brass. I don't know what it was. But *he* wanted it. *He* asked me to trade. I didn't ask him."

Such was the way with Alexi. He could make people believe they wanted what he had to give with a desperation usually reserved for the starving, thirsting, and dying.

Just look at her.

"Where'd you get the robe?" Cat doubted a monk would have traded it for anything. Then again, she'd never met one.

"You don't want to know."

Considering where he'd gotten the rest of the costume, he was most likely right.

"Why that?"

"As far away from the people we were in Freedom as it is possible for us to be," he recited.

A monk *was* as far away from Alexi Romanov, or Fedya whatever, as it was possible to be, except—

"You're gonna stand out like a—" She stared at him for a moment. "Like a monk in a saloon."

"I won't go in the saloon."

"No man with a face like yours would become a monk."

"What?" His long, supple, very unmonklike fingers fumbled with the rosary. "Why?"

"That annoying vow of celibacy."

"I don't understand what my appearance has to do with a true calling." He peered at the heavens, and the rising moon cast silver across his beautiful face, making him appear ethereal. His fingers stopped fumbling; his lips began to move as they counted the beads one by one.

"You aren't a monk," she snapped, unreasonably annoyed at his pretending to be. And at the universe for encouraging him.

"Believe me, no one will ever know."

Cat rubbed her forehead. He was right. If he could make folks believe he was a toothless old woman or a hunchbacked war veteran, a celibate, tonsured monk wouldn't require much effort. Nevertheless, Cat had a bad feeling.

"You're going to draw too much attention to yourself."

"The more attention on me, the less on . . . Mikhail."

Mikhail had darkened his face and hands with the brown goo. Changed his shirt from once white to black. Slicked his hair with grease. It didn't help. The only way to disguise Mikhail was to hide him, and they no longer had the wagons.

"Maybe we should leave him here."

"We need to stay together." Alexi's gaze shifted to the prairie behind them.

Cat's good arm went to her gun. "Something out there?"

"There is always something out there, *croi'daor*." He took a breath, let it out. "Always."

"Is it after us?"

"That is the question I don't wish to discover the answer to with Mikhail's dead body."

Mikhail snorted his opinion of that.

But they were stronger together than apart, and Cat didn't like the idea of leaving Mikhail behind either, so she stopped arguing.

"I will come in from the east," Alexi said. "You from the south. Mikhail will arrive from the north."

"I thought we were supposed to stay together."

"We will be in the same town. We will stay at the same hotel. We will watch out for one another even as we pretend not to know one another. Which would be difficult if we arrive all at once."

Cat looked over her shoulder and saw nothing back the way they had come, but she'd discovered that quite often the less you saw . . .

The more there was.

They approached Jepsum from their assigned directions, an hour apart. By the time Cat arrived, Mikhail was in his room and Alexi had gathered a crowd. Apparently Jepsum had lost its preacher, and there was a lot of marrying, burying, and baptizing that needed to be done.

While Alexi was agreeing to do all that needed doing the following afternoon, he was accepting donations tonight. The man just couldn't help himself. He wouldn't even have to buy supplies. Those folks who didn't possess coins to press upon him brought food and placed it at his feet like an offering.

As Cat rode past, her gaze met Alexi's over the heads of those surrounding him. *Lightning,* she mouthed, and he quirked an eyebrow before turning away.

No one gave Cat a second—or even a first—glance as she left her horse in the livery, then made her way to the hotel. In truth, she had to tug the liveryman's arm to get him to look her way; he was inordinately fascinated by the new monk in town.

Cat proceeded to the hotel as the crowd grew. She didn't like it one bit. A group such as that could easily turn into a mob with one wrong step.

Once in her room, she couldn't sleep, especially when she glanced outside and discovered both Alexi and the crowd were gone. Mikhail had already tapped on her door and informed her that he was across the hall and three doors to the right. She waited for Alexi to do the same. When midnight rolled around and he still hadn't, she went in search of him.

First she looked in on Mikhail, who lay on the bed, feet

hanging over the edge. He opened one eye, then set the gun he'd pointed at the door back on his chest when he saw who it was.

"Alexi?" she whispered.

He pointed with his left hand. "Two doors down."

Two doors down was empty—except for the monk's robe and that disgusting scalp. She stared at them as the moonlight filtered through the window; then she crept down the stairs and onto the street.

As Joe Enderly, she had no problem strolling into the saloon. There she half expected to find Alexi in another disguise, collecting what funds were left in town that hadn't already been "donated" through a friendly—though not completely above-board—poker game.

A poker game *was* in progress; she even joined it for a while to make certain none of the men around the table was Alexi. The only way she knew for sure that they weren't was that none of them were cheating.

She took one of the saloon gals upstairs, pretended to lose consciousness from excessive drink, searched the other rooms once the girl fell asleep herself, then moved on to the whore-house and repeated the act.

No Alexi. Only then did she begin to get nervous.

After hurrying to the livery, which was empty of people but full of horses, including theirs. Cat released her breath. She stepped onto the street, hand on her hip, the other tied down, the "lost" arm of Ethan's shirt flapping in the dry Kansas breeze.

Where was he?

Maybe he'd returned to the hotel while she'd been searching. Cat began to walk in that direction. She had just passed a window advertising barber/surgeon/dentistry when she caught a movement in the glass.

Furtive. Hell, downright sneaky. She was suspicious even before she turned her head and saw nothing but empty board-walk. But there'd been something there across the street. Right where a slight space between two abandoned buildings gaped black.

Cat walked on, waiting for a sound, a movement. A shot. She reached the end of the boardwalk, leaned against the building, tilted her head down and shifted her eyes to scan Jepsum. When she saw no one, she slid around the corner and doubled back.

On this side, nothing but the rear of buildings and a great expanse of looming prairie. The perfect place for an ambush.

As she walked past a narrow fissure between structures, Cat tensed. Anyone could be there waiting.

Nothing happened. Maybe she was—

Cat's good arm shot into the darkness. The heel of her hand slammed into a chest. Her fingers curled, attempting to snatch shirt or hair, anything to yank upon, but before she could, her wrist was encircled, and she was jerked into the abyss.

A palm pressed to her mouth. "Shhh."

Alexi.

She kicked him. They were too close for it to hurt, but she felt better at making the attempt. Her heart still thundered so loudly she could hear little else.

Leaning in, he set his cheek to hers. This opening between the buildings was very small and, without light or movement, anyone looking in would have to possess the eyes of a mountain lion to see a thing. If they did catch a glimpse, they would merely think they'd stumbled upon two men doing something no one in a small Kansas town wanted to see two men doing.

"Someone is following you," he breathed, and dropped his hand.

"Yeah, you," she whispered.

"I was following . . ." He shifted his eyes as a man with a gun drifted by their opening.

The fellow didn't see them, didn't hear them either. *An amateur*, Cat thought, though he moved quite soundlessly for one.

"I saw him when I looked out my hotel window."

Alexi always took stock of his surroundings upon arrival. Making note of the quickest and least visible exit had saved their lives on several occasions.

"He was obviously waiting for someone to come out, so I changed my clothes and did." Alexi's lips were so close to her ear, his breath tickled. "But he didn't follow me. Oh, no. He waited for you."

Cat frowned. If this fellow was looking for her specifically, they needed to have a chat. Just the two of them.

She started after the man; Alexi pulled her back. "What the—?"

Cat kneed him in the groin, and while he was gasping for the last breath he'd ever take on this earth, slipped away.

The man, moving slowly as he searched, was still close. Cat shoved her gun into his spine. "Drop it." He did. "Kick it away." He did that too. "What do you want?"

"Whaddya think?"

His voice was familiar. She tightened her hand on the gun. "Mister, I'm gonna need you to say—"

Movement behind her, she nearly whirled and shot; then she caught the scent of cool spring rain. She hadn't kneed Alexi hard enough if he was already walking without a limp and speaking above a croak.

"*Durochka*. Don't."

"But—"

"Stay dead." Then she could have sworn she heard him murmur, "For me."

But she'd already snapped, "You or her?" punctuating the words with a sharp poke of the barrel into the small of her captive's back. "Say it!"

"Y-y-"

Alexi sighed.

Cat slammed her elbow into his gut, ignoring the puff of his breath past her cheek as she closed her eyes.

Her captive blurted, "You or her?"

Cat's eyes flew open. *Not him.*

"How could it be him?" Alexi had already recovered with typical aggravating ease from anything she did to him. "He thinks you are dead. Everyone does. Or at least they did."

That *had* been foolish. But his voice—

She'd heard it before.

Cat spun the fellow around and understood why when she recognized the liveryman. That explained why no one had been in the barn when she'd checked on the horses. He'd been following her. But why? As Alexi had mentioned, she was dead. And in this disguise, before she'd opened her big mouth, he could not have known she wasn't Joe Enderly.

"What are you doing here?" Alexi demanded.

The man swallowed, gaze flicking to the barrel of the gun before settling on Alexi. "You ain't gonna shoot me, are ye?"

"Doubtful."

Cat cast him an exasperated glare. "*He* isn't the one holding the gun." She waggled the weapon. "Answer. Now."

"I was gonna rob the monk," he blurted. "People were givin' him all that money."

And here she'd thought the man had been staring at Alexi because he was so pious.

"You weren't following the monk," Alexi said.

The guy glanced in his direction, then frowned as if he'd remembered something.

Cat stifled a curse. She'd told Alexi he was too damn pretty to wear that robe. People would remember.

"You know, you look kinda—"

"Never mind that." Cat stuck the gun in his face. His eyes crossed. Amazing how the endless black of that opening where the bullet came out mesmerized folks. "Why were you following me?"

"The monk went in before I could catch 'im. Then you come out, and I remembered that gold coin you give me."

"You gave him a gold coin?"

Cat shrugged. She hadn't been paying attention. She'd been watching Alexi work.

"I figgered there were more where that came from," the fellow said. "As you had only one arm, couldn't be that hard to take it."

"You were going to rob a man of God. But when you couldn't find him, you decided to steal from a one-armed war veteran."

"Yeah." He lifted his chin. "So?"

Cat glanced at Alexi. "Yet you don't want to shoot him?"

"I didn't say I didn't want to, just that I wouldn't."

The liveryman smirked.

"I wouldn't be grinning if I were you. Not only do I *want* to shoot you. I will."

The smile faded.

"Now, now. No need for that."

Until she'd asked the question, she could have let the fool go. But she had and now she couldn't afford for him to tell everyone that Cat O'Banyon was alive and well and very close to Denver City.

"There's every need."

"No. I believe he is sorry he tried to rob a *one-armed war veteran*." Alexi emphasized the last words, then lifted his eyebrows. "Isn't that right, friend?"

"Uh . . . yeah. Sure. Weren't good of me. Him havin' fought in the war and been wounded. Nope. Not good of me at all."

It still took several seconds to understand that not everyone in every town in the country knew of Cat O'Banyon and her bizarre habit of making men repeat after her. This guy obviously hadn't. He still thought she was a crippled man, and therefore . . .

He got to live.

"How about we let bygones be bygones," Alexi continued. "You, sir, may go back to your livery. If we see you again before either of us arrives to collect our mounts, you are dead. Fair enough?"

The man was nodding his agreement and backing away before Alexi finished his sentence. He paused next to his discarded weapon.

"Leave the gun," Alexi said.

When the guy did, hurrying into the dark without another glance, Cat holstered hers.

"You need to stop asking that question."

"I don't think I can."

"Try."

Still unnerved by what had just happened, and disturbed by her own admission. Cat fired back. "Can you stop? Even when you're wearing a monk's robe, you're taking things that aren't yours."

"I take nothing that isn't offered freely."

"You took payment for doing things you aren't qualified to do."

"I don't plan on doing them."

She fisted her hands, shoved them against her temples, and fought not to shriek in frustration. "How can you not see that it's wrong?"

He stepped in close, crowding her. "How can you not see that it's death?"

She dropped her hands but refused to retreat. "I'm not dead."

"You keep saying that. Then you turn around and just beg to be killed."

"I never beg."

His eyes flared; she thought he might shake her. Then those eyes shifted, and he cursed, pushing her to the ground, following her down, pinning her there as a gun fired and a bullet whooshed over their heads.

Footsteps approached, but her right arm was pinned, the left tied beneath the shirt, as useless as she had pretended it to be.

"You have to move!"

Alexi didn't and she feared he'd been hit. Then, with a speed that impressed even her, he pulled a Colt from her holster and fired. The sound of a body collapsing to the ground echoed as loudly as the report of the gun.

Alexi stood. In the moonlight, his face shone gray. He dropped the weapon; it landed next to her with a thump. She reached for it with a hand that did not look like hers.

"I did warn him," Alexi said.

Then he turned his head to the side and threw up.

CHAPTER 19

$\mathcal{T}$he shakes followed; they always did. Alexi could barely stay on his feet.

"What is wrong with you?" Cat asked. But she kept him standing, and she got him out of there.

He should have considered that the man had another gun. Didn't everyone?

Two gunshots near midnight. It was only a matter of minutes until someone in authority arrived. Certainly the fellow had deserved shooting. However, the explanation would take time, involve a bit of lying and Alexi Romanov—King of All Liars—just wasn't capable of it right now. Besides, the longer anyone stared at Cat, and the better the lighting, the less she would appear like a man. In truth, how anyone could see anything but her beauty shining through was beyond Alexi's understanding.

Voices from the end of the street. Cat cursed and hauled him toward the fissure between the buildings, thrust him in, followed. There was barely enough room to slide along sideways. If either one of them had been any larger, they'd have gotten stuck. As it was, Cat continued to shove him along none too gently.

He'd scared her. He scared himself.

Alexi fought not to vomit again, covering his mouth to muffle the sound of gagging.

Cat pinched his arm. "Do *not*," she ordered, as if her will alone could stop him. The only thing that did was the fact that he'd already left the entire contents of his stomach next to the body.

They reached the other end, and she grabbed his hand before he tumbled into the open. Hers was warm and dry in contrast to the chilly dampness of his.

"Look first! What is *wrong* with you?" she repeated.

More than he could ever say.

Alexi peeked out. Everyone on the street at this time of night —and there were quite a few; gunfire often had that effect—were either hurrying toward the commotion or peering in that direction. He and Cat were able to slip out and blend in.

Cat threw her arm around his shoulders, nearly knocking him down before she pulled him close, weaving along with him as she began to sing—voice deep and slurred.

"Buffalo gals, you comin' out tonight, comin' out tonight, comin' out tonight?" She stumbled, almost taking them both down. Then she belched, loud and long and luscious. Anyone in their vicinity moved out of it. "Buffalo gals, comin' out tonight? To dance by the li-i-i-ight of the mo-o-o-o-n."

Her off-key rendition got them to the door of the hotel. No one stood behind the desk. The clerk had no doubt gone to see who had been shooting.

Cat pushed Alexi toward the steps. "Hurry up, before someone comes back."

He fell onto them, lay there shivering and sweating and trying not to feel the kick of the rifle, the smell of the blood, and the sound of the screams.

"No. That was then. Not now." He hadn't used a rifle.

This time.

"Alexi!" Cat shook him until he opened his eyes.

Hers were so . . . What? Concerned? Scared? Furious? Maybe

all three. He managed to drag himself to the second floor and into his room.

"We need to go."

"Too . . ." Alexi swiped at the tickle on his cheek. His fingers came away wet. He peered at them and saw blood. But when he blinked, it was gone and he was left staring at sweat.

"Too what?"

He couldn't remember what he'd said. He couldn't remember what she had.

Cat picked up his duffel. "We'll head out while everyone is—"

"Obvious. Too obvious to run away now."

"I didn't plan on running. More like sneaking. You know, the way we usually leave town?"

He shook his head and the room spun.

"I'll get Mikhail."

Alexi retched.

He's going to die.

"No," was all he managed, before he fell onto the bed and back into the war.

* * *

Captured south of Richmond, Fedya and his scout didn't have to travel far to Castle Thunder Prison. Once there, they were tossed into Palmer's Factory.

Originally, the place had housed Union deserters, and a disgusting lot they were—rough, violent, with no sense of morals or loyalty. By the time Fedya arrived, Palmer's also housed prisoners of war like himself and his companion. Within a day, he discovered it was also home to at least one spy.

Dr. Ethan Walsh.

His scout disappeared soon after they were incarcerated. As the man could easily take care of himself, Fedya didn't worry about him. By the end of the first day, he was a bit worried about himself.

Certainly, a lifetime with his otets *had taught Fedya not only how to fight but how to fight dirty. Unfortunately, the people he had to worry most about were not the other inmates but the guards. They had guns; he did not.*

At least not right away.

"Hey, killer."

As Fedya didn't think of himself as a killer, he didn't glance up at the taunt. He was a soldier. He'd done his job, done it well. Which turned out to be the problem.

Someone punched him in the shoulder. Fedya, used to such sneak attacks from his father, merely turned. He was glad he had not started swinging his fists when he saw the guns pointed at his chest by sneering guards whose eyes plainly said, "Go ahead. Fight us. Please."

"Hear you're quite the sniper." The closest man, as wide as he was tall, which wasn't very, had a squashed nose that Fedya really wanted to squash some more and protruding black eyes. He prodded Fedya in the stomach with the barrel of his Richmond rifle.

Fedya didn't answer. What could he say? Yes, I've killed dozens of your brethren. Shoot me now.

Later, he wished that he had.

"You must be the best if they sent you to kill the president and General Lee. We're gonna make you pay for that, boy. Pay long."

They hit the back of his head with a rifle. When he went to his knees, they kicked him. The other inmates did not come to his aid. Instead, they shouted encouragement and placed bets on how long until he lost consciousness. Or died.

A scuffle. Grunts. The kicking stopped. So did the jeers.

Fedya lifted his head. His scout, and another fellow he'd never seen before—much smaller, but then who wasn't?—stood between him and everyone else.

"I have enough folks in my infirmary," the stranger said. "I don't need another. "

Fedya's scout growled, then glowered, and even though the guards had guns, they backed off and went away.

But they never forgot that first day; they didn't forgive, and they made certain all three of the men involved were forever sorry for it.

* * *

ALEXI SHIVERED and sweated and moaned. Every once in a while he stiffened, and Cat feared he'd have a fit, or worse, stop breathing.

Should she fetch Mikhail? Alexi didn't want that. Then again, perhaps he'd been saying *no* to something within his nightmare and not to her mention of Mikhail.

His eyelids twitched; his mouth tightened; his fingers clutched at the sheets. He was definitely having one helluva bad dream. Cat should know.

"No!"

Cat slapped her hand over his mouth. She didn't need the law knocking on the door. If anyone saw Alexi in this state, they would think him mad. But she figured the sheriff, and any deputies he might have, were occupied with a dead body. Still, shouting would bring someone eventually, along with attention they did not need.

She lifted her hand from his mouth. When he didn't shout again, she set it on his brow. He was drenched in sweat. Which gave her something to do.

She released her bound arm, then shoved a chair beneath the doorknob. Apparently the town of Jepsum did not believe in locks, or perhaps could not afford them.

After undressing Alexi, she bathed him with the water from the basin. Tepid, nevertheless, it was cooler than he was.

When she was through, she tucked him beneath the covers where he continued to shiver, thrash, and mutter. She sat at his side and reached for his hand. At her touch, he reared up, gasping as if he'd been held beneath the water until near drowned. He dragged her across the bed, across his body, his fingers digging painfully into her arms.

"*Ne trogay menya.*" His voice deep and menacing, his eyes stared into hers, though he did not see.

"Alexi. Wake up."

"*Ya ne budu.*" His grip tightened.

"Fedya!"

Big mistake. He shook her once, so hard her head snapped back and then forward, nearly colliding with his before she could stop it. Now he seemed to see, and what he saw he did not like.

"*Svin'ya! Sobaki!*"

How could she reach him? She didn't know any Russian.

Or did she?

Cat began to recite all the words he'd said to her that had sounded remotely like his native language, and as she did so, he quieted. His fingers loosened, his eyes slid closed. He began to breathe less harshly.

The final one she remembered, because he had used it not an hour before, was—

"*Durochka.*"

His eyes, blue and lucid, suddenly stared into hers. "Why are you calling me a fool?"

"You called me a fool?" What else had he been calling her when she thought he'd been murmuring endearments?

"Sometimes I must." He glanced around the room, then back at her, seeming to realize he was naked, in bed, with Cat on top of him. He ran a hand over her ass. "In order to do this right, you need to remove all those clothes."

"Shut up." Her tone was light; he was fine.

However, when she began to roll free, he stopped her. "Stay. Please. I'm—" His voice broke. "Cold." And as if to emphasize how cold, he shuddered.

Since he'd scared her—badly—and she was so damn tired, Cat relented. "Let me take off my boots."

She stood but when she saw how he'd pressed his lips together to keep his teeth from chattering, she took off everything—as he had done when she'd been shivering in Indian Territory—then slipped in beside him.

"What are you doing?"

She set her head on his chest and wrapped her arm across his belly, pressing the length of her body to his. "You said I needed to remove my clothes."

"I—um—I don't think I can."

"You don't need to. I already removed yours and mine."

"I mean, I can't perform. I'm—"

"Shh." She stroked his chest. "You've performed enough for one lifetime." He stiffened, and she wanted to call him a fool again. Instead, she whispered; "Tell me."

He gave a shudder so deep it had to have hurt. "Tell you what?"

"Whatever you want to." She let her hand rest atop his heart. "And I think, mostly, what you don't want to." She tilted back her head. "What happened tonight?"

He stared at the ceiling. He didn't blink.

Cat considered shaking him as he'd shaken her, or at least calling his name. But which name? She was still debating when he spoke.

"I shot him."

"He deserved shooting."

"What?" He lowered his gaze; comprehension quickly replaced confusion. "Oh, him."

"Who were you talking about?"

His chest rose, then fell beneath her palm. "Mikhail."

CHAPTER 20

*C*at stiffened in his arms. Alexi waited for her to pull away, to leave—his bed, his room, his life. He'd be cold again, but that was nothing new. He'd been cold since . . .

He could not remember ever being warm. Not like this. Both outside and within. Every time a shiver escaped, Cat would move closer, press herself more firmly against him, flex her fingers, and pet him like a . . .

"Mikhail's fine." She rubbed her cheek against his chest, arched her back, practically purred. Strangely, the movement did not make him want to toss her onto her back and plunge into her again and again and again. It made him want to—

He tightened his arm around her shoulders and gently, so she would never know, pressed his lips to her hair.

Alexi didn't want to tell her the rest. She would never lie next to him like this, or any other way, again. But after what had just transpired, he thought he must.

"Mikhail will never be fine again, thanks to me."

"Mikhail adores you. He'd do anything for you."

"I know," Alexi whispered.

"Are you brothers?"

212

"No. Yes." He sighed. "It's confusing."

"Maybe you should start at the beginning."

"The beginning. Yes." Then he tried to decide when, exactly, that was.

"Mikhail said he's known you as long as he can recall."

"That's true. Except *when* he can recall isn't quite the beginning." The beginning was somewhat earlier. "I told you about Ethan, the war, Castle Thunder."

"Some."

"Where did I stop?" He knew where he'd stopped. He just needed a minute to breathe.

"You and your scout—Mikhail—were captured and sent to Castle Thunder."

"Ethan arrived ahead of us. He'd already set up a surgery, started helping people as best he could with what he had. Wasn't much. We were captives in one of the most brutal prisons of the South. Medical supplies, if there were any, went to the Confederate soldiers first, then the Confederate prisoners. What was left, they gave to us." He shook his head. "Ethan did amazing work in horrible conditions with little but his hands and some hope."

After a while, the hope had been in even shorter supply than bandages.

"What went wrong?"

"It was prison. What could possibly go right?"

"I mean between you and Ethan. When you speak of him now, you seem to admire him. When you spoke to him in Freedom, I thought the two of you might come to blows."

"I do admire him. He's a brilliant doctor."

"Why do you dislike each other?"

"He dislikes me." With good reason. Alexi's feelings for Dr. Walsh were too complicated to explain now. Perhaps too complicated to explain ever. Best just to go on with his story.

"In prison the days were long, the nights even longer.

Surviving on nothing takes stamina, intelligence, and a good dose of ruthlessness."

"Which explains why you're still here."

"*Spasibo.*"

"English."

"Thank you."

"Tell me about the languages."

"In good time. Beginning to end. Lest I forget—" He would not forget. He only wished that he could. "Because the days were long and the nights longer, nowhere to go, nothing to do but die . . ." Cat stiffened in his arms. He began to pet her as she had done him. "The guards made up games."

"Poker? Brag?"

"No, *m'anam*; those games were already well known. Our captors thought up new ones, and they made us play."

"Why would they have to make you? If you were so bored, wouldn't you want to?"

"Not these games." Alexi was putting off what he did not want to say. He knew it; she knew it. But she let him. "One of their favorites involved feeding tainted food to the most starving inmate; they would place bets. Could the victim be saved or couldn't he?"

Cat's breath caught, but he tightened his arm about her, and she remained silent. He wanted to tell as much of this as he could, while he could.

"They liked to use a prisoner's talents against him. Prove he wasn't as able as he thought. Every time a patient died, Ethan mourned, and the guards never let him forget how worthless he was at his job."

Alexi paused, uncertain where to go next. The languages now? Or the make-believe? Anything to postpone the story of Mikhail.

"We devised games of our own to keep us sane. To take us away from that place, if only in our minds. There were so many immigrants who had sold themselves into service, like me. Also those who had been born here but whose parents had not been, and the array of languages was astounding."

For a moment Alexi could hear the voices blending together in the close confines of Palmer's Factory. Then, when night would fall and the silence became far too loud—

"We started throwing out words in English, discovering how many languages we might turn them into. Someone would say an expression in Spanish, Italian, German. Whoever translated it into something else won."

"You always won." It wasn't a question.

"I am good with languages. But eventually that game wore thin, and we needed another. As a child, I'd often pretend to be someone else." It had helped when being himself was too damn awful.

"You taught your fellow prisoners to step out of themselves."

"We became so proficient, the guards would watch our performances. If we were convincing enough, our game went on and theirs did not begin."

"No wonder you're so good at being . . . anyone."

"*Oui.*"

"And you learned that becoming someone else helps you leave the broken one behind."

"We never leave the broken one behind, *chaton;* we only step away and allow him or her time to heal."

"You healed me."

"Not yet." If he had, she wouldn't still be asking her question and telling her lies.

"You saw my pain," she continued as if he hadn't spoken. "And you helped me."

"My motives were not unselfish. You wanted something from me; I wanted something from you. It was a bargain on both our parts."

That bargain had changed somewhere along the way, though Alexi wasn't sure how, or why, or to what.

"Perhaps," she said. Then, as if she couldn't bear to examine where this strange intimacy between them was going—or where it had already been—she returned to his story. "You pretended you were someone else to survive the games the guards played; you occupied your minds sharing languages."

"We did."

"And then?"

"We went mad; we died." He plucked at the covers. "We killed one another."

She shifted so she could see his face. "You were on the same side."

"Too many men shoved into too small a space with barely enough food to feed even half of them. The majority of those incarcerated in the Palmer's section of Castle Thunder were deserters. They felt allegiance to no one but themselves. In a very short time, the only side anyone had was their own."

"All right. I understand. Go on."

"Go on? Isn't that enough?"

"You're stalling, Alexi. This all began because you shot someone and puked. You, who claim to have been the best sniper in the Union. So good you were sent to kill the two most important men in the Confederacy."

"I didn't."

"You would have."

He shrugged.

"And I doubt you would have thrown up when you were through. Which means something happened between then and now to make you not only shiver and shake after firing a gun but to make you carry empty weapons so you don't shoot anyone ever again."

"Just did."

"With my gun. What happened?"

Still he hesitated. He had not spoken of this since it had occurred. Why bother? What was done was done; those who were dead were dead, and while one might hope to get them back . . .

Miracles didn't happen. At least not for him.

"They knew why I was there, what I had done."

"You didn't do it."

"Not the mission I was caught during, but all the others . . . " He rubbed his burning, too dry eyes. "Every person there had a story of someone they knew who'd been shot by a sniper. After a while, each one of them had been shot by me."

At first he'd thought that might be why he'd been brought to Castle Thunder and not killed outright—to give the guards someone to blame, to torture, to pay for what had already been done. And that might have been part of it. But, as always, what appeared on the surface was not what lay beneath.

"That's not fair," Cat said.

"Fair?" Alexi let out a short huff of breath. "In a war, there's no such thing. The guards considered it justice to make me perform greater and greater feats of marksmanship under worse and worse conditions. Nothing and no one could stop them." Certainly not him.

Cat did not beg. But Fedya had. Many times.

"You shot Mikhail during one of their . . . games?"

"Yes and no."

"Alexi—"

"I didn't shoot *Mikhail*."

"But you said—"

"Then again, I did."

She groaned. "Say what you mean."

"I was captured, along with my scout," he repeated.

"Mikhail."

"Back then we called him Mikey."

"That's what—" She drew back to look at him again. "That's what Ethan called him."

"Mikey was Ethan's brother. He was younger, but so much bigger and stronger. He had a knack for finding things. When they were children, whatever became lost, Mikey found. When they hunted, Mikey led. He could track anything."

"You're talking about them like they're two different people."

"They are."

"That's impossible."

"Tell it to Mikhail. He doesn't remember Mikey; he doesn't remember Ethan."

"But how—?" She stopped, eyes widening. "The game."

Alexi rubbed his forehead as an ache began in the center. "It started out simply enough. There was an enclosed yard between the buildings where they meted out punishments. Lashings. Executions." He closed his eyes.

Blood-drenched soil dotted with stained tufts of grass. The sound of the whip whistling through the air toward—

Alexi's eyes snapped open. "I would shoot cans or bottles from farther and farther distances. I never missed. I can understand how that would become boring. So they began to set the cans and bottles on people's heads. Much, *much* more interesting."

"Mikey," she whispered.

"Became Mikhail."

"I don't understand."

"No one does." He swallowed, his throat clicking loudly in the silence of the room. "The distance was too great. I'd never hit anything from so far away. I knew better. Especially with the rifle they furnished. A Dimick, so long and heavy. The ammunition had been made by idiots. The sight was—" He shuddered. "It was a miracle I didn't kill someone before Mikey."

"Why didn't you shoot them. They gave you a gun. Bam, bam, bam. No more guards."

"A Dimick is a muzzle loader, single shot. Even if they'd handed me a Henry . . ." Alexi's fingers flexed at the thought of having sixteen shots in a repeating rifle at his disposal. "I doubt the guards would have provided me with more than one bullet at a time. They were thugs, but they weren't stupid thugs. Even so, whenever I had a weapon, a half dozen of them kept theirs pointed at . . ." His voice faded as memories flickered—so strong they seemed real, though he knew better.

"You?"

The whispers, the scents and sounds, still beckoned. "That would have made things easier. But I was too valuable an amusement, among other things."

"Other?"

"Never mind." His value, the real reason for his presence at Castle Thunder, was for later in the story. "They kept their guns on whoever was unlucky enough to be my pedestal that day. If my aim was true, the victim lived. If not, he died. If I refused—"

"He died."

Alexi took a breath, let it out slowly. "They thought it would be interesting to see if caring about my pedestal affected my aim. Apparently, it did."

"You shot Mikey."

"No. I killed Mikey."

The brick area behind the prison was designated as the place to impart punishment on convicted deserters—lashings, executions. In truth, it was used by the guards for anything they didn't want others to see. Fedya spent quite a bit of time there.

At first he didn't mind. He'd been trained to shoot; he was good at it. Performing greater and greater feats of marksmanship gave him confidence. In this place where men were treated like animals, confidence was in short supply.

Even when the guards began to move the targets from the tops of barrels to the heads of those deserters they planned to whip, or kill,

Fedya didn't hesitate. If he could place a shot just so and end someone's life, he could as easily place it just so and save them.

Not that he actually saved anyone. If the man was condemned to die, Fedya's skill did not prevent the inevitable. The dark splotches staining the dirt and the grass of the enclosure gave testament to what happened every day after they returned him to Palmer's Factory.

"Thought you were a killer." The words, low and vicious, came from a guard equally so. Beltrane carried a whip on his belt, decorated with blood. Sometimes Fedya could swear he saw flecks of flesh stuck there as well.

Fedya was confused. Wasn't he supposed to hit the can and not the man? Wasn't that the purpose of this game?

Beltrane's face was pale and pockmarked, his hands hard and large. He appeared to be in his twenties, but most of his thin brown hair was already gone. He was short, stocky, and bowlegged. All he had to recommend him was his skill with a whip and his enjoyment of violence. Which explained his steady employment at Castle Thunder.

"You shot my cousin in the head, you fucking filth." Beltrane uncoiled the whip.

It did no good to deny such accusations. Fedya had tried before, but no one believed him. And who knew? He'd shot so many men, he might have shot someone's cousin, or brother, or friend. He had no idea.

The whip snapped, and Fedya started. Beltrane laughed around his disgustingly chewed-upon cigar. "We gotta make this more interesting. "

Fedya was already standing at the farthest reaches of the enclosure. A Confederate deserter who appeared all of fifteen years old stood on the other side. The boy shook so badly, the can atop his head shimmied. Nevertheless, Fedya had already put three perfectly placed holes through the tin.

Beltrane continued to chew, the brush of his black gaze reminding Fedya of a spider scuttling over his face in the night. He even swiped at a tickle on his nose.

"There you are." Michael Walsh hovered at the entrance to the courtyard.

Though Fedya encountered Ethan rarely—the doctor spent his days and nights treating patients—Mikey came around every so often to see how Fedya was faring.

Seen as the doctor's helper, Mikey was given free rein in the prison to scrounge what he could for the patients. And as Ethan treated all who resided in Castle Thunder—Confederate, Yankee, traitor, deserter, spy, it didn't matter—Mikey went everywhere that he wanted. On several occasions, he even took part in their make-believe. But mostly Mikey remained at his brother's side, doing everything Ethan asked.

Fedya wished he had a brother who loved him like that. Then maybe he wouldn't feel so alone. Although right now, being alone was all that Fedya wanted.

He had never mentioned what he did in the brick enclosure behind the prison. Nothing Mikey or Ethan could say would stop Fedya's performances; besides, it was best not to draw Beltrane's attention if you could help it.

Mikey glanced at the Confederate kid, then back at Fedya and his overgrown dark hair sifted over his bright gray eyes. "What are you doin' out here?"

Mikey wasn't slow, a surprise to most people who believed someone so large could not move or think with ease.

"It's not what you—"

"You don't know any of these folks." Beltrane's voice was slick, slimy, serpentine, like him. "So you don't really care if they die." The guard stared at Mikey with what was supposed to be a smile but was merely a baring of stained teeth.

Fedya's skin prickled. "Mikey, go back to the hospital. "

Beltrane flicked a finger and two guards blocked Mikey's exit.

"He should return to his brother," Fedya said.

"He will." Beltrane's smile widened. "Maybe."

Fedya stiffened at the insinuation. He always hit what he aimed at. Nothing would change that. Still, he didn't want Mikey anywhere near this man, this place, this gun.

"Just set another can on that deserter." Fedya tried not to let his

unease show at the distance across the yard. He'd made shots from greater distances than this, but he'd done so with better equipment.

The gunshot was so loud, Fedya cried out. Blood bloomed on the Confederate kid's gray coat, and he collapsed to the ground.

"You don't need a new can." Beltrane tucked the pistol back into his belt next to the whip. "What you need is a new pedestal. "

The guards marched Mikey to the wall.

CHAPTER 21

*C*at touched her fingers to Alexi's chin. "You don't have to go on. I understand."

She didn't want him to continue. From the way his voice, his body, trembled when he spoke, the memories were tearing him apart.

He squinted as if he wasn't sure who she was, before returning his gaze to the ceiling. "I doubt that."

She tried not to let his words bother her. He was right. How could she understand? Certainly she'd shot people. But they'd deserved it. Michael, Mikey, Mikhail had not.

The pictures he painted—of Castle Thunder, of Fedya, of the Walshes, the guards, his "pedestals"—were so vivid Cat could practically see them. She smelled the unwashed bodies, the dirt, the blood. She heard the cries, the shouts, the shots, even the whip. Of course, Alexi had always been able to make anyone believe anything, and his gift with words was only one of the reasons why.

She laid her hand on his chest, was comforted by the beat of his heart, even though the speed was far too hard and fast. She took a deep breath, let his familiar rainwater scent wash over, then soothe her.

"I've done things, Alexi. Things that haunt me." Like the Freedom sheriff. Clyde. And worse. "There's nothing you can tell me that will shock me. There's nothing you can say that will . . ." She paused, uncertain of how to go on.

Alexi, as always, had no trouble. "That will make you hate me as much as Ethan does?"

"I could never hate you."

"Let's find out," he said, and continued.

"No!" Fedya started toward Mikey.

Beltrane's whip cracked. Fedya stopped, expecting to feel the sting of the lash across his arm, his chest, his face. Instead, his friend cried out, and a slash appeared on the back of his once-white shirt.

"Don't move." Beltrane spat his cigar stub at Fedya's feet.

"Or what? You'll whip me?"

The guard laughed, spewing smoke-fouled breath in Fedya's face. "Of course not." Beltrane flicked his wrist again. Again Mikey cried out.

"Stop."

"No." The whip cracked.

Fedya's fingers clenched on the Dimick rifle. "What do you want?"

"The same thing I've always wanted. Some goddamn entertainment. "

The guards shoved Mikey against the wall. They set a much smaller can upon his head.

"No," Fedya said. "Please, just . . . No. "

Beltrane flipped his hand as if swatting a bug. The men—four instead of the usual two, in deference to Mikey's height and breadth— spun him around. The can flew sideways, bouncing against the brick wall with a tinny clack that made both Mikey and Fedya flinch. The guards tore off his shirt. Blood ran from the open wounds.

"Either shoot the can," Beltrane said in a conversational tone that chilled Fedya more than the words themselves, "or I'll peel every last bit of skin off his back. Your choice."

As Alexi had heard stories of those Beltrane had flayed alive, he swallowed his gorge and nodded. With him, Mikey stood a chance of leaving this place alive. With Beltrane, he would die.

Slowly.

They positioned Mikey's back against the wall, perching the tiny can upon his big, tall head. His gray eyes met Fedya's, and Fedya nearly dropped the gun.

Mikey trusted him.

When the others had trembled and begged, Fedya had merely become calmer, intent on proving to them his prowess. But now, staring at Mikey, who stood with his shoulders thrown back, gaze confident, Fedya was the one who trembled.

He accepted the bullet and loaded the gun by rote. Lifting the weapon, he sighted down the barrel. Fedya had done this a hundred times before. Why was now any different?

Because he had someone he cared about, someone who trusted and believed in him, someone whose loss would be an agony as his pedestal. The gun suddenly felt very heavy.

"Shoot," Beltrane ordered. "Now. Do it."

Still Fedya hesitated. Perhaps if he waited long enough, Ethan would come looking for his brother. Would the doctor be able to stop this?

The avid sparkle in the guards' eyes told the truth. Nothing would stop this. If Ethan arrived, he'd probably be the next man balancing a can on his head.

The whip whistled. Blood trickled down Mikey's chest. He bit his lip, but not before a single moan broke free, and Fedya knew that the only way to stop this was to finish it.

He stared into his friend's eyes. "I won't hurt you. I promise. Everything will be all right."

Fedya pulled the trigger.

"I killed him."

The lack of emotion in Alexi's voice frightened Cat more than his pale, chill skin.

"Shot him in the head. Just like all the others."

"*Durochka*," she murmured, the word a caress. "You're mistaken. Mikey is Mikhail." Although why that was, she had yet to discover. "He's here. With us. He isn't dead."

"Blood," Alexi continued as if she hadn't spoken. "Like a river across his face. I'd never . . ." He swallowed. "I would shoot, then disappear. I didn't know that head wounds produced so much blood."

Not only that, but as far as she knew, they produced a corpse. So—"What happened to Mikey?"

Alexi's sole movement was a tremble, so faint the only reason Cat knew of it was because her body was pressed the length of his. She feared he'd gone away in his head to a place long before the war, before the Walshes, before he'd become a sharpshooting boy. Although, from what she'd gathered of his childhood, she wasn't certain he'd find any refuge there either.

"Alexi?" She brushed back his hair.

His pupils were so large they'd swallowed all the blue in his eyes. Or perhaps it was just the night that had swallowed them both. Despite what had happened out there, in here Cat felt as if they were living in a world apart.

At least he knew her, because he whispered, "*Koshka*," then closed his eyes and answered the question she thought he hadn't heard. "Ethan saved him. I don't know how. But when Mikey woke, he didn't remember he was Mikey. He didn't remember Ethan." Alexi let out a long breath. "He only remembered me."

"That you—?"

"Shot him? No. Though maybe it would have been better if he had."

"Why?" That memory couldn't be good for anyone.

"He and Ethan had been inseparable. Now Mikey didn't know him."

"Is that why Ethan dislikes you?"

"Hates my guts, you mean?"

Cat didn't answer.

"He blames me for Mikey's death."

"He's not dead!"

"The only thing that remains of Michael Walsh is his talent at scouting. He was a bright young man. He had a future. Now he's—

"Fine."

"He isn't fine, Cat. He thinks he's Mikhail."

"There's nothing wrong with Mikhail."

"Tell that to Ethan."

"Why is he so angry?"

Alexi threw up the hand that wasn't around her. "I shot his brother!"

"What choice did you have?"

"*Not* shooting him."

"It didn't sound like that was one of the choices Beltrane gave you."

"I never missed before." He whispered the next sentence in the voice of a child whose world has been shattered. "Why did I have to miss then?"

"You understand that they would have made you continue *until* you missed? Wasn't that the game all along? To prove you weren't as good as you thought you were? To destroy you from the inside out? I'd think you would be smarter than to let them."

"I . . . What?" He frowned.

"They continued the game until you lost. I'm sure you lasted longer than most. How many men did Ethan save in their poisoned food game before he 'missed'? Once he did, didn't they move on to another game?"

"Yes," he said, as if the concept were a new one.

"If Ethan's so brilliant, you'd think he would have figured that out for himself."

"He believes I bartered Mikey for my freedom."

"What freedom?" As far as Cat could tell, Alexi was still a prisoner.

"I shot Mikey; then I was released the next day."

"But Mikey just happened into the situation. One had nothing to do with the other. It was bad luck."

"Bad something," Alexi muttered. "But it did appear suspect. I can't fault Ethan for doubting me."

"He had to have heard how they forced you. That Beltrane hurt Mikey. That he threatened to kill him. Didn't he see the marks on his brother's back and chest from the whip?"

"What happened, why, how, didn't matter. Mikey was no longer Mikey. The guards enjoyed making us suffer. That Ethan believed I had betrayed him, betrayed Mikey, that the relationship of the three men who could have been responsible for killing their president and beloved general was in tatters, well, they found that—"

"Hilarious."

"They definitely weren't going to do or say anything that might help us make peace."

"Ethan had to have trusted you, or at least trusted those who did. You wouldn't have even been in Castle Thunder if you weren't trustworthy enough to be included in the same plot he was. Yet he didn't take your word over that of the enemy?"

"I was the one holding the gun; his brother was the one dying. Before we had a chance to speak, I was released."

"They just opened the door and let you walk away?"

"Prisoner exchange. The Confederates had kept me alive because one of *their* most valuable assets had been captured. To get him back, they needed someone of equal value." He laughed—one short, sharp bark. "You can imagine the army's disappointment when they discovered how significantly my worth had decreased while incarcerated."

Cat tilted her head. "You couldn't shoot."

"Like my father, if I held a gun, I trembled. So, like him, I . . ."

"Taught," she whispered.

His breath blew across the top of her head, and she remembered standing in a field, Alexi at her back, showing her how to aim high, hit low, his breath distracting her then, as now. Schooling her about the kick of the gun. Teaching her to breathe in, hold, then pull the trigger. Why hadn't she noticed that he never pulled the trigger himself?

"Shooting made you throw up."

"The trouble was not so much the throwing up as the uncontrollable shaking of my hands whenever I pointed a loaded gun at someone."

"Loaded gun," she repeated. *Aha.*

"I spent the rest of the war training recruits. Probably the only instruction they ever received. By that time, both sides were just throwing bodies at one another, waiting for someone to blink or run out of bodies. They could have thrown me, but I had a reputation, and someone in command decided it might be more advantageous to send the soldiers we had left out there with more than the first gun they'd ever seen in their hands."

"Was it?"

"Perhaps. They let me continue. I was still teaching when Mikhail arrived."

"Arrived? How?"

"He escaped."

"From Castle Thunder?" Cat didn't think that was possible.

"Many did. Of course, most were recaptured. Fools would jump out the windows, break a leg when they hit the ground. Made it difficult to run."

"No doubt."

"I remember one attempt. Quite ingenious. They tunneled through a wall, came up in the stable. Unfortunately, one of the conspirators decided he'd rather have more food and less brutality, so he turned traitor. When they finally dug through the earth, a guard with a gun awaited them."

"And Mikhail?"

"During an uprising, while the guards and the prisoners were scuffling, he tossed a rope of sheets through the window, climbed down, then disappeared."

"Isn't it a bit difficult for someone of Mikhail's size to disappear?"

"One would think; yet he did."

Considering Mikhail's memory, they'd probably never know how. "And Ethan?"

"Remained. He would not desert his patients. They had no one else. Mikhail tracked me to New York, Rikers Island. Some called it Camp Astor, after a rich fellow who donated funds for training and uniforms." He waved his hand. "He insisted I was Alexi; he was Mikhail."

"Why would he think that?"

"We'd played so many parts, so many games in that place. In one we were Alexi and Mikhail Romanov, brothers who had many adventures on the road. We took care of each other."

"So you began to live the life he imagined for you?"

"I didn't have anything better to do."

"Ethan knew Mikhail was with you? And why?"

"All Mikhail talked about once he could talk again was his brother, Alexi. When Mikhail escaped, Ethan knew he'd gone to find me. When the war was over, Ethan followed."

"I bet that was a wonderful reunion," Cat said dryly.

"Fantastic," Alexi returned in the same tone. "Mikhail nearly killed him."

"He wouldn't!"

Alexi lifted one eyebrow.

"I'm sure he had a reason."

Alexi shrugged.

"You'd prefer I think Mikhail attempted to kill his brother, or that you ordered him to, rather than tell me the truth?" He didn't answer, but he didn't need to. She knew Mikhail. It didn't take long for her to add one and one and come up with—"Ethan tried to kill you."

Cat's fingertips curled inward as the urge to impart murder of her own washed over her.

Alexi took the hand balled into a fist upon his chest and smoothed it out. "He had his reasons."

"He's an ass. Didn't you explain?"

"No time. He attempted to wring my neck; Mikhail nearly broke his; Ethan left to avoid any more violence, and I didn't see him again until last week."

"How did you know where he was?"

"He wasn't trying to hide."

Cat silently performed another quick addition of the facts before speaking. "You had Mikhail keep track of him." Alexi sighed, which was answer enough. "What if Mikhail had decided to finish what he'd started with Ethan while you weren't around to stop him?"

"Mikhail doesn't just kill people. He has to be told . . ." He left out the words *by me.* "Or he has to be threatened."

"Or you have to be."

"I doubt he'd be very amenable if someone threatened you either."

Why that made Cat feel part of the family, she didn't know. Alexi and Mikhail weren't *really* brothers. They weren't family. They weren't *her* family. Her entire family was dead.

"I told Mikhail to find Ethan. He was not to approach him, talk to him, or watch him. Just locate and return."

"And he was all right with this? After all that happened at Camp Astor?"

"The things that upset him fade away. You saw him in Freedom. He had no recollection of Ethan. Not from before the—"

"Accident," she said firmly.

"Or after. By the time I sent him to find a man, he'd forgotten all he knew of that man."

"But Ethan doesn't forget."

"Why would he?" Alexi asked.

"Doesn't forgive either."

"Your point?"

"Ethan said he owed you."

"For taking care of Mikhail." Alexi's mouth twisted. "As if I wouldn't."

"But you used his gratitude—"

Alexi snorted.

Cat ignored him. "To force Ethan into doctoring me."

"He'd have done it. He wouldn't have been able to help himself."

"You let him keep his pride."

"That doesn't sound like me."

Cat thought back to the night they'd snuck out of Freedom. Ethan and Alexi in the bedroom doorway, the words spoken low, but not so low she couldn't hear.

"What will happen 'next time'? " she asked.

"Next time he will kill me."

The sheet fell to her waist as she sat up, exposing her breasts to the moonlight. The bandage that covered her wound tugged on her skin, and she yanked it free, then tossed it aside.

"Do not worry your pretty head. I don't worry mine."

"Why not?" She turned to him, slightly concerned when she found his gaze on her face and not her breasts. Did the huge, healing scar repulse him? He avoided looking at it as if it did.

"Do you believe Ethan could kill me? He's tried before, and he's failed."

"Because of Mikhail. If it were just you and him, your empty guns would be the death of you."

"You think I haven't killed since Castle Thunder?"

"Why would you? You have Mikhail for that."

He winced but recovered quickly enough, sitting up so that the sheet pooled at his waist. The moon highlighted the muscles in his belly as he moved, and Cat was the one distracted.

"You saw me shoot the stableman."

"And then puke and shake and nearly faint."

"I still did it."

"But could you do it again? *Would* you, if it were you in danger instead of me?"

"I may have difficulties shooting people, but that doesn't mean I can't stab them, strangle them or . . ." He waved a beautiful hand. "Something else."

"Have you?"

His eyebrows crashed down. "Keep asking and I'll strangle you."

"Doubtful. I don't think you'd kill Ethan either. You'd stand there and let him murder you, and you'd never once try to tell him why he shouldn't."

"There *is* no reason why he shouldn't."

"I'll give you a reason," she snapped, and kissed him.

His lips were cool, but they warmed beneath hers, as did his skin when she stroked it. He barely breathed; he did not move. He let her do anything that she wanted.

And she wanted. Desperately. With Alexi, how could she not? He was sin; he was sex. He was safety and sanity. The first she had found after—

Cat tensed, and with a sigh of acceptance, Alexi began to pull away.

Desperate again—she needed this, needed him—Cat shoved her hands into his hair and held on. She pushed every thought aside and filled her mind, her senses, her soul with the man who had brought her back from the brink. She could never repay him; he wouldn't ask her to, no matter how many times he insisted what was between them was no more than the fulfillment of a bargain.

It had begun that way, certainly, but things had changed. She wasn't sure when . . . how . . . why. She didn't care.

She left her mouth on his, lest he open it and let words tumble out. No time for talk. Talk only got in the way. Like his lips, his teeth, they kept her from his tongue.

She nipped him, and he gasped. Ah, there it was.

He tasted of the night and the wind. Despair. Desire. Destiny. He smelled of the rain after a hundred-year drought. She wanted to drink of him until her eternal thirst washed away.

She trailed her lips to the curve where his neck became his shoulder and inhaled. "The ocean." She captured a fold of his skin, suckling until she left a mark. She'd never done that before, but suddenly, she couldn't resist. "You always smell like water, like rain." She lifted her gaze. "Like things that are blue and white and new."

"Prison." He rested his shoulders against the wall. "We never got clean; we always smelled . . . bad." His hands clenched, and she took them in her own, unfurling the fingers, pressing a kiss to each palm before releasing them. "Every time I smell sweat, or dust, or filth, I . . ." He swallowed, then raised his eyes.

The honesty in his expression, his words, humbled her. He'd bared his soul, and she'd bared her breasts. If she were half the woman that he was a man, she'd tell him everything. But she'd never claimed to be much of a woman.

Instead, she gave him what she could of herself. Tossing the sheet to the ground, she bared both of them to the night and each other.

"Cat." Alexi groped for the covers.

She caught his hand, drew it to her. "Catey."

"What?" He was still inordinately concerned with the damn sheet.

She curved her own hand over his, squeezing her breast, lifting the weight, rubbing the delicious grain of his palm against her nipple until it peaked. "Call me Catey."

He tried to yank away, but she wouldn't let him. He gave an impatient sigh. "And who should I be? The czar? A prince? A pauper? What are we pretending tonight, *mein Wunsch*?"

Cat considered asking what he'd just called her, then decided she didn't want to know. His *something*. That was good. That was right. She *was* his. Just as he was hers.

For tonight.

"Pretend whatever you like. Whatever gets you through the night, through the pain. You taught me that, and I thank you for it."

"You . . . thank me?"

"I wouldn't have survived without you."

He turned his face away. "Don't say that. People die because of me; they don't live."

"*Durochka*." She waited until he turned his face back before whispering, "I did."

They remained motionless, barely breathing, his hand still on her breast, hers still upon his. Was this real or wasn't it? She wasn't sure herself.

"Catey?"

Her heart took one hard, fast leap at the name. "Yes?"

"Call me . . ." He seemed to struggle.

Was he Fedya? Was he Alexi? Did it matter? Not to her.

She welcomed him into her arms. No more words. No more names or pasts or memories. Only the two of them. Whoever they were.

His skin no longer cool, he didn't shiver or shake or moan. Then. Later, of course, they both did.

He kissed her as only he could—until she forgot where they were, what day it was . . . hell what century. Then he trailed that clever mouth across skin that flamed—crackling, snapping, ready to blaze.

He tasted of her breasts, drank of their tips as if he were thirsty too. Made her writhe and clutch, then murmured comfort in a dozen languages against her belly, laid his cheek upon it, let his breath cast across the damp trail.

Gooseflesh rose, chasing the heat like lightning chased the sky. Like she chased the wind.

He became distracted by her wound. It was very hard to miss. "Does this hurt?"

"There are things that hurt much, much more."

He pressed his lips to the ravaged flesh just once before he moved on. She tangled her fingers in his hair and let him. He teased; he tormented. He went from gentle—tongue taunting, tickling, then plunging, mimicking what was to come—to rough. His teeth grazed the cusp of her thigh, the beginnings of a beard scraping skin that had never been scraped so before.

He brought her to the edge; then he pulled her back. His lips caressed the muscles as they tightened and released in her legs, her stomach. His eyelashes fluttered across her hipbone like the wings of a butterfly. He took a fold of flesh into his mouth and worried it with teeth and tongue, marking her as she had marked him.

Returning to a place that hummed, he made it howl. Arching, gasping, still she did not beg. She didn't have to. He knew what she needed, wanted, desired without a single word. He always had.

He rose above her as the moon fell. He plunged into her, rocked against her, riding the wave, holding himself in check, eyes closed, belly quivering, or maybe that was hers. His face, so beautiful and still, she had to touch it. When she did, he opened his eyes.

Stark with an emotion she couldn't place, she felt her heart hammer once and seem to pause. She whispered, "Darling?" before she could stop herself. It was what she'd called him when she'd been Meg, when he'd been Jed. But she wasn't Meg now; she was—

"Catey?"

She stiffened and the movement caused him to gasp, to arch, to thrust so deeply she felt him where she never had before. Where she hadn't realized she'd wanted to.

Then she was clutching his shoulders, lifting her mouth, devouring his as they shivered and shook, as they moaned. When he collapsed atop her, his slick chest slid across hers, chiding her nipples, making her catch her breath as another tremor threatened. What was it about this man that made her body respond to the slightest glance, the softest word, the briefest touch?

His cheek was damp; she rubbed her lips across it. "Alexi," she began, and he sighed, then fell onto his back.

"What happened to 'darling'? "

Something in his voice made her glance at him, and again his expression was not one she recognized. "I . . . uh . . ." She found herself grateful for the night, so he couldn't see her blush. She'd never been so caught up in the act that she blurted endearments.

Until now.

He shifted onto his side; she followed. Their noses nearly touched. She set her hand on his hip, rubbed her thumb along the dip there.

"When you become this woman, the one no one can resist." His voice dropped. "The one I can't."

She stopped rubbing, but she couldn't remove her hand; she couldn't look away.

"When men rise over you, plunge into you, taste and taunt you, do you think of dead William? Is that how you manage?"

At the mention of her husband, she removed her hand. Not because his words had brought back Billy, but because, until he'd uttered them, she hadn't thought of Billy at all. And she realized something.

Instead of leaving the bed, the room, his life, she moved closer, until her breasts brushed his chest, her nose brushed his face, and her breath, when she spoke, mingled with his.

"When I let other men touch me, when I let them grind and

LORI HANDELAND

buck and sweat, in order not to scream, so I won't cry or kill them before I find out what I need to know . . . "

He held her gaze; he didn't flinch. He never would, which was why she told him the truth.

"I think of you."

CHAPTER 22

*A*lexi managed not to laugh, or perhaps he managed not to cry. Instead, he smiled gently, touched her face; he kissed her brow and drew her back into his arms, where she sighed, settled, then slept.

God, she was good. Better than he could ever hope to be.

She could lie next to him naked, her hand upon his hip, her thumb gently stroking, after he'd just been inside her so deeply he'd thought they were truly one at last. Until she stared him in the face and told him one of the biggest lies he'd ever heard. And he'd heard a lot.

Had he begun to suspect when she used the word *darling*? Or perhaps it had been when she'd invited him to call her "Catey." If she'd wanted him to believe this was real, she should never have said that. The question was: Why had she?

If she hadn't gone to sleep in his arms, Alexi would think she'd meant to slip out after he did.

Again.

But her breath puffed against his chest in a slow and steady rhythm. Her heart, too, thudded evenly against his ribs. To be certain, he ran a fingernail along her spine. She slept on. Unless, of course—he narrowed his eyes on her face—she didn't.

Doubting himself was new. Alexi understood what he was and what he was not. He was aware of his limitations, and he worked within them. Until tonight, until her, he would have been confident that the woman in his arms slept. Satisfied. Sated. Seduced. Now . . .

He just didn't know.

Alexi slid from her embrace; she did not cling. Had she ever? Her fingers limp, her face slack but no less beautiful. Her skin was like ivory; the wound just above her breast made him ache.

His fault she was marked and always would be. She didn't seem to care, or even notice. But then, like him, Cat understood the worst scars could not be seen.

He moved to the window. Before he exited a room, as soon as he entered another, he always had a peek at the street.

Alexi glanced out, then back at Cat. She hadn't moved except to breathe. He'd taken one step toward the door when his mind saw what his eyes already had.

Someone was out there.

* * *

CAT AWOKE, and she knew she had to run.

The scent of rain surrounded her and with it the memory of what had happened last night became as fresh and clear. She'd told Alexi something she shouldn't have. Of course he would probably say the same for himself.

He'd never asked her why she'd deserted him the first time. If he had, she would have told both him and herself that she'd left to become Cat. But if she were being truthful—and after the revelations of last night, why not be truthful about every damn thing? —she would admit that she'd left because she'd begun to feel something other than nothing.

And that she could not afford. Not then. Not now. Perhaps not ever.

Last night, when Alexi had pulled her close, kissed her brow, said nothing, thereby accepting everything, she'd known she would have to leave again. Instead, she'd fallen asleep in his arms, squandering her chance to escape. How would she flee now when she could smell the approach of dawn along with the rain? If she'd meant to get away, she should have done it in the dark.

Slowly Cat opened one eye, expecting to find Alexi staring right back. Instead—

Both eyes snapped open. She was alone. And that scent of rain?

Droplets chased down the windowpane, gathering along an opening at the bottom, hanging there like lace until they became too heavy and full, then tumbling downward to join the ever-expanding puddle on the floor.

Alexi must have gone back to his own room. Which meant she still had a chance.

Cat leaped out of bed and snatched a shirt from the floor. She left her "amputated" arm loose beneath the fabric, but it wasn't until she was struggling to button the buttons with her one remaining hand that she realized she'd put on Alexi's garment and not her own.

A thorough search of the remaining clothing revealed her boots, socks, and pants. But, apparently, Alexi had been in such a hurry to leave that he'd put on the wrong shirt and not even noticed.

She didn't have time to find another, and for her purposes, it didn't matter. She had to escape Jepsum before Alexi or Mikhail woke, but she couldn't afford to let anyone see her out of her costume, or guess that she was a woman in man's clothing.

Cat O'Banyon was dead, and Alexi had been right about keeping her that way. She was going to finish this once and for all. Her best chance of doing that was as a ghost no one saw coming.

She'd allowed herself to be seduced by the magic of Alexi, the camaraderie of Mikhail, the security she felt when the three of them traveled together. But *she* had to kill the man who haunted her. Her and no one else. That was the only way to make things right.

Cat crept into the hall. She needed to slow down her companions or they'd be on her trail so fast she might as well not leave them behind. A quick glance toward their rooms revealed both doors ajar. There was something so wrong about that Cat pulled her Colt and crept closer for a peek. Not only were the men not in their beds, but the rooms were empty. Not a saddlebag in sight. No clothes. No signs of a struggle, no blood, no note. Nothing.

Cat hurried to the livery and questioned the new man in charge.

"Yeah." The old fellow turned his head and spat into a bucket. The resulting *ping* caused the nearest horse to shuffle and snort. "Big man come in when it was still full dark. Kept mumblin' somethin' 'bout a cat. Lost one. Mebe left one behind."

"He was alone?" Cat's gaze scanned the remaining horses; Alexi's wasn't there.

"Yeah."

"Anyone else leave in the middle of the night?" He shook his head.

What was Alexi up to? He'd taken his horse, probably while the stableman was occupied with Mikhail. Why the secrecy? Had her admission scared him so badly he not only had to escape, but he had to do so in the dark? Or had it been his admission that caused him to run?

Either way, he was gone, and she had no doubt if she tried to track him, she would discover two trails that crossed each other, wove here and there, then disappeared. Considering she'd been in the process of deserting him, she should be happy to discover he'd already deserted her. Instead she felt . . .

Abandoned. In a way she hadn't since she'd buried Billy.

The stableman rubbed his unshaven cheek, the sound reminiscent of a dust storm casting against the walls of a prairie house. "You wanna point me to your mount? Fellow who usually works here got hisself dead, and I don't know whose is whose."

Or, apparently, how many there had been in the first place.

Cat indicated the horse she'd rode in on, and the man spat into the cistern again before retrieving the animal, then saddling it too, as she was still one-armed Joe.

"You hear the news?" he asked.

Cat grunted. She didn't want to hear anything but the hooves of her mount carrying her away from Jepsum in the direction of Denver City.

"Cat O'Banyon was in town."

Cat, who'd been fastening her saddlebag, dropped it. "Who?"

"The bounty hunter woman! Has everyone say *you or her?* 'fore she kills 'em."

Cat had to press her lips together to keep from correcting him. She didn't kill people. Unless, of course, they asked for it.

"I heard she was dead," Cat said. "Shot in Injun Territory. Buried there too."

"Guess not. Horace—the usual stableman—said she made him say the words."

"I thought Horace got hisself dead. How'd he say anything?"

"'fore he was dead," the fellow said as if talking to an idiot.

And how right he was. Cat knew better than to assume someone was dead and not make sure of it.

"She had him say the words," the stableman continued. "Then she shot 'im."

Horace was a liar. But Cat could hardly blame the man. Who wouldn't want to die at the hand of a legend rather than that of her companion, who could barely hold on to a gun without puking?

"He didn't die right away. Told the sheriff 'bout it first."

"Sheriff catch her?" Cat asked in an attempt to keep the conversation going. She needed to know what else Horace had seen and told.

"He did."

Cat, who'd been in the process of mounting her horse, slid off.

"Here now. Let me give ya a boost."

"Wait. He caught her?"

"Sure enough. Heard tell there was a woman in man's clothes creepin' around after Horace got kilt. Sheriff walked right into her when he went a-lookin'."

"Wouldn't anyone who'd shot Horace just get the hell gone?"

Why, oh why, hadn't she?

"You'd think." The old man's face creased. "But it had to be her. How many women wearin' men's clothes and a gun belt are there?"

You'd be surprised.

"Where is she now?"

"On her way to Denver City with the sheriff."

"Already?"

At least the woman wasn't hanging from a rope on yonder tree. Cat might be able to rescue her yet.

"Why wait?"

Cat couldn't think of a single reason.

She caught up to the Jepsum sheriff a few hours before the next dawn. It wasn't hard. He'd been bound hand and foot, gagged too.

Cat stared at the man as the light from the fire—he was lucky his captor had left one to keep the critters away—trickled over his furious face. She leaned down and removed the gag. "What happened?"

Cat didn't bother to disguise her voice, and she'd shoved her arm back through her sleeve rather than leaving it concealed beneath the material. Made it easier to ride.

"Who are you?"

"No one of any consequence." Cat used the barrel of her gun to indicate he should go on, even though he hadn't yet started.

"I never saw so many women pretending to be men in my life."

"Bet not."

"Ain't ya gonna untie me?"

"Depends on what you say." Cat lowered herself to his saddle, which rested nearby. Unfortunately for him, his horse was gone.

Silence descended, broken only by the crackle of the fire and the snorts and shuffles of Cat's mount.

"I can sit here all night," Cat said. "I can leave you the same way I found you in the morning and follow the trail myself. Up to you."

The sheriff cursed a blue streak before he commenced. "I was takin' Cat O'Banyon to Denver City."

"Where is she?"

"Where do you think? She tied me up and went there herself."

As the woman he'd captured *wasn't* Cat, why would she go to Denver City? "You sure?"

"Yes! I'd tied her. Tied her good. Gone to sleep. Next thing I know, she's got a knife to my throat askin' where I aim to take her." He made a disgusted sound. "I don't know where she had that knife. I searched her right thorough for weapons."

Cat, who'd been considering the woman might have been Alexi, narrowed her gaze. "How thorough?"

"Very."

Which meant the woman had been a woman. Probably. At her continued silence, the sheriff lifted his chin. "I didn't do nothin' wrong."

"Didn't do much right either. Or you wouldn't be where you are."

His scowl deepened.

"Why'd she care where you were taking her?"

"Said she was sick of bein' hunted. Planned to end it once and for all."

It made no sense—the woman *wasn't* Cat O'Banyon—but Cat would worry about that later. "Where were you taking her?" He hesitated, and Cat cocked the Colt. "I don't wanna kill you. I will. But I don't want to."

"What's to stop you from killing me after I tell you?"

"Not one damn thing."

He stared at her for several seconds, then sighed. "Deserted warehouse near the stage stop in Denver City."

"Which deserted warehouse?"

The sheriff shrugged as best he could with his hands tied behind his back. "Suspect there's only one."

"Where'd you get your information?"

"Folks talk. At first the bounty was just rumor. Whispers here and there. But a few weeks ago, a wanted poster showed up."

Cat wondered why Ben hadn't mentioned that—although not every poster made it to every sheriff. What she'd like to know was how there'd come to be a wanted poster in the first place. She still hadn't done anything that warranted a bounty. Of course money talked, and whoever was after her appeared to have plenty.

"Picture? Description?"

"No picture. Description was pretty much what we already knew. Woman who dresses as a man. But she's also real good at pretendin' to be others just to catch whoever she's after. So really . . . could be anyone."

Cat stifled a smile, but as he continued, her urge to smile faded.

"Taller than most gals. Dark hair. Green eyes."

Green eyes were rare. But Cat knew from experience that people often lumped all those with light eyes together—gray, blue, green. She couldn't count the times she'd been compli-mented on her *pretty blue eyes.* She doubted whoever the sheriff had captured in her place had possessed green eyes. She doubted he'd looked, or if he had, that he'd cared. The promise of money could make anyone color-blind.

The sheriff squinted at Cat's face; she didn't bother to retreat out of the range of the firelight. If he figured out who she was now, it didn't really matter. By the time he could tell anyone, she'd either be dead or the one most interested in the knowledge would be.

"What else?"

"Anyone who captured Cat O'Banyon, dead or alive, was supposed to contact the telegraph office in Denver City for instructions. I got an answer in less than an hour sayin' where to take her."

How many women had been dragged to that deserted ware-house in Denver City, and what had happened to them when they'd proved to be the wrong woman? For that matter, how many women had been killed before being dragged there just to make things easier on the one doing the dragging?

Cat stood. Time to make sure no one else paid for her mistakes with their lives.

"You said you'd let me go if I told you."

"No. I said I'd kill you if you didn't. You're still breathing."

"I won't be, if you leave me like this."

As that was true, she drew her knife and cut the bonds on his hands. While he was busy unlacing his feet. Cat mounted her horse and galloped away.

Ten days later, Cat crossed Cherry Creek. Denver City sat between her and a mountainous horizon beyond which the sun had just begun to set. Many of the older structures had been fash-ioned of pine or cottonwood, but not as many as Cat would have expected. The majority were made of brick; several were two story, some even three stories high. Dust was everywhere, probably because the few trees in the city proper were spindly and small, doing nothing whatsoever to keep the prairie from blowing through the streets.

Cat walked her horse down roads ripe with rooming houses, dance halls, whorehouses, gambling halls and watering holes. She left her mount outside a saloon, went in, ordered a drink she didn't touch, and asked about deserted warehouses nearby. There *was* only one.

The area near the stage stop boomed. Many of the local businesses had moved onto the lots surrounding it in order to service travelers. Though Denver had recently laid track of their own to connect with the Union Pacific, the majority of arrivals and departures still used the stage.

Cat left the saloon and followed directions. Moments later she stood on a silent, shadowed boardwalk of stores, staring at the two-story brick building to which she'd been directed. Didn't look abandoned to her. Too many lights.

She tried to come up with a plan to get inside, wondering if the other Cat had.

"Surrender. Or—" Cat drew her Colt. "Not."

She'd taken only a single step forward when the door she'd been staring at opened and two figures stepped out.

CHAPTER 23

*A*fter seeing the sheriff coming toward the hotel, Alexi had tossed on some clothes and stepped into the hall. He reached the head of the stairs in time to hear the lawman asking the clerk about them.

He cursed his unsteady hand, which had deposited a bullet in the stableman's chest and not his head. Head shots nearly always ensured there would be no talking about who had shot you. Chest shots allowed more leeway. Why hadn't he made sure the man was dead?

He'd been too busy shaking and throwing up. Which had led to the sheriff learning their descriptions, then asking around. Someone had remembered the drunken singing and tattled.

Panicked, Alexi had searched desperately for a way to draw the sheriff away from town. Away from Cat. He'd glanced down, saw that he'd put on her shirt—or rather Ethan's—and a plan had unfurled. By the time the sheriff found him, he was her.

The first night out of Jepsum, Alexi had slipped the sheriff's bonds with ease. He'd once traveled with a man who could escape from anything. During rainy afternoons the Remarkable

Rudolph had shared several tricks of his trade with Fedya, the sharpshooting boy.

The ties around Alexi's hands and feet had not lasted five minutes after the sheriff began to snore. The man's resolve to keep their destination a secret had lasted even less time once he'd seen Alexi's face.

And his knife.

Upon arriving in Denver City, Alexi had taken a moment to stand on the bank of the South Platte River and remember the last time he had been here, over ten years before.

Pikes Peak or Bust! had been the rallying cry of the gold prospectors that had poured into the area. His father had been one of them.

Kazmir Kondrashchenko hadn't come to pan for gold. He would never work so hard. But he'd followed the sparkle. Kaz always did. He wasn't the only one.

The number of people that crossed the flat land of Kansas to stake claims on both sides of the river allowed Fedya and his father to make a good bit of money. They stayed on as the settlements grew and began to push, shove, and shoot at each other.

General Larimer controlled the collection of lean-tos, tents, log cabins, and tepees on the east side of the creek. Larimer, despite his imposing title, was a land speculator whose only military experience at the time was a stint in the Pennsylvania militia. He named the settlement Denver City, in hopes of currying favor with James Denver, the territorial governor of Kansas. By the time Larimer discovered that Denver was no longer the governor, the settlements on both sides of the water had become Denver City.

The place nearly turned into one of the many ghost towns in the territory when gold was discovered in the mountain settlement of Central City. Thousands of residents scurried there only to scurry right back after a taste of the mountain winter.

Bummers arrived—prostitutes, gamblers, and shopkeepers—to reap the rewards of the prospectors' earnings, then stayed on as Denver City grew, a supply hub for those mountain gold camps.

Alexi marveled, as he always had, at the contrast between the land on the east side of Denver City and the west. It was as if God had used his hand to flatten Kansas, then dug deep to create a river before plopping what had been gouged out on the other side and producing the Rockies.

The last time Alexi had been in Denver City, it had still been part of Kansas Territory and he'd still been Fedya. How they had both changed. Yet in many ways they were quite the same. He might now be Alexi Romanov—suave and always clean, able to pretend he was anyone, at anytime, anywhere—but he continued to make his living in the way his father had taught him—not the shooting, but the show. And while the city was still a ramshackle boomtown in certain areas, it was also the capital of the Territory of Colorado.

Before heading to the spot revealed to him by the Jepsum sheriff, Alexi rented a hotel room. He used it for only an hour while he shaved and performed a few other necessary ablutions.

When he tapped on the appointed door a short while later, a young man with blond hair and one lazy eye peered out. "What?"

"I was told Cat O'Banyon should be delivered here." The boy squinted, first at Alexi, then at the street, obviously confused.

Alexi reached for the sky, and his shirt tightened over the breasts he'd recently put back on. "I surrender."

"Surrender?" the kid repeated. "Huh?"

"Just take me to him," Alexi said in his best Cat O'Banyon voice. "I wouldn't want to be you if I got away."

The youth blinked, frowned, then motioned him inside. "I gotta search ya."

Alexi was once again glad he'd stopped to shave his beard,

apply makeup, as well as his breasts, not to mention pad his ass as the boy groped him everywhere.

Or almost. If he'd grabbed Alexi in the crotch he'd have found a big surprise. As he believed Alexi a woman, he didn't bother. Which was why Alexi had concealed a knife in that general vicinity.

The kid took his guns—useless, as they were still unloaded— and the extra knife Alexi had stashed in his coat pocket. Best to give folks what they expected—a visible gun, a hidden knife— then they didn't look very hard for anything else.

The youth shoved him between the shoulder blades. "You first."

Alexi went up the steps and into a large, seemingly empty room. No lights, the only illumination came from the lantern still swaying in the hall.

"She says she's her." The boy spoke to the far gloomy corner. "She surrendered."

No response.

"Took her guns. A knife." At the continued silence, the kid shrugged and went downstairs. The door opened and closed.

Someone moved in the darkness. "I suppose you want me to say *you or her?*"

Alexi didn't answer, keeping his eyes cast down. He could dress like Cat, walk and talk like her too, but he couldn't change blue eyes to green no matter how good he was at make-believe.

"You don't recognize my voice?"

Alexi's ears crackled. "Turn around."

Alexi turned. Shoes scuffled; the air stirred. When warm breath hit his neck, Alexi whirled, grabbing the man's wrist and twisting with one hand, snatching his throat and slamming him into the wall with the other.

The gun clattered away. The fool's skull thumped against the plank. Their eyes met.

"You," the fellow exclaimed at the same time Alexi said, "Ben?"

The surprise was so great, Alexi stilled. Then he rapped Sheriff Ben's head against the wall again, just for the hell of it. "Start talking."

Chase tried, but Alexi had also increased the pressure on his throat—he couldn't help it; Cat had *trusted* the man—and the sheriff couldn't force a word past the fingers digging into his skin.

Alexi retrieved the knife from his pants, eased up on his grip, and lifted both the weapon and his eyebrow before stepping back. "What have you done?"

"I told her to stop." Chase rubbed his neck as he trained a wary eye on both Alexi and the knife. "That if she kept going the way she was, she'd get killed. But she wouldn't leave it be."

"So you put a bounty on her?"

"I don't have that kind of money." The man's shoulders slumped. "If I did, I wouldn't be in this mess in the first place."

"You sold her to him."

"No." The sheriff sighed. "I owed her to him."

Alexi tightened his hold on the knife—whether in preparation for using it, or to keep himself *from* using it, he wasn't sure. "Go on."

Ben stared at his feet. "I was sent west before the war. My daddy had no patience for a boy who played cards."

Alexi could read beneath that easily enough. Daddy Chase hadn't sent his son west for playing cards; he'd sent him west for playing cards badly. If Ben had possessed any talent at the game, his father would never have discovered the habit.

"I wanted to make a new start. I wanted to stop. But I . . ."

"Didn't." Why was it that those who couldn't play well were the ones who couldn't stop, and the ones, like Alexi, who could, had little interest in continuing?

"I meant to. I tried. But I was in debt to a very bad man."

"His name?"

The sheriff lifted his gaze, hesitated, gave in. "Larsen."

"First name?"

"I never heard him called anything but that." Ben's mouth twisted. "Or *sir*. Larsen had a private poker game. Since I couldn't gamble in any of the saloons in Rock River or leave town for long since I was the law, Larsen invited me to his table."

"I bet he did." Suckers were easy to spot. For those who knew how to spot them.

"I kept trying to climb out of the well I'd dug. I'd get halfway up; then I'd slide all the way down. And then some."

"He played you." Alexi should know.

"I was always good for some of it. I had a job. I got paid every month."

"Exactly. If you hadn't had money, he wouldn't have bothered. What happened?"

"I missed a payment, and he decided I needed a lesson." The man's voice lowered, and his next words came out just above a whisper. "How could I know what he'd do?"

Alexi wanted to ask: How could you not? If Larsen hurt Ben, his payments would have been delayed while the sheriff recovered. If he killed Ben, no more payments. Ben's brother, on the other hand . . .

Was expendable.

Alexi turned the knife so that the blade caught the faint light from the hall and cast shadows over the other man's face.

"Don't" was all Ben said, and Alexi blew an annoyed burst of air past his lips. He was right. Alexi hadn't come here for him; he'd come for Larsen. If the sheriff died now, before he told Alexi where the bastard was, this would never end. Cat would never be safe.

"You owed the man so much it was worth killing for?"

"For Larsen," Chase muttered, "Tuesday is worth killing for."

"I assume you learned your lesson over your brother's dead body." Alexi relished Ben's wince. "Why does he still want her?"

"Because she won't stop!" His words bounced off the walls and ricocheted around the empty room.

"How is it that you got involved in making her stop?" The sheriff's sigh caught in the middle, more of a sob really, and Alexi understood. "Even losing your brother wasn't enough to keep you from his table."

"I owed too much to ever pay."

"Only Cat's death will clear your debt." Alexi didn't even attempt to keep the disgust from his voice.

"She's been trying to die since Billy did. I'm just giving her what she's been begging for."

Alexi was sorely tempted to give Ben what he was begging for. But not yet. "Where is he?"

Chase shook his head. Alexi showed him just how sharp the knife was.

"Shit." Blood trickled down the man's neck. Alexi considered where to cut him next. "Hold on." The sheriff struggled to get away, but his back was against the wall.

Alexi allowed a smile to blossom. He was enjoying this too much. "Where?"

"You'll never get in alone."

"I got in here alone."

"Larsen isn't stupid. And *he* isn't alone. No one will get near him but me. And whoever I say is Cat O'Banyon."

"Why?" Alexi asked.

"There've been some brought in who aren't. With the size of the bounty . . . well, folks are grabbing females off the street. Mistakes are made."

How many dead women had been brought to Denver, their bodies tossed aside when it was discovered they weren't the right body? How many had been killed for the same reason?

"I wouldn't think he'd care about mistakes."

"He doesn't. But he started to get nervous that so many

bounty hunters were seeing his face. There are others looking for him besides Cat. He's not what you would call a decent man."

"He's not what I'd call a man."

"He sent for me, then got out of town. I'm to identify her, then bring her to him. He wants to make sure she's really dead, either by killing her himself or seeing the body."

"Why didn't you run?"

"He'd find me." Chase swallowed. "He found her."

"Not really." If Alexi had his way, Larsen would be finding nothing but his own unmarked grave long before Cat showed up.

"I'll take you to him," Ben said. "I'll say you're her."

"What's to keep you from telling the truth the instant we're there?"

"I want free of him. He kills you, she's still out there. This doesn't end. If you kill him, it does."

"Why didn't *you* kill him?"

Ben paled. "I . . . uh . . ."

"Never mind." Some men were killers; some were not. Chase, most definitely, was not. How he'd managed to become a lawman was a mystery, though he hadn't been a very good one.

Alexi didn't trust Sheriff Ben, but as killing the man who haunted Cat's life was why Alexi had come, he lowered the knife. "After you."

* * *

"WHAT THE HELL?" Cat murmured, as her brother-in-law headed up the street, holding the arm of a woman who couldn't be Cat O'Banyon, even though she might look a whole lot like her.

And Ben should know that. Which meant . . .

Cat had no idea. Was this the woman who had escaped the sheriff? Another one? Was that Alexi in disguise? She didn't think so, but she'd been mistaken before.

If Alexi were here, Mikhail would be close by. A quick scan of the street and the rooftops revealed that nothing moved but the two figures ahead of her. Which didn't mean that Mikhail wasn't here. He hadn't become one of the best trackers alive by allowing himself to be seen by his quarry.

If that were Alexi with Ben, and Cat wasn't yet certain it was, she had a pretty good idea what he was up to. As he'd told her, just because he couldn't kill with a gun didn't mean he couldn't use a knife or his hands. She needed to stop him before he proved that and ruined everything she'd spent years working toward.

After the incident with Frank Walters, Alexi had implied that her brother-in-law might be feeding information to the man whom Cat was hunting. She had not believed him. She hadn't wanted to. She'd trusted Ben—not completely but enough. She'd obviously been wrong.

Then again, Ben wasn't taking *her* by the arm and leading her to her doom. He was taking someone he had to know wasn't Cat. As she needed to discover why, she followed, keeping to the shadows of the buildings, staying far enough back so Ben and his companion did not suspect.

The two disappeared into a stable across the street. Should she confront Ben now? Have him release the false Cat and take the real one wherever he was going? Before she could decide, two horses trotted out, then galloped for the distant mountains.

"Dammit!"

Inside, the stable was deserted, its appearance suggesting it had been unused for years. Not a horse remained to beg, borrow, or even steal. By the time Cat retrieved her mount from the front of the saloon, those she followed were nothing but specs on the gray, moon-shrouded horizon. Fortunately, she'd learned something about tracking from Mikhail. She wasn't as good as him, but Ben wasn't trying to hide.

Unfortunately, the terrain slowed her down. Rocky, hilly— perhaps that was where the *Rocky* Mountains had gotten their name—the up-and-down nature of the trail, when there *was* a trail, allowed the pursued to stay well ahead of the pursuer. But Cat kept going. She didn't have any choice.

Around midmorning of the fourth day, the trail seemed to disappear. Cat climbed from her horse, then followed a very faint sign to—

The ground fell away into nothingness just a few feet ahead. Cautiously she approached and peered at a deep gully. A creek ran across the bottom, and several tall pine trees provided shade for two figures and three horses.

Much of the gulch was shadowed by scrub. She didn't see another person; though, considering the extra horse, one must be there. She had to find a way down.

However, the drop-off was, indeed, a drop-off. If Cat tried to descend from here, she'd be at the bottom in no time.

With a broken neck.

Cat led her horse along the edge of the abyss and, within minutes, uncovered a trail.

* * *

"DEVIL'S HEAD MOUNTAIN."

Ben cast Alexi a quick glance. "You know it?"

Alexi nodded. The area was covered in thick timber, full of gulches and caves, making it the perfect place to hide. Rumor had it, the mountain was not only the hideout for every outlaw no one could find, but the final resting place of the same.

There were also dozens of legends about the missing treasure those outlaws had buried and never returned for because they'd been buried themselves. Though Alexi had spent a lot of time searching the location as a child, he'd never found a single stash. He hadn't even found an outlaw. Nevertheless, those rumors remained. Alexi could probably sell a dozen land claims to imaginary gold stashes.

Something to consider if he got out of this alive.

As they'd pushed through the forest, Alexi had detected movement now and again; once he'd even heard a horse whinny. But he'd never seen anyone. Still he was fairly certain Larsen's men patrolled the perimeter.

They'd entered the box canyon through a long, narrow rock alley, guarded by a sniper who didn't have the sense to shade the barrel of his rifle from the sun. The man had waved them past with hardly a glance, proving, if their safe passage thus far hadn't already, that Ben Chase was well known to both Larsen and his cohorts.

Alexi cast his companion a worried look from beneath the brim of his slouch hat. The sheriff's hands shook; he was sweating and far too pale. If they weren't careful, this dodge would be over before it had even begun.

Ben dismounted, indicating Alexi should do the same with a flick of his head and a tilt of the gun he'd pulled before they got too close to curious eyes. When Alexi stood on the ground, the sheriff poked the barrel against his side hard enough to leave a mark.

Alexi gritted his teeth. His time would come.

"Hello?" Ben called. "Larsen?"

"That her?" The question came from the shoulder-high scrub on the far side of the creek.

"Sure is." The man's voice was too high, the words too fast.

Alexi hated working with amateurs.

"We're square now." Ben peered at the scrub, but there was no indication, beyond the voice, that anyone was there. "Right?"

"Right. Get out."

Without so much as a good-bye. Sheriff Chase mounted his horse and did as he was told.

Alexi kept his gaze on the scrub, hat tilted to the sun so Larsen could see nothing but darkness beneath. If he could just keep the fellow believing Alexi was Cat until Larsen got close enough to touch.

And he would get close enough. Men like him always did. They just couldn't help themselves.

When the shot rang out, Alexi started and glanced down, expecting blood to bloom across his chest. He even patted himself, searching for the hole, waiting for the pain.

A ripple of laughter emerged from the overgrowth. "Did you think I wouldn't know?"

CHAPTER 24

*T*he descent was steep; Cat left the horse behind. Those on two legs could traverse it faster than those on four. Besides, horses were herd animals. The instant hers caught sight or scent of theirs, it would call out. That she did not need.

The path twisted sharply downward, eventually flattening out. Cat paused at the mouth of a narrow alley of rock. She caught the flash of sun off a gun at the top.

"Fool." She could only hope his aim was as bad as his ability to hide. Though—

Her gaze wandered over the towering gray walls. Anyone who walked between them was begging to die. Even if the sniper missed, the ricochet wouldn't.

She hadn't encountered any guards on the way in, which concerned her. She'd thought there would be more hanging about. However, considering the area, they could be anywhere.

The gunshot had Cat ducking and covering her head, but the sound of a body hitting the ground made her look up. A figure lay crumpled halfway through the narrow passage. The man's hat had tumbled off when he died, and his blond hair shone in the sun.

Ben.

She waited for a trickle of sadness at the sight of Billy's brother lying dead on the ground. It didn't come.

She and Ben had never been close; Billy's death had only pushed them farther apart. Considering what she suspected—what Alexi had suspected all along—that Ben had sold her out, she could only be glad that someone else had dispensed justice before she had to.

"There's someone out here!"

Cat hissed with annoyance as her presence was announced by the sniper.

"I had thought there might be." The words were said too loudly, and they weren't the right words. Still, the voice *could* be his.

Suddenly the bush under which the sniper had been concealed shook, then shook some more. The barrel of the rifle jerked backward. Cat didn't think; she ran, expecting to hear the echo of the report an instant before, or maybe after, a bullet slammed into her back. She reached a curve in the rock alley and slipped around it unharmed.

Cat set her shoulders to the wall just outside the wide-open space. She'd planned to do some sniping of her own, sneak close, put a bullet in his brain before he put a bullet in someone else's. Now that he knew she was here, that plan had fallen apart.

Should she go in, guns blazing? There was a good chance everyone in the canyon would die if she tried it. Would she risk an innocent life to have her vengeance?

No.

Would she risk Alexi?

Never.

She'd done a lot of things she wasn't proud of, but Cat still had a line she wouldn't cross. Until today she hadn't been quite sure of that.

"Send the woman out," she shouted.

"I suppose you want to trade? You for her?"

Those words were similar enough. Cat didn't even have to close her eyes to know.

It was him.

"Yes. I agree."

Her throat had gone tight. She swallowed, then rubbed her sweaty palms against her legs. She could not let him see or hear how finding him at last affected her.

She was no longer Cathleen Chase; she was Cat O'Banyon, and Cat was never afraid. If she could only make him, and herself, believe that.

"Come on in."

"Not until you send her out."

He laughed. "Ain't gonna happen."

"But you said—"

"I said that I supposed you wanted to trade. Didn't say I was going to."

Cat tightened her lips over vile obscenities. If she left now, he'd kill his captive. She'd already decided she wouldn't sacrifice innocence, or Alexi, for vengeance. She'd have her retribution—she'd come too far to give up now that she'd found him—but she was going to have to fashion a better idea. And the only way to do that was to go inside.

Cat stepped into the light, half expecting a bullet to the chest the next instant. Instead, she stared at an ugly little man. Large nose. Pockmarked skin. Lips far too wide for his face. Paunchy. Bowlegged. Bug-eyed. He held a gun to Alexi Romanov's head.

She should have known. She *had* known on some level. She just couldn't understand why. Alexi wasn't the type to sacrifice himself for anyone but Mikhail.

But times had changed. *They* had changed. Would those changes be the death of them?

"Toss your gun belt behind you," the man ordered.

Cat tossed.

"The knife too."

Cat complied.

"Step away from them both."

As she didn't have much choice with that blasted pistol so near Alexi's clever brain, Cat inched away from her weapons. "Let him go."

Alexi rolled his eyes heavenward. She'd obviously ruined his plan—though it hadn't been a very good one, considering the gun to the head.

"Larsen—" he began, but the other man shushed him, gaze locked on Cat.

At least now her nightmare had a name; Larsen. A face: ugly. However, neither the name nor the face changed anything. The only way anything would change was if he died.

"Where's your idiot henchman?" Larsen asked.

Alexi's lips tightened. He never took it kindly when people called Mikhail an idiot. Cat didn't much like it either. Although she had been wondering the same herself, minus the idiot part.

"I sent him on an errand."

Cat heard what Alexi wasn't saying. Mikhail would never have allowed Alexi out of his sight. He would never have allowed him to attempt a dodge like this. If he were anywhere near, he would have joined her, helped her. Which meant—

Alexi *had* sent Mikhail away. They were on their own. No one would ride to their rescue anytime soon.

Well, she'd managed tricky situations in the past. She wasn't certain how she'd manage this, but she wasn't going to give up without a damn good try.

"What kind of woman are you?" Larsen's voice twisted with hatred and anger. "I kill your husband, and instead of crying—"

"Oh, I cried."

"Most women, after what I did, would have killed themselves."

"Not until I kill you." Although the idea of killing herself no longer held much appeal. She'd survived this long, and there was no way she was going to let the bastard win. If she had to strangle him with her bare hands or maybe . . .

The creek was definitely deep enough to drown him in. If he would just lift that gun away from Alexi's temple.

"Are you that poor a shot you need to keep the barrel up against his head?"

Alexi cast Cat an exasperated glance at her pathetic ploy, but Larsen did what she wanted. With a curl of his lip, he shoved Alexi in Cat's direction.

He probably thought Alexi would sprawl on the ground, maybe knock Cat down too, but he underestimated the man's grace. Alexi didn't even stumble. Cat caught him by the arm anyway, then stepped between the two of them. She allowed her lip to curl the same way his had. "I thought you'd be taller."

Alexi made a strangled sound—between a laugh and a cough —and Cat had to fight not to laugh herself. She was furious to find him here. She was also so glad to see him she was having a hard time not pulling him close and covering his face with kisses.

In view of the situation, and who stood in front of her, she should be shaking and trying not to puke. Oddly, she had no desire to do either one. Alexi was near. He hadn't left her. She wasn't alone. Together, they could accomplish anything. Even this.

"Why did you do it?" Larsen demanded.

"You think I'd just let you kill Billy and move on?" Cat inched forward.

Alexi muttered something in Russian and followed. She wanted to tell him to stay where he was, but that would alert Larsen to their movements. The man glared at Cat's face so intently she didn't think he'd noticed, and she wanted to keep it that way. If she could just get close enough to—

"I meant, why'd you send him?"

"I didn't." She advanced another tiny step. "I followed Ben and someone I knew wasn't me."

If Larsen thought she'd come for Alexi, that she'd go to great lengths to make sure no harm came to him, Alexi would be dead.

"I couldn't let Ben sacrifice what I thought was an innocent woman in my place." Which begged the question: "Why did he?"

Larsen knew what Cat looked like; he wouldn't be fooled by another woman. He hadn't even been fooled by Alexi for long.

"Ben knew," Alexi said. "That it was me."

"Then why—?"

"He thought the foreigner would kill me, and he'd be free," Larsen interrupted.

"Free?" Cat was so confused.

"Ben has—" Alexi sighed. "*Had* a gambling problem."

"He *sold* me?"

"*Oui.*"

"Ass."

"*Oui.*"

"Did you think I wouldn't know?" Larsen spread his hands. The contrast between his stubby, clumsy digits and Alexi's long, graceful ones was so great they appeared two different species. "You might walk and talk like her. You might even look like her for the first minute. But when a man's been as close to a woman as I've been to Cathleen Chase . . ." His chuckle was hellfire billowing out of a crevice. Cat swore she smelled brimstone. "He knows."

Alexi growled.

Cat threw out an arm to keep him from charging forward. "Stay."

"You didn't tell him? And here I thought you fools were in love. Him trying to save you, you trying to save him. Then again . . ." He licked his thick lips, and his gaze crawled all over her. "Love might have nothing to do with it."

Cat, who was still amazed she hadn't felt ill just being in the man's presence, suddenly felt ill at the thought of what he meant to reveal, what he already had.

Alexi had taught her how to become someone else. His method had worked very well to keep Cat moving forward and not falling back, to keep her sane and not a shrieking lunatic. She was Cat O'Banyon—a woman without a past. Cat had not been in that farmhouse. She had not heard the shot that killed her husband. She had not listened to him die as the man who killed him tore off her clothes and did things she remembered only in nightmares.

But Larsen wasn't going to allow her to pretend anymore. He was going to torture her with words before he no doubt tortured her with the same deed. She wasn't sure she'd survive this time. And maybe that was okay. As long as Alexi did. She would not stand idly by while another man gave his life for hers.

Alexi moved in front of her. "She didn't have to tell me."

In the process of stepping in front of *him*, Cat froze. "What?"

He shrugged. "I knew."

"You . . . what?"

"Why do you think I taught you what I taught you?"

"I asked you to."

He lifted an eyebrow, and she understood. He was not a man who did anything merely for the asking. Alexi Romanov required something in return. The question was why, if he'd known the truth, he had asked for her.

Cat tried to come to terms with this revelation. She still could not quite believe it. Alexi had never given any indication, by word or deed, that he'd known she was ruined. Then again, so was he.

"What was done *to* you does not define you, *il mio piccolo assassin*. What defines you is who you became because of it."

"What did you just say?" Larsen demanded.

Alexi's lips twitched, a smirk begging to break free. Cat had no idea how he could remain so calm when they were both going to die soon if she didn't do something.

"I called her my little killer." Alexi's gaze went hard as it settled on Larsen. "She will kill you; I will watch."

"Jesus," Cat murmured. "Shh."

"He's coming," Alexi said calmly. "He will soon be foolishly close."

Cat spun even as Alexi tried to shove her out of the way. Her hand brushed cool metal. Without thought, her fingers closed around it and she twisted.

The gun went off. Alexi grunted. Crimson crept across the front of his shirt.

Though the explosion, and the result, were not as planned, Cat still managed to turn the pistol in the other direction and cock it. Larsen was already running hell-bent for the narrow rock exit. She sighted, took a shot, missed. Then Alexi toppled over, and she got distracted.

She lifted her gaze from the man at her feet, who needed her help, to the one speeding away, who needed a bullet.

Cat dropped the gun and went to her knees.

"What are you doing?" Alexi tried to push away her hands as they unbuttoned his shirt.

"Undressing you."

"Later, *mo chroi*. Don't you wish to go after the man who ruined your life and shoot him too?"

"I didn't shoot you. He did." Or at least she thought that was what had happened. Things had been confusing with both her and Larsen holding the gun.

"Does it matter who shoots, once the shot hits home?"

She'd thought so, but—

Another shot rang out. They both glanced toward the narrow rock entrance.

"His men are simpletons," Cat said.

"That wasn't his man."

Her lips curved. "Mikhail didn't go anywhere."

Which explained Larsen's odd dearth of companions. Mikhail had been eliminating them one by one.

"He did have an errand." Alexi's answering smile told Cat her assumption had been correct. "Which he completed and now he is up there."

Which meant Larsen was as dead as Ben. She wished she had time to think about that. Instead, Cat yanked on Alexi's shirt, to which he'd somehow attached fake breasts, spraying buttons across the ground. The wound was high up on the right side, more a glancing blow off his shoulder, though far too close to his pretty face for comfort.

She tore free a strip of her own shirt and pressed it to the seeping hole. "Speaking of simpletons. What if Larsen had shot you on sight?"

"I would have died on sight."

"Alexi " she began.

"A man like that . . . once he had you to himself . . ." He turned a palm faceup. "He wouldn't have wanted you dead right away."

"You were willing to bet your life on that?"

"Better mine than yours."

"No!" Cat stood, then found herself captured by the blood on her hands. Alexi's blood. Blood he'd shed for her. She wiped her palms against her pants, but she could still feel it there, see it too—shiny and bright, like him. "It was supposed to be me this time," she whispered.

Not the man she—

Her heart lurched. Oh, no! When had that happened?

"I'm not Billy, *bebe*."

She set the heel of her hand against her chest and rubbed at the sudden ache. "I know who you are."

"You think I'd die and leave you alone?"

Cat swallowed. "No."

"Damn right, no." Alexi sat up, the muscles in his belly rippling beneath a trail of blood. He reached into his pants, the movement a bit obscene, considering the location, then withdrew his long, skinny knife. Apparently, he'd not only stolen her shirt but also her habit of adding a concealed pocket for weaponry.

"I was going to get in close and stick this through his heart. Then watch as the light left his eyes forever. Because of what he did to you, he deserved nothing less."

"I wanted to kill him."

He stared at her for a moment. "Would you have strangled him with your bare hands, or shoved his face into the water and held it there until he stopped struggling?"

How did he know her so well? Because they were two of a kind. That used to bother her, but it didn't any longer. The world was a difficult place. Only people like Alexi, like Cat, survived.

"I hadn't decided."

"You are magnificent." His gaze warmed her. Cat hadn't realized she was cold. "Strong and capable. Smart and canny. Willing to risk everything, do anything, to have your vengeance."

I wasn't willing to risk you.

Unable to remain still any longer, Cat crossed to the creek, tore off another section of her shirt and dampened it. She came back and began to wash the blood from his skin.

"I woke up," she said quietly, "and you were gone."

"How did you like it?"

"I didn't."

"I could no longer bear the lies."

"Lies?" She frowned, confused. "You mean what Larsen said? I couldn't—I didn't—"

He made a sound of exasperation, then took the now-bloody rag from her hand and tossed it over his shoulder. "I am not a fool. From the moment I found you standing on my doorstep in the rain, I knew."

"If you knew . . ." She stared down, gathering her courage before once again meeting his eyes. "How could you touch me?"

He lifted a hand to her cheek. Her breath, the very air around them, stilled at all she saw in his eyes. "How could I not?"

For an instant Cat wasn't sure what to say and then—"Wait a second. You knew what that bastard had done to me, yet you made it a condition of helping me that I sleep with you? That's . . . That's . . ."

His hand dropped away. "Wasn't it better to face what you feared? Not doing so only makes that fear loom larger."

"Says the man who carries empty guns."

"We aren't talking about me."

"We will," she muttered.

"Aren't you better now?"

"Better?" she repeated, as if the word were foreign.

"You think I was wrong to require your body as payment for my help? You think I did so because I couldn't resist your allure?"

"Well . . . yeah."

"*Durochka,* when you arrived in Omaha you were a skinny, hollow-eyed wreck. I could have resisted you."

"Why didn't you?"

"You were so brave, so determined to make things right. Or as right as they could be, considering nothing would ever be right again."

Cat swallowed. He'd taken one look at her, and he'd known everything. Yet still he had touched her. Protected her. Been willing to give his life for her. Even while she was doing her best to die for a dead man, Alexi Romanov had stood by her. Did that mean he loved her too?

She wasn't sure how to ask.

"Besides, I thought I could fix you."

"With make-believe?"

"It had worked for me. Why not for you?"

"You still puke when you shoot a gun."

"You still pretend to be anyone but yourself when I touch you."

There was something in his voice that made her sharp retort die. "Is that what you meant by the lies? Is *that* why you left?"

"I couldn't stand it anymore. I wanted you to *see* me. To *touch* me. And not Jed or the prince of Persia or whoever else you pretended I was."

Cat bit her lip. She could let him continue to believe that, or she could take a chance and tell the truth.

"My parents called me Catey."

"What?"

"I was born Cathleen. Billy and his family always called me that. But *my* family called me Catey."

His eyes darkened from sapphire to midnight as what she had said sank in; his smile slowly blossomed. "You weren't pretending."

She shook her head.

The moment stretched out. They were on the edge of something new, something frightening, but also very important.

"I meant to leave," he said. "Would have. Then I saw the sheriff coming into the hotel, heard him asking questions. I saw I'd put on your shirt and—"

"You became me."

"It is what I do best." Alexi got to his feet, nearly fell back on his ass, would have if Cat hadn't helped. Once upright, he kept his arm around her shoulders, and she kept hers around his waist.

"You could have died." The thought of what might have been caused Cat to tighten her grip, to hold him even closer. They'd been given another chance, so she took it. "I don't think I could live in a world without you in it, Alexi."

He said nothing. Had she misjudged everything? Then he smiled and in that smile, she once again found hope.

"I guess the dead bastard was right." At her curious expression, he continued. "Only love could make us behave like such fools. Practically tripping over each other to be the first in line to die."

Cat's chill returned at the memory of how close they both had come.

"I've never loved anyone before."

"I have." Cat released a long, sad sigh, and with it she let go of Billy. It was time. "I didn't think I could love again."

"There are a lot of things you didn't think you could do again."

"You taught me differently."

He stared at the creek, but she didn't think he saw the flowing, muddy water. "I'm not sure if I know how to be the man you need."

"Alexi." She waited until he met her eyes. "You already are."

Together they walked between the towering rock walls that led out of the gorge. As soon as Mikhail saw them, he pulled back from the edge and headed down to meet them. Bodies lay strewn in their path. The only one Cat was concerned about was Larsen's.

He'd been shot in the head. Alexi was a very good teacher.

She liked looking at him this way a little too much, and that made her realize something else. "I was wrong."

"Again?"

Cat cast him a dry glance before returning her attention to the lovely hole in Larsen's head. "You were right."

"Not only were you wrong, but I was right. How lovely. What was I right about?"

"It doesn't matter who killed him." Cat stepped over Larsen's dead body and moved toward the sunlight at the end of her darkness. "As long as he's dead."

EPILOGUE

A month later, Cat stared at the ceiling and tried to count backward. However, as she and Alexi had just finished a rousing bout of "princess and the pauper," she was having difficulty remembering anything, let alone anything backward. But she was fairly certain that she'd been wrong about more than Larsen.

Alexi kissed her, then rolled out of bed. The sun had set, and it was time for him to work.

They'd ridden out of the Rocky Mountains and into the first decent town they saw, bought a square of main street, and opened a gambling hall. While Alexi was a gifted cheat, he was even better at spotting those with the same talent. With Mikhail as the strong arm, they became known quite quickly as an honest house.

Cat filled in where she was needed—behind the bar, dealing poker, even sweeping up when the night was through. She'd considered taking a bounty or two when the urge arose. But just as Alexi had thought he would never be able to stop the dodge, then suddenly, he did, Cat's urge to help the helpless had faded. Her being wrong might have something to do with that.

"You'll be down soon?" Alexi reached for his pants.

Cat set her hand on his wrist, and he glanced up, curious. Even with the permanent crook in his nose, he was still so beautiful he made her breath catch.

She hadn't married him yet. She probably should.

"Sit." Cat patted the bed.

He frowned. But he sat.

Cat stroked his shoulder, her fingers sliding over his wound. It really had been no more than a scratch. But the thought of what could have been had kept her up several nights after they'd left Devil's Head Mountain.

"I was wrong."

Alexi's lips curved. He loved it when she admitted that. "What were you wrong about this time, *moya zhizn'*?"

Annoyance flared. That had been happening a lot lately, and for very little reason—or so she had thought. "Is now really a good time to call me a silly fool?"

"I may have made a slight mistake in the translation."

"How slight?"

"*Moya zhizn'* means . . ." He cupped her cheek. "My life."

Life. Cat set her hand atop his. Just what she wanted to discuss.

"Remember when I said I was barren?" Cat asked.

Alexi's eyes went wary. "Yes."

Cat lowered his hand from her face to her stomach.

"I was wrong."

The End

Are you ready to discover the truth about Ethan Walsh?
AN OUTLAW IN WONDERLAND
Once Upon a Time in the West
Book #2

AN OUTLAW IN WONDERLAND

Once Upon a Time . . .

A Spy Was Born

Convinced his actions will save countless lives by shortening the war, Union doctor Ethan Walsh agrees to share with his government what he learns while working undercover in Chimborazo Hospital, deep in the heart of Dixie.

Confederate nurse Annabeth Phelan lost her entire family, save one brother, to the war. When that brother goes missing due to information gleaned by a spy, she swears to discover the culprit.

But spying is a dangerous game. Lives change, lives end once the truth is discovered, and falling in love amid the chaos of conflict doesn't stand the test of time.

Separated by tragedy, the two fall down rabbit holes they never could have imagined. Reunited years later, now an outlaw and healer, Ethan and Annabeth must ask themselves . . .

Can a love born amid desperation and lies survive?

AN OUTLAW IN WONDERLAND

DEAR READER

The *Once Upon a Time in the West* trilogy was originally published under the pen name Lori Austin, but I'm re-releasing them now under my own name.

As a child I fell in love with gritty westerns—John Ford? Sign me up. John Wayne? Okay! Clint Eastwood? First in line.

As a reader I devoured the westerns of Maggie Osborne. As a writer, my very first attempt was a western. And my first published novel?

A western.

But one of my proudest moments as an author was when a book I loved more than almost any other I'd written, BEAUTY AND THE BOUNTY HUNTER, was not only purchased for publication by the editor of Maggie Osborne herself, but that editor told me during our first conversation that my writing reminded her of Maggie's.

Be still my heart!

I hope you'll agree that I captured a bit of the Wild West and of Maggie's original and unusual heroines too. (If you haven't read Maggie Osborne's westerns, or pretty much anything she's ever written . . . Run! Don't walk!)

Word-of-mouth can really help an author out, so if you enjoyed this book, I'd love it if you shared that with your friends.

In the same vein, reviews are critically important. If you're so inclined, I'd appreciate a Review (it can be as short as you'd like) on the platform where you purchased it. I would appreciate it very much!

I love hearing from my readers and can be contacted via my website (LoriHandeland.com), through Facebook (Lori Handeland Books) and on Instagram (Lori Handeland Books).

Subscribe to my NEWSLETTER for all the latest updates. Learn about new books, sales, and the occasional freebie.

I look forward to seeing you there!

Lori Handeland

ABOUT THE AUTHOR

Lori Handeland is a five-time nominee and two-time winner of the prestigious RITA™ Award from Romance Writers of America, as well as the New York Times and USA Today bestselling author of over sixty novels spanning the genres of paranormal romance, urban fantasy, contemporary romance, historical romance, historical fantasy and women's fiction. Her novel *Just Once* received a coveted, starred review from Library Journal and was optioned as a feature film by Catalyst Global Media.

Lori set her sight on being an author at the age of ten. She remembers sitting at a typewriter before she knew how to type, pecking out a story about a family who went into space. As an only child her summers were spent with that typewriter, television, and, above all, books. As a young adult, she got sidetracked by the need to make a living. She worked as a waitress and later enrolled in college to become a teacher.

Lori lives in Southern Wisconsin with her husband of over thirty-five years. In between writing and reading, she enjoys long walks with their rescue mutt, Arnold, and visits from her two grown sons, awesome daughter-in-law and perfectly adorable grandchildren.

MORE BOOKS BY LORI?

I have written over sixty novels, novellas and short stories across multiple genres. But whether you read a contemporary or a historical, a women's fiction or a paranormal, you will always find my signature voice, along with a little humor, a little angst and the depth of characterization and fast-paced plot lines I love to read as well as write.

You can download a complete LIST of my novels on my website.

COPYRIGHT